TIPS FOR MAGICIANS

CELESTA RIMINGTON

Crown Books for Young Readers

New York

Text copyright © 2021 by Celesta Rimington
Jacket art and interior art copyright © 2021 by Chelen Ecija

All rights reserved. Published in the United States by Crown Books for Young Readers, an imprint of Random House Children's Books, a division of Penguin Random House LLC, New York.

Crown and the colophon are registered trademarks of Penguin Random House LLC.

Visit us on the Web! rhcbooks.com

Educators and librarians, for a variety of teaching tools, visit us at RHTeachersLibrarians.com

Library of Congress Cataloging-in-Publication Data
Names: Rimington, Celesta, author.
Title: Tips for magicians / Celesta Rimington.
Description: First edition. | New York : Crown Books for Young Readers, [2021] | Audience: Ages 8–12. | Audience: Grades 4–6. | Summary: When his mother, a professional singer, dies, twelve-year-old Harrison moves to the southern Utah desert, where he continues learning card tricks, makes new friends, enters an art contest, and finds a way to pay tribute to his mother.
Identifiers: LCCN 2020046333 (print) | LCCN 2020046334 (ebook) | ISBN 978-0-593-12126-9 (hardcover) | ISBN 978-0-593-12127-6 (library binding) | ISBN 978-0-593-12128-3 (ebook)
Subjects: CYAC: Grief—Fiction. | Moving, Household—Fiction. | Friendship—Fiction. | Magic tricks—Fiction. | Deserts—Fiction. | Utah—Fiction.
Classification: LCC PZ7.1.R565 Ti 2021 (print) | LCC PZ7.1.R565 (ebook) | DDC [Fic]—dc23

The text of this book is set in 12.5-point Sabon MT Pro.
Interior design by Jen Valero

Printed in Italy
10 9 8 7 6 5 4 3 2 1
First Edition
GFV

For Victoria and Maxwell, my muses

CONTENTS ✛ ✛

PART ONE: TIPS FOR MAGICIANS

PART THREE: TIPS FOR MUSICIANS

PART FOUR: HARRISON'S TIPS FOR LIFE

Part One

TIPS
FOR MAGICIANS

Magic is within the story you tell.

—LEO ABBOTT, STAGE MAGICIAN

CHAPTER 1

TIP ONE:
NEVER REPEAT A TRICK

You never really know if you're ready to perform a magic trick until you give it a try. I shuffle the cards and think through the steps of this new trick one more time. The sunlight shines through the living room windows, creating boxes of light on the blue carpet. I remember Mom wanted to replace that blue carpet.

Kennedy, who isn't my babysitter, pours what's left in her cup of water into the soil of Mom's withering houseplant. I have been watering it, and I put it in the sun every morning. I've done that for a year, but right now it's not doing well.

"Maybe we should pick up some plant food from the garden store," she says, giving the plant a look of pity. People look at me that way sometimes. It makes me want to change the subject.

"Maybe we should go to the pool," I say, shuffling my cards again. I use the overhand technique.

Kennedy smiles. "Harrison, your skin is still sunburned from the last time I took you and your friends swimming."

I look from her dark-brown skin to the bright-pink tint all over my white arms. "I'll wear more sunscreen."

Kennedy is starting college at the end of the summer. She's practically a grown-up. She has a car and a job working for her mom's talent agency. But even though Kennedy is like six years older than me, she's one of my best friends. And she's been hanging out with me a lot since Mom died last year.

"Mmm," she says, sitting on the couch and checking her phone. "Maybe I'll just put my feet in." She glances up and gives me a serious expression. "But you and the guys have to promise not to splash me."

"Okay," I say. Kennedy's black hair is smooth and much straighter than it was the last time we went to the pool. She's told me that it takes a long time to get her hair done that way. "Are you ready for this one?" I hold up my deck of cards.

She sets her phone down. "Ready. What is this trick called?"

"Topsy Turvy Cards."

I use the coffee table, and Kennedy watches as I

spread out the cards, to show they're all facing the same direction. She looks at the cards and then at me. I think she's wondering if I'll give away the secret.

I follow the steps as I remember them, turning the cards over in my hand like the video showed. I make it seem like I've turned half of the stack faceup and half of the stack facedown. But by passing a "magic" card through the center of the deck, suddenly the cards are all the same direction again.

Kennedy grins. "Wow, Harrison. I totally didn't see how you did that," she says.

"Is that sarcasm?" I let out an awkward laugh.

"No, not at all. I don't know how you did it." She leans forward. "Lemme see it again."

I gather up my cards in one hand. "No way."

"Pleeeease."

This is a test. I'm sure of it.

"A magician never repeats a trick," I say.

"Because?" She raises one eyebrow.

Yeah, she was testing me. Kennedy knows what happened last time I showed a card trick to Creed and a few of the other kids at karate.

"Because someone will figure out your secret and ruin the mystery."

Kennedy pumps her open hands toward the ceiling. "I think he's got it!"

The air-conditioning clicks on and blows the curtains

by the sliding glass doors. Sometimes, when the air is blowing from the vents, I still smell whispers of Mom's hairspray and perfume.

"But can I make one suggestion?" Kennedy pulls out her phone again and motions for me to come closer.

"Sure," I say.

Kennedy types the words *magician persona* in a search on her phone. I've been watching YouTube tutorials for how to do these card tricks, but I've never seen those words together before.

"You and I know a lot about show business because of our moms, right?" Kennedy's mom was my mom's talent agent and friend. I like how Kennedy brings up my mom in regular conversation, like it's no big deal. When Dad talks about Mom—or I mention her in front of him—it feels like a big deal.

"Well . . . you know about show business from *both* of your parents," she says, waving her hand like that wasn't her point. "What I'm saying is, to be a good magician, you've got to bring in some performance quality to your tricks."

"Okaaay," I say. "Like what?"

"Look here." Kennedy shows me the website for a stage magician named Leo Abbott. "This says, 'A magician persona is a character you play as the magician. Your audience might be impressed by how well you do the magic tricks, but you add to the wonder by the way you present yourself.' "

I read the list on her screen. "'Magicians can be mysterious, scary, funny . . .'"

"'Decide on your style, and then perform *with* the trick,'" Kennedy says. She drops her phone on the couch and points across the room toward the fireplace. "Go over there like you've just walked onstage in front of a huge audience. They are waiting. A completely silent crowd, holding their breath in anticipation. Waiting for *your* magic."

I've learned not to argue with Kennedy. She's usually right anyway.

I take my deck of cards and stand in front of the fireplace, facing her.

"Now, who are you? You feel those stage lights warm your face. The music is quiet. It's just you: a magician and your cards."

I take a deep breath. I can't imagine I would ever be in front of a huge audience. Kennedy widens her eyes at me, and I start laughing.

"You're making this too serious," I say.

She smiles. "Okay, so maybe you're a comedic magician. You make people laugh with your tricks."

"I don't think so. I just feel weird standing here like this."

"Face the other way, then. Pretend I'm not here. Imagine performing as a magician. How will you act?"

I turn toward the fireplace. The hearth still has a clay sculpture on it that Mom made. She thought it was terrible, and only made it because her sister, Maggie, was visiting, and Aunt Maggie gets everyone to try art projects. The sculpture is supposed to be me and Mom together. I asked to keep it, even though she didn't think it was very good. The memory feels heavy enough to make my shoulders slump. It makes me feel like I don't want to go swimming or see my karate friends today.

Suddenly, I know what my magician person-thing will be. It'll be mysterious and keep my audience from knowing too much. It will be impressive and confident. It will push away this sad feeling.

"Harrison?" Kennedy says. "Don't make it too hard. You can try out some different ways."

I think of all the times I saw Mom perform onstage. Even when I watched her from the wings, I noticed what Kennedy is talking about. Mom had a way of being bigger and braver than her usual self when she was in front of an audience.

I can be like that.

I turn back toward Kennedy and give her a smile.

"What will you call your magician self?" she asks.

That one is easy. "Harrison"—I pause for effect—"the Magnificent."

CHAPTER 2

TIP TWO: CHOOSE A GOOD MAGICIAN NAME

"Lavender's blue, dilly dilly, lavender's green . . ." Mom sat on the edge of my bed and sang.

"Mom?" I lifted my head from my pillow and interrupted her. "How can lavender be blue and green? Isn't lavender light purple?"

"It's referring to the lavender plant, Harry."

"Oh."

She continued the song. "When you are king, dilly dilly, I shall be queen . . ."

Mom's voice was what the reviewers called "a clean, clear soprano that rises from the stage and takes audiences to the heavens with it." Or something like that. Some people said her voice was magical. To me, though, Mom's voice was the sound of home.

"Who told you so, dilly dilly," she sang, "who told you so?"

I joined her on the last part, my voice able to match her notes.

"'Twas my own heart, dilly dilly, that told me so."

Mom leaned over and kissed my forehead. She smelled like peaches and lime-flavored lip balm. She hadn't washed off her stage makeup, and her long eyelashes tickled my face.

She tucked the sheets around me and whispered, "Never stop singing, Harry. It's a gift."

I sighed and nodded, too sleepy to answer. I'd waited up for her, something I always did on her show nights, so we could have a good-night song before bed. She always met with her audiences and signed autographs after her shows, but she kept the meet and greets short and hurried home to sing me to sleep. That was our thing. That was Mom.

She sang one more song—one from her show. It was called "You Are." I closed my eyes and listened, happy to have her home.

"I sang that at the Red Cliffs Amphitheater the summer we lived in Muse," she said. "Do you remember?"

I was only five when we were there, but I still remembered a few things about that summer in the Utah art village. I remembered walls of red rocks and the buzz-

ing of bugs in the desert. I had made a friend named Chloe, and I remembered that, too.

I was getting sleepy. "Yes," I whispered.

"That place is full of magic, Harrison. We'll go back to visit again sometime."

"Okay," I mumbled.

"Good night, Harrison the Magnificent."

Mom often called people names that sounded like magicians. So I was Harrison the Magnificent, and Dad was Calvin the Incredible.

"Good night, Mom."

✦   ✦

Kennedy drops me off at home after karate, like she does every Tuesday and Thursday. I wave at her from the porch as she backs her car out of the driveway.

"Put some ice on that elbow!" she calls out the car window.

My elbow got bent back a little too far in a move called Breaking Twigs today. I didn't want to make a big deal about it in front of Creed and the rest of the class, but now, it's pretty sore.

I wave at Kennedy with my good arm. "I will!"

"And tell your dad!" she adds.

I nod at that one. Kennedy keeps nudging that Dad and I need to "communicate." Dad doesn't say much, so I guess I don't, either. But we used to have a lot of fun together.

I push the front door open and lug my karate bag inside.

"How was class?" Dad asks from behind his laptop on the living room couch. He's home a little early from his job at the National Theatre in Washington, DC.

"It was fine," I say, not wanting to bother him about my elbow. "How was work?"

Dad runs his hand over his unshaven face. He sometimes goes days without shaving—just one of many things that have changed since Mom died. "We need to have a talk as soon as I finish this."

"Okay." I can't tell if this is good or bad news. I leave my bag by the door, holding my throbbing elbow. Dad didn't used to work all the time. We used to go hiking along the Potomac in the fall. In the hot summer months, he always found time to take me kayaking at Lake Ridge Marina. But not this summer. I've missed time with Dad. It's weird to miss someone who is still here.

I grab my deck of cards off the top of the dusty piano and practice my one-handed cut. My hands are still a bit too small to cut the deck, spin the top section, and put it back together with only one hand. But I'm getting better at it.

"I'll be back," I say as I head to the kitchen.

I pocket my cards and grab a bag of peas from the

freezer. I return to the living room with the frozen peas on my sore elbow and sink into the orange armchair. Dad closes his laptop.

"I wanted to ask you . . ." He leans forward, resting his elbows on his knees. He stares at the glass coffee table as though he might develop superpowers and cut through it with his laser vision. "What would you think about going to visit Aunt Maggie?"

"Aunt Maggie? *Really?*" Of all the things to follow the words "We need to have a talk," I didn't expect something this great.

My aunt owns an art gallery in a town called Muse, where we lived that summer Mom had a performing contract there. It's in the southern Utah desert, and people come from all over the world to tour the national parks and hike the red cliffs. Aunt Maggie has come to visit us a few times, too. The last time we saw her was at Mom's funeral, but even then, it was comforting to have her around.

"Yes! Dad, that would be awesome!" If we went to Utah, Dad and I could go on those amazing hikes, and he'd have time to do things with me again.

Dad doesn't seem as excited as he should be. I'm about to remind him about the parks and the hikes when he says, "Well . . . there's an opening in the Dorian Striker show, and they've asked me to stage-manage."

"In Utah?"

Dorian Striker is a performer that Mom and Dad

knew before I was born, when Mom was touring as a professional singer and Dad was her stage manager. Dorian Striker plays guitar and sings. He has a full band and big sets and special effects. I saw ads for his show on TV just last month.

Dad still stares at the smudged, dusty glass of the coffee table. I don't remember the last time we used a cleaner on that glass. "It's a national tour, Harrison."

I know right away what this means. Mom used to tour before I was born. It wasn't a life like I have, with a colonial-style house and Christmas wreaths in the windows and a backyard forest. It was a life of different cities every week, sometimes terrible food, hotel beds, lots of vitamin C, and lots of travel.

"Oh." My fingers are icy from holding the bag of peas. My skin burns with the cold, but it gives me something else to feel besides the thumping in my chest. Dad didn't mean he would be coming to visit Aunt Maggie *with* me.

"Life on tour isn't something I want for you. But I also don't want you to be alone so much."

I wonder how much Kennedy tells him.

"I'm not alone that much," I say, lying.

Dad looks up, finally. "I think it would be good for you to be with family and to meet new people. And if you went to live with Maggie, I could take this stage-managing job and know you were okay while I was on the road."

I let the peas drop to the floor.

"Wait . . . I'm going to *live* in Utah?"

"Did you hurt yourself at karate?" He's noticed the peas.

"I'm going to live in Utah *without you?*"

"What happened to your arm?" Dad says, concerned, and stands up from the couch.

I shake my head. "It's fine." I bend and straighten my elbow a few times. "See?" It feels like it's creaking, from being frozen.

Dad relaxes a little and walks to the front window, looking out at the cherry tree in the golden sunset. It's nearly the end of summer, so the pink blossoms are long gone.

"I think we should sell the house, Harrison." The spring in the old clock clunks as it unwinds. I feel the noise in my chest, almost as if it's hitting my heart.

"I need a fresh start," he says. "And I think you do, too."

"But what if I don't want a fresh start?"

"This place reminds me of your mom." Dad looks darkly at the room, like he can't stand it here. It hits me like a kick to the stomach.

"Can't we have a fresh start *together?*" I suddenly feel like I'm sitting in a stranger's living room. I take the cards from my pocket, fumble, and drop half the deck.

Dad turns at the sound, his expression stiff. I can't

tell if he's mad at me for dropping cards, or if it's my card tricks in general that irritate him.

His face relaxes after a minute. He steps over my spilled cards and helps me pick them up, and I catch a glimpse of what Dad was like before Mom died. Calvin the Incredible who needs a shave.

"You still working on that new trick?" he asks. "What do you call it?"

"I have two I'm working on," I say quietly. Harrison the Magnificent should be bolder, but I can't do it right now. "The Ambitious Card and the Four Burglars. I'm not quite ready to show them yet."

"You'll get it," he says. "Keep practicing. I'd love for you to show them to me before we leave. Production meetings start in Las Vegas in six weeks. And I want to get you to Aunt Maggie's in time to start school there."

"Isn't there a job you can do in her town?" I think of Dad and me in another place, in a house I imagine from my aunt's description—adobe-style, with cactus and rocks in the yard and red cliffs rising behind it. I imagine us exploring desert caves. Following a different plan. I imagine Harrison the Magnificent performing a spectacular trick to make all the dusty sadness disappear. Like a bright light shoving out a heavy fog.

"In Muse?" Dad stands and paces the room. "Not the kind of work I'm good at, Harrison. That theater where your mom performed used to have a professional crew and stage management, but Maggie said it closed down a few years ago."

"Maybe you could get it running again."

"Harrison . . ."

"Or I could go on tour with you!"

Dad shakes his head.

"But I don't see why it's better to split up. We used to be three of us. Now we're two. And if you leave me in Utah, we're not really like a family. It's me by myself, and you by yourself, and that's not any better."

"The tour is only for six months," Dad says, using *his* new trick of not showing emotion. He's worked hard on that talent—almost as hard as I've worked on my card tricks. One of the ways he stays emotionless is to never play Mom's recordings. I haven't heard her sing for over a year. "I need the work, and it'll be good for you to live with Aunt Maggie."

I can tell I'm not going to win this discussion right now. I notice that Dad is standing directly in front of the fireplace. On the hearth behind him is the clay sculpture Mom made of her and me. I think about how Muse is a place Mom has been, a place she's performed. It's a place I've been with her, even though I don't really remember it. Maybe I could feel close to Mom there, but I won't have those painful aches that creep up and take your breath away when you round the ice cream aisle in the Food Lion.

I try the one-handed cut again. For the first time ever, I split the deck with my fingers, spin the top section, flip it over, and combine the deck together again in one piece. With one hand. Without dropping a single card.

That has to mean something important.

And I decide right then. If Dad is sending me to live in Muse with Aunt Maggie, then I have to figure out a way for Dad to be there with me. A fresh start in a place Mom has been.

CHAPTER 3

TIP THREE: LEARN FROM OTHER MAGICIANS

When you're practicing magic tricks, you need a good supply of cards. You might be surprised how quickly magicians will go through their decks. I've used up plenty in the one year I've been working on my magic skills.

The day I held my first deck of cards was the day of Mom's funeral. The entire stage crew from her show formed a line and shook my hand one by one and whispered how sorry they were that she was gone.

"What an incredible loss."

"How tragic."

"Such a talent."

I can't remember which hand slipped the box of cards into mine and said, "Your mom loved my magic tricks. She always said that magic is real, and it's our job to find it. Here's a fresh deck, so you can learn some tricks of your own. It gives me something to do when I don't know what to do."

I held the cards and mumbled something I can't remember. I probably said thanks.

Someone else from the stage crew shook my hand and told me, "Harrison, your mom always said you have a voice to match the angels. I hope you'll never stop singing."

That night, I went home with Dad to our empty house with the colonial windows on the edge of a forest in Woodbridge, Virginia. Mom loved to hang wreaths in those windows at Christmastime. She loved the trees. And she loved to sing. But the house was quiet with her absence, and the silence hurt my ears and my heart. So I started to sing "Amazing Grace."

And Dad said, "Please don't do that now."

So I went up to my room. And I almost searched some of Mom's recordings on my tablet. But I thought of Dad, and instead, I typed into YouTube "How to do card tricks."

And I haven't sung since that day.

✝   ✝

It's a lot of work to pack up an entire house. Our last five weeks in Woodbridge have been a blur of boxes and choosing what goes with me and what goes in storage.

Dad brought a bunch of his theater friends to help with the big stuff. Since I'm going to live with Aunt Maggie, and Dad will be on the road, Dad sold a lot of our furniture and gave the rest to people we know. That was weird. Now, all Dad and I have left is what we put in our suitcases. The house is empty. I hate seeing it like that, so I've been spending most of my time at the pool with Creed and Josh. Kennedy's been really nice about taking us while Dad has been training his replacement at the National Theatre. And yesterday, she took a group of us to get milkshakes after karate.

Dad woke me up early today. For a minute, I forgot what was happening. We've been sleeping on the floor, since our beds are gone, and I thought we were camping. Then I remembered. We're moving away today. Sometimes, I get a little feeling of excitement about going to Utah and visiting that red-cliff desert with Aunt Maggie, but then I realize it isn't a vacation. We aren't coming back here.

"The Jacksons are here," Dad announces from the living room.

That's Kennedy and her parents. They said they'd come over to say goodbye.

"And we brought *doughnuts*," Kennedy calls down the hallway toward my room.

I shove my pajamas into my suitcase, thinking how this is the last time I'll ever be in my room—this place where Mom sang me to sleep. I dig through my suitcase to be sure I still have Mom's clay sculpture of us. It's there, safely wrapped inside one of my T-shirts. I also check to be sure I have my deck of cards. I put those in my pocket.

Kennedy is sitting at the table with everyone when I join them in the kitchen. She's listening to our parents talk. She even joins in and knows what to say about the Striker show and Dad's new job. It's cool how Kennedy is like a kid and a grown-up at the same time. She can be both. But mostly, I think of her as being on my side—like she understands things my dad doesn't.

Kennedy notices me. "Hey there."

I don't think I can do this goodbye stuff. I don't want to get to the part where everything is the last time. The last time sleeping here, the last breakfast in this kitchen, the last time Kennedy comes over.

"Hi."

"You want some chocolate milk?" Dad asks, offering me a cup.

I shake my head.

"You want to go for a walk?" Kennedy asks.

"Sure."

Instead of heading outside, Kennedy walks around the empty house with me.

"Did you do what we talked about?" Kennedy asks.

"What? The saying goodbye thing?" I pull my deck of cards from my pocket and shuffle them.

"Yeah. Did you do it?"

"It seems weird to say goodbye to a house," I say. "I feel weird doing it."

"I think you'll feel betterrrr if you tryyyy it." Kennedy stretches out her words to be funny. "I'll go first."

She bounds up the stairs, and I follow her. She stands at the top, where you can look over the banister to the family room. She holds her arms open wide.

"You think of the ways this place has been good for you." She glances at me really quick. "It *has* been good, don't you think?"

"Yeah, it has. It's my home."

"*Was* your home," she says. "We're trying to let it become something else. Now, work with me here."

"Okay." I'm confused, but I let her keep going.

"You remember what has been good, and you say thank you." She looks around at the bedrooms behind us and the main floor below, keeps her arms spread wide, takes a deep breath, and says in a strong voice, "Thank you."

"Just like that, huh?" I smile at her, because this is ridiculous.

"Now, you do it."

I roll my eyes, spread my arms a little, and mumble, "Thank you?"

"What was that?" Kennedy nudges me. "Come on." She opens her arms wide again, like it's a dance move— sharp and strong. "Give it a good effort."

I copy what she did with her arms, stretching as wide as I can. "Thank you." I say it louder.

"You need to mean it."

"Thank you!" I yell, and my voice echoes off the walls of the empty house.

"You're welcome!" Dad hollers back from the kitchen below and cracks himself up. He hasn't done that in forever. He laughs, and Kennedy and I laugh, and Kennedy's parents laugh. Our voices fill the rooms.

"Are you making him say thank you to the house?" Kennedy's mom, Lorraine, calls up.

"Yep," Kennedy calls back down.

"Can I put my arms down now?" I ask.

"Bring them in. Like this." She demonstrates by wrapping her arms around herself.

I shrug and copy her.

As we stand there like that, she says, "You have to imagine you are soaking in all those good memories and keeping them with you."

I nod.

"Let this house be something else to someone new. You can find what this house gave you in a new place. And you can make some new friends, too. You just have to be brave."

I think about that idea of taking all the good with me. I'm not able to take much else. But the good memories are sometimes the most painful. They make me miss Mom even more. And I realize this is going to hurt too much if I let them in. I drop my arms.

"I have to be Harrison the Magnificent," I say softly, more to myself than to Kennedy.

"Well, if Harrison the Magnificent helps you be brave, then . . . okay." She thinks about it a moment. "But be sure to be *you*, too."

I don't know if I can be plain old Harrison and move across the country without Dad and without Kennedy and Creed and Josh. I don't think I can be plain old Harrison and start seventh grade in a new middle school in a new town.

"Do you want doughnuts now?" Kennedy asks.

"Yeah," I say with a slight grin.

We head back to the kitchen. Kennedy asks to see the new phone Dad bought me to keep in touch with him and everyone while I'm in Muse. Kennedy and I have already texted each other, so I have her number saved.

"Smile," she says.

I turn with a mouthful of powdered doughnut, and she snaps a picture. She takes a few with me and Dad. Then she holds the phone out in front of her, reverses the direction of the camera, and takes a few of us together. She shows me how to make one of our pictures show up when she calls me.

When the taxi arrives to take Dad and me to the airport, I imagine myself as Harrison the Magnificent and leave the house without looking back at the empty rooms.

"Maybe we can work it out for Kennedy to come visit in Muse," Dad says as he loads our bags into the taxi. I can tell he's trying to help.

"We'd all love to come visit, Calvin," says Kennedy's mom. "Let's talk about it once you know your schedule with the Striker show."

"Will do. Thanks for everything, Lorraine." I can tell Dad means a lot with his thank-you. Lorraine may have been Mom's talent agent, but she was also her friend. Dad shakes hands with Kennedy's dad, and we get in the car.

Kennedy and her parents stand by their car and wave as the driver backs the taxi down the driveway. Although I've already said goodbye to Kennedy, I want to do one more thing. I roll down the window, open my arms wide like we did in the house, and I think of all the good I want to remember.

And I yell as loud as I can, *"Thank you!"*

CHAPTER 4

TIP FOUR: PAY ATTENTION TO THE DETAILS

Aunt Maggie rushes out her front door, wearing a pair of shorts and a tank top, as soon as Dad and I pull up in the rental car.

"Calvin! Harrison!" she hollers like we've just won money on a game show. "You're here!"

Her brown hair is in a messy style on top of her head, with strands falling loose as she runs. She practically leaps across the rocks in the front yard. In Aunt Maggie's town, most of the homes don't have grass around them. Instead, the yards are filled with pebbles and colorful desert plants. Metal sculptures staked in the gravel spin and make patterns in the breeze.

Dad and I get out of the car, and Aunt Maggie hugs

us one at a time. She has what Mom called a "sun-kissed glow." Her skin is light like mine, but with a gentle tan and a flush of pink in her cheeks.

"Harrison, you've grown!" she says, holding on to my shoulders and looking me up and down. She doesn't pat me on top of my head, which I appreciate.

"Not enough," I complain. I've always been short for my age, but this summer, Creed and Josh grew so much that I started to look like their little brother instead of someone in their same grade. After Dad told me about the move, I hoped I would at least grow enough to not be the shortest kid in seventh grade.

Aunt Maggie laughs. "You can't help your biology, kiddo. But don't worry—being tall isn't a talent. It has nothing to do with what makes you interesting, you know?"

I shrug. She must not remember what it's like in middle school.

"Let me help with your things." She takes one of my suitcases, and Dad takes the other. Since we flew across the country, this is all I brought: two suitcases, a backpack, and my pillow.

"Thank you again for doing this, Maggie," Dad says as the two of them walk toward the front door. He sounds even sadder than usual, especially in comparison to Aunt Maggie's level of normal.

"Like I said, it's my pleasure. I love the kid. I'm really

looking forward to this, to be honest. I have this house all to myself, and it'll be nice to share it with someone."

"Make sure you give him some chores, okay? Give him some responsibilities and have him help out. I want this to be like normal home life."

It's weird to hear Dad say those things, because nothing since Mom died has felt like normal home life. I decide not to follow them inside just yet.

Aunt Maggie's neighborhood is surrounded by reddish-orange cliffs that rise like giants into the bright-blue sky. Rocky orange sand stretches out to the cliffs, with patches of surprisingly green plants, yellow and purple wildflowers, and small trees that somehow survive the desert heat. It's seven o'clock at night here, and still heat rises from the ground and from all the rocks around me. It was hard to say goodbye to Virginia and to our house, but now that I'm here, this hot desert feels like it's wrapping itself around me to make me part of it. I only wish that Dad would stay.

On the airplane, I showed Dad every trick I know except the one that makes the cards scatter all over. I didn't want to lose any cards. He seemed impressed. I think I'm getting pretty good at being Harrison the Magnificent, because people across the aisle were interested in the tricks, too. It helped pass the time. Being Harrison the Magnificent helped me stop thinking about our house and Kennedy and my friends. It helped me not feel sad about leaving behind the last place we were with Mom. But now that we're here in Muse, I remember the feeling of being here with Mom, too, and I wish Dad didn't have a job that took him away.

Dad comes back outside. He walks down the porch steps and joins me in the gravel front yard.

"They call this desertscape," Dad says, leaning over to pick up a handful of rocks and letting them run through his fingers.

"At least they don't have to mow the grass," I say.

"True."

"And look at those." I point at the metal sculptures. The moving parts on one of them are designed like the wings of a butterfly. Another one is a flower with spinning petals that create a kind of dizzying vortex.

Dad nods. "Mm-hmm."

"And those cliffs," I say. "Wouldn't it be great to go hiking in the canyons? We saw all those signs for trails on the way here, and I was reading about these ancient lava tubes from a dormant volcano that have hollowed out—"

"Harrison." Dad tilts his head the way Kennedy had looked at Mom's withering plant. "I know you want me to stay, but I can't. I need to be in Las Vegas for production meetings early tomorrow morning. I've got to drive down tonight."

"I wish you'd just work here," I say, shuffling my cards and wondering if I could ever perform a trick good enough that it would keep Dad from leaving on a six-month tour.

"All of your ideas sound great. They really do." Dad places his arm around my shoulders. He hasn't done that in a while. "But they will have to wait until I have a break between shows. I promise to come for a visit as soon as I can, okay?"

I do a one-handed cut. "When will that be?"

"I believe the first break is in October. It'll still be great weather for hiking here then, don't you think?"

"Probably. I mean, does it *ever* get cold here?"

"Maggie says it does."

I touch one of the large red boulders in the desertscape yard. It's hot from absorbing the sun's rays all day. "I'll believe that when I see it. Feel this."

Dad touches the boulder with his hand. "Wow."

He used to love exploring the outdoors with me. I can still see that part of him.

The information Kennedy and I found about magician skills said that magicians pay attention to details, and I'm noticing one right now. Dad seems to have a sort of shadow around him. Even here, with the sun shining on us by these hot rocks and desert cliffs.

"Are you two going to come eat some dinner or what?" Aunt Maggie is leaning out the open front door. "Or are you going to soak up the heat some more first?"

"I'm done soaking," Dad says. "How about you?"

I shoulder my backpack. "Yep. I'm hungry."

Dad and I walk toward the house, the rocks crunching under our shoes.

"Hey!" he says. "I remember you had a friend when we lived here."

"Chloe," I say.

"Maybe Maggie can help you connect with her again."

"Nah," I say. "She's just a girl I knew when I was five. I hardly remember her."

That's not entirely true. I remember some good things about Chloe, but I'm not sure she'd remember me or want anything to do with me. People change.

"Well, school starts next week. So you'll have a chance to make some friends there, too."

I don't think Dad remembers what it's like in middle school, either. It isn't actually that easy.

At the top porch step, he wraps his arm around me again and says, "I'm going to miss you, Harry."

Harry was Mom's nickname for me, but I don't mind hearing it from Dad, especially when he says it like that.

CHAPTER 5

TIP FIVE: GIVE TO YOUR AUDIENCE, AND THEY'LL GIVE SOMETHING BACK

Mom knew a lot of people. You'd think that's because she was famous. But really, some of her favorite people didn't know she was famous at all. She had friends "on the Mall." The National Mall is the big central spot in Washington, DC, where people walk between all the museums and monuments. Some people live on the Mall. I guess they either don't have homes, or in the case of Sylvania, who didn't ever use a last name, they don't want to go home. Mom was friends with a lot of people on the Mall. When I was in fifth grade, she took me to meet them.

"That's a handsome boy you have there, Tess," said *Sylvania, who was sitting in the sparse winter grass and*

leaning against a tree. She had some big plastic bags next to her, full of clothes and blankets.

"This is Harrison," Mom said. "Harrison, this is Sylvania. Sylvania the Astounding."

Sylvania smiled and held out her hand to shake mine. Mom nodded, and I took Sylvania's hand. It was November, and she was wearing fingerless gloves, but her fingertips were cold. My hands are always warm, even in winter, so I held her fingers in mine to warm them up.

"What a fine boy," Sylvania said, smiling. "Do you go to school?"

"Yes."

"I bet you're smart, too." Sylvania gave my hands a thank-you pat and placed hers back in her lap. "What do you like to do best at school, Harrison?"

I liked dodgeball and being outside the best, but I didn't think that was what she meant.

Sylvania's eyes were green. The greenest I'd ever seen. Her face was wrinkled into creases like thin tissue paper. Otherwise, she didn't seem old enough to have wrinkles like that.

"Um . . . I like PE and art."

"Art, huh? There's magic in that. Just ask James."

Sylvania motioned across the grass to a thin man sitting on a bench. He had a guitar leaning against the bench next to him, and he was making something with knitting needles and colorful yarn. "James! Come meet Tess's boy!"

James glanced over at us when Sylvania called his name. He shaded his eyes from the sun and took a second look. He set his project and knitting needles inside a bag and strolled over to the tree where we stood, bringing his guitar and bag with him.

"Hey there, Tess," James said. He was very tall. He wore a big green coat and a knitted hat, but his curly red hair was long enough to peek out from underneath. He had a red beard and pale skin with a lot of freckles.

"Hello, James," Mom said. "It's nice to see you again. This is Harrison."

"It's a pleasure to meet the son of Tess Winterrose," James said.

"Hi," I said. It felt as though Mom and I had stepped into Sylvania and James's living room. Even though we were outside, we had come into their space to visit.

Sylvania noticed a leaf stuck to James's coat. She peeled it off and tossed it loose into the breeze. "Harrison said he likes art at school, and I was thinking he might like a glimpse of your magic."

"My magic, huh?" James smiled. "Follow me."

"What are they talking about?" I asked Mom quietly as we followed James and Sylvania toward the National Gallery of Art.

"James has been working on an outdoor exhibit," Mom said.

"Of magic?" I asked. I figured he meant magic tricks or illusions.

James must have heard me, because he turned around and said, "Do you know about muses, Harrison?"

"Like in Greek myths?"

"Mmm, kind of like that," James said. "But a bit different."

We'd learned about the goddesses called Muses at school. All I remembered was a story about a guy who challenged the Muses to a contest. When he lost, they blinded him and took away his singing voice. I also remembered they had something to do with arts and science.

Between the National Gallery and one of the Smithsonian buildings was a sculpture garden. I'd been there on a field trip with my school once. But this time, a sign outside the sculpture garden's fence said The Art Collective. Large upright panels had been installed into the ground, and people were drawing and painting on them. Paints, brushes, chalk, and pencils were spread on a big sheet, and everyone shared the supplies as they worked.

James paused in front of the panels and said, "Do you ever get ideas that are too big to hold inside you?"

"I don't know," I said.

"Well, this is a place where all of us can share those big ideas."

"Oh," I said.

Sylvania, who was a little hunched when she walked, shuffled over to the supplies. "Do you want to try it, Harrison?"

I looked at Mom, expecting her to say we couldn't stay that long, but she was already picking up paints and brushes.

"Come on, Harry," she said, waving me over. She headed for a spot with a partially finished painting of a sunset and a familiar signature. I moved closer. The signature was Mom's: Tess Winterrose.

"I think a muse lives in this place," Mom said. "Maybe not the Greek myth kind of muse, but something that inspires people. Because coming here is like pushing a reset button for me. It feels like that summer in the red cliffs. There's a muse there, too. And it grants wishes."

"In Muse?" I asked, noticing for the first time that Aunt Maggie's town had the same name as the Greek goddesses.

"Yes. I don't know how it works. I just know that it does."

I watched her squeeze some color from the paint tubes onto one of the available trays.

"This is where I come when I feel like my singing is getting dull."

Sylvania laughed. "Your music will never be dull."

"Well"—Mom turned to her—"you make certain of that."

I wondered how visiting Sylvania or painting this sunset helped Mom with her singing. It didn't make sense to me.

Then James stood at the corner of one of the art panels and began playing his guitar softly. I thought I saw a tiny bit of green and blue light leave one of the panels and float across to another. For a minute, it seemed to cover the artwork. A boy at the other end of the panel saw it, too. He was sitting with a girl, and they were sharing a cup of pretzel bites from one of the food stands. They were drawing something together near Mom's sunset.

"Did you see that?" I asked the boy.

"I'm not sure," he said.

I wasn't sure, either. But as James played his guitar and moved through the crowd, the green and blue light slipped over one panel and then another. I looked around for something that might be casting light in this direction. I couldn't figure it out.

The boy and I gave each other looks that said neither one of us wanted to explain what we saw.

"Do you sing, too, Harrison?" asked Sylvania. She had found a big dog sitting in the grass. She scratched it behind the ears, and it pressed against her hand, begging for more.

"Maybe you could sing a song for Sylvania," Mom prodded, holding her paintbrush in the air and turning around. She winked. "I may have told her what a wonderful singer you are."

The boy eating pretzel bites raised his eyebrows at

me. I wished Mom wouldn't ask me to sing for people in the middle of the Mall. Just beyond the Art Collective and the sculpture garden, people were hurrying to their government jobs or rushing to pack in a day of sightseeing. I didn't want to be one of the sights.

But Mom smiled like she knew something I didn't. She set down her paintbrush and came close enough for me to smell her peach shampoo.

"We can sing together, Harry," Mom said softly, so only I could hear. "How about 'Amazing Grace'?"

I nodded.

"You start, and I'll join you with some harmony after a few bars."

I glanced across the grass at the people rising out of the Metro station from the escalators. They were angling across the sidewalks to their busy lives. Most of the people drawing and painting nearby were focused on their creations. The boy had gone over to the collection of art supplies and was selecting paint colors. But Sylvania sat next to the big dog, rubbing her fingers through its fur like she was content to wait for as long as it took me to decide to sing.

And something happened. It was the way Sylvania waited and the gentle strumming of James's guitar and the strange idea that maybe I had really seen a blue and green light dancing over the art panels. And it was the feeling of Mom beside me.

I took in a breath and began. "Amazing grace . . ."

My voice sailed clear and strong over the chatter of people and birds.

"How sweet the sound, that saved a wretch like me. . . ."

I closed my eyes and held out the note, feeling it come from that open space Mom had taught me to find. It was a thrill I hadn't expected—like the music had power. I had no idea it would feel this way to sing outside. To use Mom's word, it was magnificent. I didn't know that the birds would stop chirping, as if they were listening, or that the noise of cars and buses would melt away.

"I once was lost, but now am found . . ." Mom had come in now. She started a little softer than me, gliding into the song and blending her notes with mine. James joined us with his guitar, playing just the right notes to fit. I belonged there so completely, right at that moment, singing for Sylvania with Mom.

Something touched my fingers. I opened my eyes and Sylvania was reaching for my hand. Light reflected off tears on her cheeks. Our music made her happy, but it also seemed to make her strong. Her happiness put power into the world. She smiled, took a breath, and joined in with us.

"Was blind, but now I see."

CHAPTER 6

TIP SIX: WORK ON YOUR PERFORMANCE

"With this trick, I'm going to read your mind and figure out which card is yours," I say to Aunt Maggie.

Dad called after he made it safely to Las Vegas last night. It's just me and Aunt Maggie now. I shuffle the cards using the overhand technique, giving her a confident smile with a hint of mystery—Harrison the Magnificent. "And remember, I borrowed this deck from you. So this is a regular deck, and I couldn't possibly have placed the cards in any special order."

"I'm looking forward to this," Aunt Maggie says, leaning over the kitchen counter and tucking a wisp of hair behind her ear. Her hair is dark brown, but it turns reddish when the sunlight hits it. As usual, she has it up in a messy bunch on top of her head. She also has a bit of dried clay on her cheek from working at her pottery wheel this morning.

I make sure to peek at the bottom card as I finish my shuffle. Queen of spades. Then I fan the cards out facedown. "Take any card, but don't show it to me."

She takes a card from the center left.

"Study it and remember your card," I say. A strange sound is building outside the house, and the sun is way too bright in the kitchen. I try to ignore it and focus on the trick.

She smiles. "Okay. Got it."

I split the deck and hold the half with the queen of spades on the bottom in my right hand. I hold out the other half of the deck in my left and tell Aunt Maggie to place her card there. The sound outside the house grows louder. It's a weird kind of rustling beyond the living room windows.

With her card facedown on the deck in my left hand, I place the other half of the deck on top of that. The queen of spades is now next to her card. As Penn and Teller teach: "You don't need to know the card; you just need to know the card *next* to the card."

"Now," I say, shuffling the stack and being careful not to upset the middle. "Think very hard about your card. I'll read your mind and find it."

I turn the deck over and show her the cards faceup, passing them from one hand to the other slowly for effect. When I find the queen of spades, I move past it a few cards, watching Aunt Maggie as though I'm reading her mind. She looks a lot like Mom. The memories tug at me and threaten to take over, so I focus on my act and the trick I need to finish. I move the cards back the other way, passing the queen of spades one more time. Finally, I drop Aunt Maggie's card in front of her. The one *next* to the queen of spades. The four of hearts.

"*What?*" She slaps the counter. "Harrison! How did you do that?"

"A magician *never* reveals his secret." I give her my confident but mysterious smile.

She picks up the four of hearts, drops it back on the counter, and laughs. Her laugh is much louder than Mom's. "That's incredible. I love it!"

A fine mist rises into the air from a diffuser in the kitchen, and the room smells like flowers. According to Aunt Maggie, it's a mixture of lavender and geranium. *Lavender's blue, dilly dilly . . .*

"You know, Harrison, since you like magic so much, you're going to *love* what Muse has in store."

"What do you mean?" I walk around the kitchen island and sit on the stool next to her.

The reddish-orange cliffs outside the kitchen window rise like giants beyond the house. The desert daylight is like staring directly into stage lights, even from inside. But then something in the sky blocks the sun.

"Well, you're here in time for festival season," Aunt Maggie says. "We have a lot of festivals and art events in Muse. A sidewalk chalk event called Walk and Chalk is coming up in September. You can claim a space on the street and make your own chalk art alongside a village full of artists."

I'm waiting to find out how that has anything to do with magic.

"They have food trucks and live music. And, of course, it's good business for the gallery. But the Muse Art Festival in October tops them all," she says. "And *that's* where the magic comes in."

I'm expecting her to say there's a festival for magicians next.

"There's an art contest that's part of the Muse Art Festival," she continues. "Your mom wanted to enter it once."

I think of the clay sculpture Mom made of the two of us and Mom's sunset painting on the panels at James's Art Collective. "But she didn't ever do it?"

Aunt Maggie shrugs. "She said that I have the gift for visual arts in the family and she'd stick with performing." She sips her weird-smelling green drink. "You can enter a piece of your own artwork in the contest," she continues, "and maybe have a chance to win a wish."

"Win . . . a *wish*?"

Something rustles again outside the windows.

"Who grants the wish?" Mom had said something

about a muse in the red cliffs. And she'd said something about wishes, too.

Aunt Maggie takes another sip of her drink.

"The people here voted to change the name of the town from Red Cliffs to Muse twenty years ago, because they noticed how inspired everyone is to create here. You know what a muse is right?"

A tingle creeps over my arms and up my neck. Because of mom's friend Sylvania and James's guitar playing and the memory of green and blue light on the art panels, I'd never forget about muses.

"They're from the Greek myths," I say.

"Yes, there are the Muses in Greek mythology. I believe there are nine of them. They inspired mortals in music, art—even astronomy. But in this town, we don't believe muses are only in Greek myths. They may not even be in the form of goddesses like the stories say. I think many parts of the Earth are inhabited by magical beings, and there's a powerful muse in this canyon."

I remember Mom sitting on the edge of my bed, talking about this town and the nearby Red Cliffs Canyon. "Mom always told me there's magic here."

"Well, she was right." Aunt Maggie nods.

"A guy we knew on the Mall in DC—James—he talked about muses, too. Mom liked to go to this spot on the Mall where people painted pictures outside. I went with her one day, and she was painting a sunset, and I saw something. . . ."

My aunt leans forward in her seat. She doesn't seem to notice the flapping noises and the shadows outside the windows. "Go on."

"It was a green and blue light, but it moved around. Another kid saw it, too. It showed up on the art panels. I noticed it when James started playing his guitar."

Aunt Maggie sits back and wipes at the dried clay on her cheek with the back of her hand. "I'm not an expert on muses of the world, but it sounds like you've unofficially met one."

"I haven't ever told anyone else about it. I thought maybe it was an illusion."

"Did you feel different when you saw it—like you could do something you never thought you could before?"

"Maybe. Somehow it made me feel good about singing a song for Mom's friend Sylvania—even in a park in front of all those people. I don't usually do stuff like that."

Suddenly, the noise outside spikes, and it becomes flapping and squawking and shadows sailing past the windows. Aunt Maggie's house is under some sort of attack.

She jumps up from her stool and grabs her cell phone from the counter. "Blast those birds!"

"What *is* that?" I shout over the noise.

"Birds in my orchard. They're eating my fruit. I've got to call pest control."

She taps the screen and holds the phone to her ear.

"How does pest control get rid of birds eating your fruit?" I follow her to the front door as she steps into her sandals.

She points at my shoes on the floor and says, "Put your shoes on if you're coming to watch. The concrete is hot enough to fry an egg out there."

I wriggle my feet into my tennis shoes, and something slams into the side window.

Aunt Maggie startles. "Oh! They always do that, and it scares me every time!"

"What happened?"

"These starlings fly right into the glass." She shakes her head.

"Doesn't that hurt them?"

"I've never seen one fall to the ground. Maybe it just dazes them." Then into her phone she says, "Byron? Yeah, it's Maggie. Can you come right away? I've got a flock in the orchard."

After she hangs up, she says to me, "It's called 'bird abatement.' It's pest control by birds, for birds. Byron and his son send a hawk flying over the orchard, and all the pest birds flee for their lives."

"Wait, *really*? Someone has a trained hawk?"

"Yep. They're on their way. I'm going to spray birds with the hose until Byron gets here. You wanna help?"

"Yeah, I wanna help," I say, suddenly excited about being in the desert, even if it means Dad isn't here with me. For now.

I follow Aunt Maggie into the blinding sun and the blast of dry heat. It's not even nine in the morning, and it feels like a hundred degrees already. We head down the porch steps and angle across the desertscape yard toward the squawking of the birds. The sky is so vibrant blue here it almost doesn't seem real. And everywhere you look, the red-orange cliffs rise against the cloudless blue sky like they should have their own movie soundtrack. This place feels powerful, like maybe—just maybe—it *could* be inhabited by a muse.

CHAPTER 7

TIP SEVEN: ANIMALS CAN BOOST YOUR ACT

Aunt Maggie unrolls a long hose from the house and twists on a sprayer nozzle. She turns the faucet and motions for me to follow her. I pick up a back section of the hose and help her drag it to the orchard on the unfenced side of the house. Her orchard has peach and apple trees, and all of them are full of birds.

"What else do you know about this magical contest?" I ask.

"I have some firsthand experience with it. I can tell you about that later." Aunt Maggie pulls the hose into the center of the orchard. "But you should know that a wish hasn't been granted for a few years. People think something has gone wrong, but they don't know what. The latest talk at the gallery is that the muse has grown tired of the same types of art and is waiting for something truly special. I thought maybe you'd want to give it a shot."

Aunt Maggie sends a spray of water into a peach tree. The birds scatter, swarming into the sky as the water hits the branches.

"Starlings are hard to get rid of," she says. "But if you don't do something, they'll pick the fruit to pieces, and there'll be nothing left that's worth having."

"What do you have to do to enter this magic contest?" I holler over the squawking birds and the water showering on the leaves.

"Entry forms are due at the end of September. You can choose from lots of different categories. I'll help you if you like."

I've never entered an art contest in my life. I don't know how I'd have a chance of winning—even *if* this muse exists and starts granting wishes again. But what if I could have magical help to find a way for Dad to live with me instead of on the road? I also wish I could see Mom again, but the way things used to be—and no wish can possibly do that. Still, what if a wish could help Dad and me feel better somehow?

The starlings gather above us, moving together, circling around, and diving for the orchard again as Aunt Maggie sprays another tree.

"What if we turn up the pressure?" I ask, taking a step in the direction of the garage and the water spigot.

"If we spray too hard, it'll knock the fruit out of the tree," she says. "Swift Bird Abatement is pretty fast. They'll be here soon."

"They'd *better* be fast if they named their company that!" The birds have grown so loud that I have to yell to hear myself.

My aunt aims the hose at a peach tree, and the starlings leave its branches for a moment. Mist hits me head-on. I gasp in surprise, but the water feels so good in this dry heat.

"Sorry!" she says.

I laugh as the water drips down my shirt.

Aunt Maggie laughs with me. "Feels good, huh?"

I wipe my eyes with the back of my hand. "Yeah, it does."

"You should go for a swim in the pool later!" She sprays me again. We both let out another laugh, but mine is more of a sputter. "There you go," she says when I'm completely soaked.

I lunge at her to grab the hose, but she pulls it out of reach. I scramble around the other side of the trees, scattering a few birds picking at fallen apples. She turns to spray me again, but I grab the hose and fold one section, pinching off the water flow. She looks at the sprayer for a second. I let go of the hose at just the right moment, and she gets a face full of water.

"Good one, Harrison!"

A white van pulls up in front of the house. "Oh, hooray! They're here," she says.

The side of the van is wrapped with an advertisement.

SWIFT BIRD ABATEMENT,
featuring trained Harris's Hawks and Saker Falcons
Let OUR birds eliminate YOUR bird problems

Aunt Maggie pulls the hose over to me. "Turn the water off and roll that back up on the hose reel, would you? I need to talk to Byron."

I drag the hose toward the house, watching the guy Byron get out of the van. A dark-haired kid gets out of the passenger side. He and Byron both have light-brown skin that looks like it tans easily. I think the kid might be close to my age, but he's taller than me—like Creed. I immediately stand as tall as I can, wrap the hose over my shoulder a few times, and carry it the rest of the way. I roll the hose up on the hook and take a few steps toward the van in the street.

The kid slings a bag over his shoulder and pulls a long T-shaped pole from the van. Then he opens the door to a large container and reaches inside. When the kid turns around, I get a perfect view of the brown-and-red bird perching on his gloved hand. The bird is the size of a crow, but much more impressive. I stop in the middle of the gravel yard.

The kid raises his arm a little, and the bird flies from

his hand to the pole, perching on the top bar. I wonder why the bird doesn't fly away. The kid picks up the pole and carries it toward the orchard, with the bird settled high above his head as he walks. I follow him.

Suddenly, in a startling burst of speed, the hawk flies into the sky. I shade my eyes from the sun and follow the hawk's red and brown feathers against the bright blue. It soars for a moment and then dives straight down, scattering the flock from the trees in a noisy black cloud. They're like a giant version of the bug swarms in Virginia. The hawk snatches a starling from the air with its sharp talons.

"Whoa!" I exhale in surprise.

The kid runs to the spot where his hawk lands with its catch. He grabs some red meat from the bag he's carrying and holds it in his glove. The hawk flies to his hand and begins tearing apart the meat as the kid sneaks the dead starling into his bag. The hawk doesn't seem to know or care that its catch is gone.

"What did you give it to eat?" I ask the kid.

"Jackrabbit," he says. It takes him a few extra seconds for the word to come out. His face tightened up, sort of pained, like the word was stuck behind his teeth. But then he got past the *j*, and the rest of the word came. "And this is Pepper. He's m—male." This time, he drags out the *m* sound.

"Oh." I've never heard someone talk this way before.

Pepper's sharp, curved beak has blood on it from the raw meat. It's gross but still amazing. This kid is holding a real live hawk.

I want to ask him more questions about his bird and how he trained it, but I wonder if it's awkward for him to answer me when his words get stuck like that. So I just say, "That is really cool."

The kid smiles and nods.

Pepper finishes the meat and flies back to the perch. I follow the kid as he carries his hawk back to the van. He slowly tilts the T-shaped pole until the perch is lower than his hand. He holds his fingers just above Pepper's talons, and the hawk steps up.

I forget my earlier thought to not ask more questions. "What's your name?" I say.

The kid places Pepper back inside the large container and shuts the van door. His forehead wrinkles up, and his lips look sealed together while he tries to answer me. He makes an *m* sound. It only lasts a few seconds, because the man Byron moves closer to us and says, "His name is Marco."

Marco stops the process he was going through to tell me his name. The pained expression leaves his face, but now he seems embarrassed. Marco pulls the glove from his hand and clenches it tight in his fist. He strides around the van and gets in the other side next to his hawk's container.

"Marco's stutter makes it difficult for him to get his words out sometimes," Byron says.

Aunt Maggie glances at Byron like she's about to say something, but instead she opens the front passenger door and pokes her head inside. "Thanks, Marco! You and Pepper make a great team."

Marco nods and gives her a little smile. But he doesn't look back at me again. I'm not off to a great start with making friends in this town.

My aunt pays Byron, and the Swift Bird Abatement van drives away, looping around the cul-de-sac and turning right onto Coyote Way. I'm trying to learn the street names since I'll be walking to the bus stop on Monday.

"Well." Aunt Maggie lets out a big sigh. "That was an eventful morning. The gallery opens at ten. Come on. Eli Taylor is supposed to drop by this morning with a new painting. Maybe you can get reacquainted with his daughter, Chloe, before you start school together."

"Chloe?" I'm not sure I'm ready to meet her again. This day is already off to a weird start. Maybe it would be better to wait until, I don't know, never?

"Oh, come on. You remember Chloe, right? You two played together that entire summer when you lived here."

We walk across the red gravel, and a light breeze spins the metal sculptures.

"I remember Chloe, but we were *five*." What I do

remember is that we got into trouble sometimes by getting into her dad's art supplies, and that I had a crush on her. A five-year-old crush. I feel like never leaving the house again when I think of it. What if she remembers that?

"Oh, I bet if you really tried, you could remember *some* details from when you were five. That was when your mom performed at the Red Cliffs Amphitheater. You remember that, right?"

There *is* something about the amphitheater that I remember. It came to me when Dad and I drove into Muse two days ago. Mom took me into the tunnels below the stage and showed me where the performers would cross underground from one side to the other so the audience wouldn't spot them. There was no "backstage" because the theater was in the open and the canyon cliffs were the backdrop. Down there, somewhere in the tunnels, Mom let me place my handprint next to hers on a wall. I remember the sticky paint and the cold cement. I remember Mom's hand holding mine.

But I don't want to talk about this—or about Chloe—so I do my best to be Harrison the Magnificent and stay mysterious.

"I really don't remember."

"Oh," Aunt Maggie says, holding the front door open for me. The air-conditioning chills my wet clothes. "Well, trust me. You and Chloe were best friends that summer. Two little mischief-makers. Anytime you two got into my clay or into Eli's paints at his studio, the joke of the gallery was that you'd always say, 'Chloe did it.'"

"Aw," I groan. "Stories like that aren't going to do me any good when school starts."

"I won't mention it again, Harry." She drags a finger in an X across her heart. "Promise."

I smile.

"Dry off," she says, pointing upstairs to the guest room that's now my bedroom. "But hurry. I don't want to keep Eli waiting."

I change into dry clothes and discover that I absent-mindedly put Aunt Maggie's deck of cards in my pocket before going out to the orchard. Her cards are soaked. Magicians really do go through decks quickly. I rub a towel over my wet hair and meet my aunt in the kitchen.

"I had your cards in my pocket out there," I say, placing the wet pile on the counter. "I'm sorry, but they're ruined. I can't do tricks with warped cards. I'll buy you another deck."

"Don't worry about that. I'm just sorry you don't have a deck you can use today. Those magic tricks of yours are a great way to break the ice."

I think she means it's a good way to start a conversation with Chloe, and I've already thought about that. I pull my own cards from my pocket, smiling. "I've got these."

"Oh! You asked to use *my* deck so I wouldn't think you'd put the cards in order or something. Right?"

"Right. Have to make it convincing."

We get in Aunt Maggie's car, and she drives us to the end of Joshua Circle and turns left onto Coyote Way. We pass a new housing development, or what *will* be a development once more houses go up. A large sign in front of a sales office says:

LIVE YOUR ARTISTIC DREAMS
AT CACTUS GULCH

Lots and custom home design
by Muse's premier homebuilder,

BECKHAM DUNN

The sales office has flags and an artificial waterfall in front. More flags and another sign advertise a model home down the street. Something about the home pulls at my heart and floods my head with memories. It's the front door. I'd recognize that cozy, soft reddish-brown color anywhere.

It's Mulberry Silk. I remember going to the paint store with Mom and choosing samples to take back to the Woodbridge house. We sang along with show tunes blasted from inside the house and ate raspberry sherbet on the steps when we were done.

I immediately memorize how we got here and where we drive next. I want to come back to the house with the Mulberry Silk front door.

CHAPTER 8

TIP EIGHT: OPEN WITH AN ICEBREAKER

Aunt Maggie's art gallery is located halfway around a curved road called Oasis Lane—the main street through the art village. We park in a small lot at the entrance to the street, and we walk past a café called the Prickly Pear, a pottery studio, a tourism office, and a path to a botanical garden. The gallery is called Gallery 29. A giant number twenty-nine hangs over the front door, which dings when we open it.

"Eli texted and said he's on his way over," Aunt Maggie says. I don't remember being here before, but I remember the smell of wood mixed with spices and plants. The gallery is full of wind chimes, paintings, and sculptures.

One of the sculptures on a glass tabletop appears to be broken, but when I get closer, I realize that the artist designed it in multiple pieces. It looks as though a woman is sitting in a lake and the glass tabletop is the water. Her head and shoulders are one piece, and her long hair "floats" behind her on the glass. Her two bare knees sit a few inches away and are two more pieces. The way the sculpted pieces are placed, it seems like the woman sank right down into liquid glass.

"Isn't that brilliant?" Aunt Maggie asks, noticing that I'm staring at the sunken woman.

"I thought it was broken." I kind of want to move the pieces around, but instead, I pull my cards from my pocket and do an overhand shuffle.

Aunt Maggie shows me a small table in the corner. "What do you think of these?"

The table is covered with colorful stones.

"You can pick them up if you like," she says. "Minerals and gemstones have different properties that people can find useful. Some of our customers buy the larger ones to place on a nightstand. Some want the smaller ones to carry with them."

I pocket my cards and pick up a shiny black rock that reflects like a mirror when I turn it over in my fingers. "What's this called?"

"Ah, that's a great one," she says. "That's obsidian."

I turn the obsidian over with my fingers. I like how smooth and dark it is.

"How about this one?" I pick up a crystallized white

rock. "This is like the formations inside Luray Caverns in Virginia."

"Oh yeah?" Aunt Maggie leans in and examines it. "That's calcite crystal. Luray Caverns has a lot of this, huh?"

I nod, remembering our family trips to the caverns. We'd take a picnic lunch and eat at a table in the woods before going inside. And the inside was amazing. Cathedral-sized rooms, underground lakes, and an organ that made music by gently tapping stalactites until they rang through the acres underground. Mom sang with the organ last time we were there, finding harmonies with the stalactite sounds. It was eerie and awesome at the same time, until Dad discovered he had a tick on his shirt from our lunch in the woods. Everyone laughed while he tried to get it off and capture it in a bag.

Aunt Maggie is staring at me.

I put the obsidian and the calcite crystal back on the table.

"You can have those if you want, Harrison." She presses her lips together the way she did at Marco's dad, Byron—like she wants to say something else. Instead, she looks out the window.

"Eli should be here any minute," she says, walking to the other side of the gallery. "I'm excited for this new series he's been working on."

The obsidian and the calcite crystal are small enough to carry around, so I slide them into the pocket of my shorts with my cards. Just then, someone pounds on the glass side door and yells something. It's a girl holding the leashes of several dogs. She's about my height. She has dark-brown skin, but it's more bronze than Kennedy's. Short, coily black curls frame her face. She widens her eyes and points at my pocket.

"What are you doing?" she yells through the glass.

I shrug at her.

"You just stole those! Don't steal from Maggie!"

My aunt has gone in the back somewhere, and I'm standing alone in the gallery. The girl runs around the front of the building with her many dogs. She holds their leashes with one hand and yanks the front door open with the other. Propping the door with her foot, she stays outside with the dogs and points at me again.

"Who are you, and what are you doing in Twenty-Nine?"

"Twenty-nine?"

She points at the sign above the gallery door.

Oh, right, I think. *The name of the gallery.* The girl has pretty brown eyes, even when she thinks she's yelling at a thief. She also points a lot.

"I'm Maggie's nephew. I'm here with her," I say, my voice sort of crackly.

"You're stealing from your own . . ." The girl stops. "Wait."

A man with a short goatee and buzzed black hair approaches the gallery door. His bronze-brown skin closely matches the girl's. He's carrying something large beneath several padded blankets. "Chloe, I wish you hadn't brought the dogs," he says. "They're such a handful."

This is Chloe? I'm suddenly embarrassed, even though I didn't do anything wrong. I hurry forward and help hold the door open as the man, who I'm pretty sure is Eli Taylor, steps into the gallery with his artwork.

"Thank you, young man." He smiles and then does a double take as he steps inside. He looks at me like he knows me. "Harrison? Is that *you?*"

"Yes," I say.

"*You're* Harrison?" Chloe's eyes go wider.

"Hi, Chloe." What do you say to someone you haven't seen since you were five? I can't think of anything.

Aunt Maggie shows up behind me. "Oh, Eli. I can't tell you how excited I am about this!" Then she adds, "Hello, Chloe. I see you've met Harrison. Again." Smiling at the two of us, she jerks her head at me like I'm supposed to do something.

"It's nice to have you back in Muse, Harrison," Mr. Taylor says. He balances his padded artwork against his side and gives me a solid grip on the shoulder. "I was sure sorry to hear about your mom."

"Thank you." I forgot that people in Muse knew

Mom—and not just the people she performed with at the amphitheater.

Mr. Taylor has a kind smile. "I hope to see you around often."

"Thanks," I say again. "I promise not to make a mess of your paints this time."

Mr. Taylor laughs, and it fills the gallery. "Well, no hard feelings about that." He carries his blanket-covered frame to an empty table, and Aunt Maggie eagerly watches as he unwraps it.

"I wasn't sure I'd be able to finish this in time for the art show we booked for next week," he tells her.

"I never doubted for a minute," she says.

"Inspiration doesn't come as easily as it did before the muse stopped showing up."

I wonder why the town would have had a muse that granted wishes and then why the muse would've left. Did it leave the whole world, or is it just not showing up to the art contest anymore? I notice a flyer taped to the wall by the gallery door. It's about the Muse Art Festival Contest in October. It says BRING BACK THE MUSE. Now I wonder how they think they're going to bring it back.

I'm still holding the door open, but Chloe leads the dogs backward. "Come on," she says to them. "Sherman, Matisse, you can't go in there."

The dogs are weaving in and out of each other, panting and wagging their tails. It's probably a good thing Chloe didn't let them inside. I count six dogs. Although

I'm curious about Mr. Taylor's new painting, and whether or not he has anything more to say about the muse, I follow Chloe outside.

"So, uh, how are you doing, Chloe?"

One of the dogs, the largest one, runs around the other dogs. He tangles all the leashes. "I'm great. Sorry I yelled at you before. I mean, I didn't recognize you." Chloe untangles two leashes and waves the back of her hand at the energetic dog. "Back up, Sherman."

Sherman turns his head sharply and backs up.

"Sit," Chloe says, holding out a closed fist toward Sherman. Sherman sits.

"Wow," I say. "You're good at that."

"Thanks." Chloe smiles really big. I remember that.

"And don't worry about before," I say. "I guess I didn't recognize you at first, either."

Chloe nods. "Haha, true."

She bends down to pet a small terrier with perky ears.

"Is it okay if I pet them?"

"Sure," she says. "They're all friendly."

"I asked my mom and dad for a dog, but we never got one. How did you convince your parents to let you have *six*?"

"Oh." Chloe laughs. "These aren't *all* my dogs. Just Sherman. We adopted him from a lady who couldn't take care of him anymore. I walk the rest of them. It's my summer business."

"People pay you to walk their dogs? That's a smart idea," I say. I kind of wish I had thought of that. Except I don't think I would know how to handle all these dogs myself.

"It's pretty great, isn't it, Sherman?" Chloe speaks to him in a funny voice like she's talking to a baby. She rubs Sherman behind the ears and on his head. Sherman leans into Chloe and closes his eyes, like it's the best feeling ever. "So what *were* you doing in there?" she says to me. "I did see you put those rocks in your pocket."

I pull the calcite and the obsidian from my pocket and hold them out. "My aunt was showing them to me. She said I could have them."

"Oh." Chloe laughs. "Sorry again." I remember her laugh, too. It reminds me of eating grilled cheese sandwiches and watching cartoons when we were little kids. "Well, I need to get these dogs a drink. You wanna come?"

All of the dogs are panting. The sun beats down overhead, and I can only imagine how hot they are. Especially Sherman, who has the thickest fur.

"Sure." My first reaction when I meet someone new lately has been to pull out my card tricks. It's interesting that I didn't need to do that with Chloe. I didn't need to be Harrison the Magnificent with her. "Let me tell my aunt Maggie, though."

I poke my head inside the gallery. Mr. Taylor is hanging his painting on the wall below a permanent metal sign with ELI TAYLOR etched on it in cursive. His painting has the orange and red shades of a canyon, and a small town in front. A shadow spreads over the canyon in the background—the only darkened spot in the painting. On one side of the shadow, light-green waves flow toward the town. On the other side, lightning strikes the cliffs. It looks like the shadow might swallow the town, but maybe the green waves will protect it.

"Cool," I whisper.

Mr. Taylor turns around. "Do you like it?"

"Yeah," I say. "Is that supposed to be the muse?"

Mr. Taylor takes a few steps to view the painting from a different angle. He tilts his head. "Maybe a little too on the nose, huh? Maybe I should've gone with something more subtle."

Aunt Maggie studies the painting with her hands on her hips. "I think it's perfect, Eli. Don't second-guess it."

I hurry to agree with her. "Yeah. I mean, I don't know anything about art."

"But you know what you like and what you don't," Mr. Taylor says.

I nod.

"Aha!" Mr. Taylor exclaims. "Then that's all you need to know."

I'm not sure what to say to that.

"I hope you'll enter the Art Festival Contest, Harrison. We need all the fresh ideas we can find."

"And you think the muse will come back?" I ask.

"Something has to change," Mr. Taylor says, "or nothing changes."

I'm not sure what to say to that, either.

"If you have an idea for an entry—anything at all— I'm happy to help you. I mean, you will make the art. I'll help you know how."

"Um, thank you." I wonder why Mr. Taylor is so eager to help me. Does he think I can fix the muse problem? Maybe he thinks I could win a wish, and he figures I really need one.

"Are you coming, Harrison?" Chloe has opened the door a crack, and some of the dogs are barking at people entering the gallery.

"Sorry about the dogs, Maggie," Mr. Taylor says, shaking his head.

"May I walk the dogs with Chloe?" I ask Aunt Maggie.

"Sure." She smiles at her customers. "You have your phone?"

"Got it."

"Don't go wandering off the paved paths into the desert, and text me first if you want to leave the village."

"Okay." I love that my aunt is trusting me like this.

Mr. Taylor hands me ten dollars. "You and Chloe

can stop at the Prickly Pear and get Royden Lemonade Supremes."

I'm about to ask what Royden Lemonade Supremes are when Chloe hollers, "Harrison! Matisse got away! Can you help me catch him?"

CHAPTER 9

TIP NINE: KNOW HOW THE ILLUSION LOOKS TO YOUR AUDIENCE

C hloe holds the leashes of the five other excited dogs. And I follow Matisse—a little white dog with a stubby tail—across Oasis Lane. Cars would probably fit on the streets in the art village, but no one drives through this part of town. They walk. That's lucky for Matisse. His leash drags behind him, so I just need to get close enough to grab the end of it.

He runs through a chalk drawing, his paws picking up blue dust and leaving prints behind. He's headed for a crowd of people gathering outside the Prickly Pear café. Just before I catch up with him, a man in the crowd sees me chasing Matisse and lunges to grab him.

Matisse darts sideways. He runs through some bushes in the botanical garden and out to the parking lot.

"*Matisse!*" I yell, my throat scratchy and dry from running in this heat.

The little dog stops to sniff at the potted plants around the parking lot's edge. It gives me enough time to get close, but just as I lean forward, he darts away. I've never tried to catch a dog before, but it seems like tiny dogs are especially crafty. He's running down a row of parked cars when a shrill note pierces the air.

Chloe's here with the other dogs on their leashes, and she's holding her thumb and finger in her mouth to make the loudest whistle I've ever heard outside of a Nationals baseball game.

Matisse stops running. Chloe whistles again, and Matisse turns and runs toward her. When his leash drags close to my feet, I grab it and hold tight. Matisse trots in front of me like he's had the best day ever.

"Why . . ." I'm gasping. "Why didn't you just whistle for him like that before?"

Chloe is a little out of breath, too. "I've never called the dogs with a whistle before. I just thought I'd better give it a shot, since he was about to run across Coyote Way."

"You just learned to do that this minute?"

"No," Chloe says. "I've been practicing for a long time. I'm not always able to get it. I guess I got lucky."

"Sorry I didn't catch him sooner." I hand her the end of the leash.

Chloe takes it and holds her closed fist out to Matisse. He sits, and she gives him a small treat from her pocket. The other dogs gather at her feet and also sit for treats.

"You're really good at that," I say. Chloe handles these dogs the way Marco Swift handles his hawk. With some serious skill.

Chloe pulls on the dog leashes a little and says, "Come," and we start back through the botanical garden toward the restaurant.

"I've only met two kids from Muse, and you both are master animal trainers."

"Well, I'm not a *master*. You make it sound like a martial art or something."

I shrug. "I was taking karate back in Virginia. And I've been learning card tricks. I guess that's the first thing that came to my head."

"Karate and card tricks?"

"Yeah."

"That's cool. You should show me some of that sometime."

"The karate or the card tricks?"

"Both," she says.

"Okay." I'm starting to think Chloe's pretty great.

We pass the Prickly Pear's patio seating. Lights are strung across the patio, which is shaded by the buildings, and music plays from outdoor speakers.

"So who else did you meet?" Chloe asks.

"What?" I forgot what we were talking about.

"You said you've met two kids in Muse so far. Who was the other one?"

"A kid with a hawk. His name's Marco."

"Oh, I know Marco! I've never watched him with his . . . Wait, you said he has a hawk? I thought he was a falconer. Don't falconers have . . . falcons?"

"Could be both, I guess."

Chloe leads the dogs around the side of the restaurant by the bathrooms and stops at a water fountain.

"Did you talk to Marco?" she asks.

"Um, yeah. A little." I don't want to talk about Marco's stutter. I once overheard Creed and Josh talking about me after Mom died, when I didn't want to hang out with them for a while. It doesn't feel good to know people are talking about things you can't change.

"He gets stuck on his words sometimes." But that's all Chloe says about it. She pulls six flat discs from her small backpack. She presses her thumbs into one of the discs, and it pops open into the shape of a bowl.

"You wanna help me with these?"

I hold out my hand. "Sure."

Chloe gives me the first bowl, which I fill up at the water fountain. When every dog has its own dish, I ask, "So what's the deal with this town anyway? My aunt Maggie told me something about an art contest." I feel funny asking Chloe about the muse.

Chloe sets a water bowl in front of Sherman.

"Okay, so what you have to know about *that* is that people get pretty crazy about the contest. It's everything."

"Okay."

"No. I mean ev-er-y-thing." Chloe drags out the word.

"Okay." I nod.

"It's been years since anyone has seen the muse"— Chloe leans against the restaurant wall—"but that doesn't stop the town arts council from trying to make the event bigger and better, to get its attention. And people still hope they'll be *the one* to bring the muse back and win a wish."

"So it really *was* granting wishes?"

Chloe nods. "My dad says it was."

Sherman lifts his head from his bowl. Water drips from the tan fur around his mouth.

"Do *you* believe the stories?" I figure I'd better be clear on this, so I don't embarrass myself.

Chloe smiles, and a dimple shows up below her eye. "I know it sounds kind of *out there*—but yeah, I believe them."

Wind chimes hang above us from the beams that form the roof overhang. A slight breeze blows, and the chimes clink together, ringing out different tones.

"What has Maggie told you?" Chloe asks. One of the dogs, a medium-sized one with golden-brown fur, keeps pushing his bowl around with his nose. Chloe be-

gins picking up the dogs' water dishes. I help by collaps-
ing them back down.

"She didn't say much," I say. "We kind of got interrupted."

"Well, this is the tricky part around here. Try to get
her to talk about it more. My dad says that Maggie actually won a wish years ago."

"Do you know what she wished for?"

Chloe shakes her head. "The people who've won
don't talk about it very much." Chloe starts walking,
and the dogs run forward until their leashes stop them.
"I'm going to take them back to their owners. Do you
want to come?"

"Yeah," I say, wiping sweat from my forehead. "But
your dad gave me money for us to buy some kind of
lemonade special."

"Oh, awesome! Royden Lemonade Supremes!"

"Yeah, that was it."

"Do you want to hold their leashes this time, and I'll
run into the Prickly Pear and get the drinks?"

I look at the six dogs, who just had a pretty good
run and a long drink of water, and they're a lot calmer.
"Sure. Do you trust me with them?"

"I think you got this. Just don't let go of any leashes,
and keep a close eye on Fresco." She points to a short-
haired dog with floppy ears. "He likes to eat bird poop."

"Gross."

I give Chloe the ten-dollar bill, she hands me the dogs' leashes, and she hurries into the restaurant.

I watch Fresco, like Chloe told me to, but there doesn't seem to be any bird poop lying around. The dogs and I are standing near a turnoff that goes behind a photography studio. Where the pavement curves, another chalk drawing creates an optical illusion on the ground. The artist drew it with angles and shading that make the ground look like it has cracked open and the pavement is crumbling deep into the earth. From here, it looks like Sherman is about to fall over the edge. Sherman stares at me.

"Hi, Sherman," I say.

Sherman wags his tail. He trots over to me—right over the edge of the chalk drawing's cliff—and he presses against my leg like he wants me to pet him. So I do. I really think I'd like to have a dog.

"Hey," Chloe says when she returns with our drinks. "You all survived."

"Yep," I say. "And Fresco didn't eat any bird poop."

"Well, there you have it. You can handle dogs just fine." She gives me a tall cup of what I think is lemonade, but it has some small green things floating in it.

"Thanks. What's in it?"

"It's lemonade with vanilla, coconut, and mint."

"Oh, the green stuff is mint?" After watching Aunt Maggie make her green vegetable drink this morning, I need to know what I'm getting into.

Chloe takes a big drink and sighs. "It's so good!"

I drink almost half of mine without stopping. I didn't realize how thirsty I was, and it tastes amazing. "You're right! I've never had lemonade like this before."

"Ready to go?" Chloe asks, reaching for the dogs' leashes. "You can walk a few of the dogs, too, if you want."

"Okay, but first, can you take a picture for me with my phone?" I feel a little strange asking, so I explain. "I want to send a picture to my friend Kennedy in Virginia. I mean, I want to show her what I'm doing—you know, to keep in touch."

"You have a girl back home that you want to send pictures to?" Chloe gives me a sly smile that makes me want to crawl into that image of crumbling pavement.

"Yeah. I mean, no. It's not like *that*. She's not our age. I mean, she's an older friend. She used to hang out with me when my dad was at work."

"Oh, like a sitter?"

Creed and Josh used to tease me that Kennedy was my babysitter, until they met her. And then they were jealous they didn't have someone as cool as Kennedy to hang out with nearly every day.

"No, just a friend. A friend with a car. She drove me to karate, and I used to show her my card tricks. And she took my friends and me to the pool sometimes."

Chloe nods. "She sounds great. Where do you want to take the picture?"

"How about over here—with this cool chalk drawing."

77

"Oh yeah. That's perfect."

Chloe and I finish our drinks, and then I hand her my phone with the camera on.

"Do you need me to hang on to the dogs?" I ask.

"Yeah. I don't think I'll take a very good picture while I'm holding on to them"—she rubs the fur on Matisse's back—"and I don't want to lose anyone else today."

So that's how I got a picture of me standing on the top of a very tall cliff with the rest of the earth crumbling away. And that's why the six dogs in the picture with me look like they're somehow floating in the air with their leashes in my hand. Like I magically kept them afloat.

I text the picture to Kennedy with the caption *Harrison the Magnificent levitates six dogs over art village ruins.*

As Chloe and I lead the dogs back to the edge of the art village, she lets me take Fresco and another one of the calmer dogs, named Pearl. I text Aunt Maggie to ask if I can go with Chloe to take the dogs home. She says it's all right.

The road in front of us, Coyote Way, branches off in two directions. On the right, it leads back toward housing developments. The left heads away from the town. I pause at the edge of the road, squinting at the cliffs in the bright sun.

"What's out that way?" I ask Chloe, pointing to the left.

"That goes into Red Cliffs Canyon."

"Is the amphitheater down that road?"

"Yeah, it is. But it isn't open anymore. I mean, they don't have shows there anymore, if you were thinking of going."

With no cars coming in either direction, Chloe and I lead the dogs across the road to a paved path. It curves with the land around sharp black rock piles that Chloe says are lava clumps from an ancient volcano. We head right on the path, back toward Aunt Maggie's neighborhood.

"The amphitheater is the reason you were here that one summer, isn't it?" Chloe says. "I remember your mom was a singer."

I like how Chloe just comes out and says things.

"Yeah, that's right," I say.

"I'll bet you miss her."

I nod. That's right, too.

Chloe takes in a deep breath. "You smell that?"

"What?"

"It's the desert." Chloe smiles at me. "It smells good, doesn't it?"

Mostly, I'm feeling the sun burning the back of my neck. But when I take in a deep breath, I smell hot rocks and dirt, and a peppery smell that's probably the desert plants. I also smell Fresco, because he is a slobbery sort of dog.

"I smell Fresco's breath."

Chloe laughs. "I know what you mean—it's strong! But I mean the rest of it. Do you smell the plants and the red cliffs out here? The sun really brings it out."

"Yeah, I smell it."

"Well, I was thinking that maybe when you feel sad about your mom, you can come out here and know that she smelled this same desert."

I hadn't thought of that before. It makes something tingle on the back of my neck, and I place my hand over it to keep the sun off. "Thanks, Chloe."

"I hope you don't mind that I said that."

"I don't mind," I say. "It was nice, actually."

We reach the end of the paved path and a side street. The Cactus Gulch sign is on the corner. From here, I can see the model home with the Mulberry Silk front door.

I suddenly have that feeling I would get sometimes in Virginia. I'd be doing something that I would normally think was fun, but all of a sudden, I'd want to be alone for a while.

"Do any of your dog clients live that way?" I point at the new development.

"No. Why?"

"I have something I want to do." I pause, holding Pearl's and Fresco's leashes. I shouldn't say I'm going to walk with Chloe and then change my mind, but I really can't help this all-of-a-sudden feeling.

"It's okay, Harrison," Chloe says. "I walk these dogs along this road all the time."

"Are you sure?"

"Yeah. It's no problem." She takes the leashes from me and says, "Come on, puppies. Let's get you home."

"Thanks, Chloe."

"You'll be at school on Monday, right?" she says.

"Yep. See you there."

Chloe crosses the side street with all six dogs, and I stay on the corner by the sign, wondering if maybe I hurt her feelings with wanting to be alone.

I pull the crystallized calcite and the smooth obsidian from my pocket. The sun beats on me and the rocks, and I feel part of the desert by holding them. I'm just thinking I should text Aunt Maggie again when Kennedy texts me back.

Kennedy: Harrison, this is awesome! Who took that picture for you?

Me: Chloe. She's a girl I knew when I lived here before.

Kennedy: Cool! And where did all the dogs come from?

Me: Chloe walks the dogs to earn money. It's kind of her own business.

Kennedy: Smart girl. I hope you and Chloe have fun.

I look up from my phone in time to notice a small tortoise right in the middle of the road. It inches forward, stretching its neck and opening its mouth as it creeps along. I move closer. Its wrinkled little legs move toward the dirt and the desert bushes. I'm curious whether or not it'll be able to climb up and over the curb, but a big SUV is coming down the street. It's going to turn, and it will hit the tortoise if I don't do something fast.

CHAPTER 10

TIP TEN: FIND A GOOD PRACTICE SPACE

The lady driving the SUV is wearing sunglasses, and I can't tell if she sees me waving wildly at her to stop. I race to the tortoise and carefully lift it with one hand on each side of the shell, keeping it low to the ground and running up and over the curb.

The lady slams on the brakes. She rolls down the window. "I'm so sorry! Are you okay?"

"Yeah," I say. "This tortoise was in the street. It wasn't going to make it across in time." I place the tortoise gently in the dirt, facing away from the road.

"Oh dear!" The lady lifts up her sunglasses. She has really long eyelashes and bright-purple eye shadow that stands out against her fair skin. "That was kind of you to rescue the tortoise. There's a reserve not far from here, and it must've gotten out. I'll call the wildlife service and let them know. I should watch more carefully." Her big eyes look frightened. She may be thinking what would've happened if she hadn't seen *me* in time. "Do you live around here? I don't think I've met you before."

"I just moved here," I say. In Virginia, I'd never tell a complete stranger where I live. I'm not going to start now.

The lady smiles and nods. "Oh. Well, welcome to Muse. Have a nice day."

"Wait," I say before she rolls up her window. Although that fancy lemonade was refreshing, I've been out in the sun long enough that I really need some water right now. Not telling this lady where I live is one thing. Dying of thirst is another. "Do you know where I can get a drink of water?"

She points at the Cactus Gulch sales office. "I'm headed to work right there. We have bottled water if you want to come on over."

"Okay, thanks," I say.

"My pleasure." She dials a number on her cell phone, and I watch the tortoise continue its slow steps into the desert. The lady tells the wildlife service where to find the tortoise as it disappears behind a large rock. Then she drives her SUV to the office and waves me over before heading inside the building. I cross the street, past the flags and the waterfall, to the sales office door.

It's air-conditioned inside and smells like new carpet. A dish full of saltwater taffy sits on a desk by a nameplate that says TABITHA. The lady is in another room, with large drawings of homes on the walls. All the homes are one-story designs with a rectangular shape and a flat roof. Their colors match the rocks and dirt of this desert. Lots of orange and brown. Along the back wall of the room is a counter with baskets of snacks and a small fridge.

The lady opens the fridge and says, "Help yourself."

"Thanks." I take one of the bottles and guzzle the cold water until I have to stop to breathe.

"Take another one for later," the lady says.

"Are you Tabitha?" I ask, pulling another bottle from the fridge.

"Yes, I'm Tabitha. I'm the Realtor for the Cactus Gulch homes. You know anyone who wants to buy a house?" She laughs.

"Maybe," I say. If I want Dad to move here with me, we'll need a house of our own.

Tabitha picks up a brochure from the table and hands it to me. She has long painted nails. "Well, you can take that and have a look at the model home down the street if you like. Tours inside the model are scheduled with me, so have the interested people give me a call. My number is on the back there."

I take the brochure. It shows people living in houses like the ones pictured on the walls: an older couple with golf clubs, a man painting in his studio, a mom and a dad with some kids.

"Do you need anything else? Need to use the phone to call home?" Tabitha asks. "I wouldn't want you to get lost wandering around the desert by yourself."

"No, I'm okay. I have a phone." I finish off the first bottle of water and hold it out to Tabitha, and she nods at a recycling bin. I drop the bottle in there. "My aunt knows I'm out here, and I know my way back to her house."

Tabitha tilts her head, and her big eyes seem to peer right through me. "Wait a minute. . . . Who's your aunt?"

I pause. Tabitha is nice enough, but she's still a stranger to me.

"Wait. A. Minute. You look so familiar." Tabitha does a double take and covers her mouth with her hand. Then she slides her hand down and rests it over her heart, like she's holding a feeling in there. "Are you . . . Tess's boy?"

I wasn't prepared for this. I breathe deep against the ache and straighten my shoulders. Harrison the Magnificent doesn't feel sad.

"I'm sorry. I should introduce myself better," Tabitha says. "I knew Tess when she performed at the Red Cliffs Amphitheater. Maggie Winterrose is a friend of mine. We worked together on the town arts council for a few years."

"Oh. That's nice," I say. "And you're right. Tess is my mom."

Tabitha smiles, but her eyes are shiny and soft, and I recognize the way she tilts her head. I can tell she knows something about what happened to Mom, and I know what's coming next. "I'm sorry she—"

"Thanks," I say quickly, to keep her from finishing.

Tabitha clears her throat. "Does Maggie know you're here?" The air-conditioning clicks on, and a cool fruity-scented air fills the room.

"I can text her," I say, pulling out my phone.

Me: I'm not walking home with Chloe anymore. I'm at Cactus Gulch with your friend Tabitha. Is that ok?

Maggie: Yes. Thank you for letting me know. It's fine so long as Tabitha agrees. Is everything all right with you and Chloe?

Me: Yes.

Maggie: Ok. I'll be able to leave the gallery in about an hour. We need to go to the school to finish your registration.

Ugh. Going to a new school on the last Friday of summer vacation is the last thing I want to do. But I send off an *ok* to Aunt Maggie. I reach into my pocket for my cards.

"Would you like to see a card trick?" I ask Tabitha.

Tabitha's long eyelashes blink twice, and she smiles. "Absolutely."

I take the cards from my pocket and ask her to

examine the deck and shuffle them. When she's satisfied, I take the cards back and divide them into three piles, facedown, on the table.

"Now," I say, "pick up the top card on this center pile and place it faceup on either of the other piles."

Tabitha turns over a card and places it on the pile on my left.

"Good. Now, pick up the next card from this center pile and place it faceup on the other pile."

She does. "Do I have to memorize what they are?"

"Nope," I say. "The next card in the center pile is going to be your card. Pick up that card. Don't show it to me. Look at it, memorize it, and then you can place it facedown on any of these three piles."

Tabitha takes her card and follows my instructions. The posters on the walls and the construction sounds outside fade away. I focus on the cards and being Harrison the Magnificent.

We get to the part of the trick where people are always sure I've messed up and gotten it wrong.

"Okay, hold out your fist."

She gives me a pitying look, but she holds out her fist. I turn her hand so her thumb is on top and tell her to use the knuckles of her first two fingers to pinch a small pile of cards that I give her.

"Pinch it tight," I say. "Don't let them drop."

"Got it." She squeezes tight and stares at the pile in her hand.

Then I slap the cards she's holding, and all of them fall to the ground except one.

"Your card," I say, nodding at the card still pinched between her fingers. She turns it over.

"*What?*" Her genuine shock is my favorite part. "How did you do that?" Tabitha says.

I smile and give a little bow.

"That's amazing!" She laughs, looking in disbelief at the card in her hand and the cards I knocked to the floor. I love how a well-performed magic trick can make someone so happy.

"Thank you," I say. And then I add, "You can call me Harrison the Magnificent."

"Harrison," Tabitha repeats, nodding. "I remember you."

The front door of the sales office opens, and Tabitha hands me her card. "Keep doing those tricks. You're very good at that." And she leaves the room to greet the visitor.

I gather all my cards and place them back in my pocket. Tabitha is saying, "Yes, we have several lots still available with a southern view. The model is this design here, and it's unlocked at the moment. You're welcome to go over and have a look around."

I pick up the second water bottle and step into the lobby. The guy at Tabitha's desk has light-brown skin and dark, curly hair. He's wearing glasses and a business suit.

He says to her, "I wanted to see what lots you had left, but I'll have to come back later to tour the model."

I pass Tabitha's desk as I head for the door, hold up the water bottle, and whisper, "Thanks."

"You're welcome," she says to me. "You can come back and show me more of those tricks anytime."

"Okay," I say.

She types something into her phone, her painted fingernails tip-tapping against the screen. Then she opens a book on her desk and shows her customer the design examples.

I leave the sales office and step into the sun. I walk past the splashing waterfall and down the driveway. A weird insect buzz rises from the desert, and the sound of hammering bounces off the cliffs as construction crews build the frame for another flat, rectangular house down the street. One chocolate-brown house near the model home looks nearly finished. The outside of the model home is rust-colored, like the rocks.

Thinking of Mom and the Mulberry Silk–colored door of our Virginia house, I angle across the street.

I look behind me, and the guy hasn't left the sales office yet. I hurry past the flags and through the desertscape yard to the front door of the model home. Glancing back again and seeing no one around, I try the door handle. As Tabitha said, it's unlocked. If I stare only at the door color and nothing else, I feel like I could walk inside and find Mom in there, singing show tunes.

I tell myself I'll only stay a minute. The living room is bright and has a wall covered with windows that reach from the ceiling to the floor. It has a perfect view of Red Cliffs Canyon.

I explore the whole house. The living room leads to a dining space and a big kitchen. Behind the kitchen, a hallway goes to a large bedroom and bathroom and an art studio. On the opposite side of the house is another bedroom, bathroom, and a study with a small fireplace. The living room has a fireplace, too. The back of my neck is still hot from the sun, and I can't understand why they'd need fireplaces in this desert. It's hard to imagine it would ever be cold here.

Every room is decorated with matching furniture, brightly colored rugs on the wood floors, and vases of fresh flowers. The new smell is so different from our old colonial house on the edge of the forest, but the floral scent reminds me of Mom.

I wander to the windows and peer out at the canyon, trying to find the amphitheater. But the theater is probably hidden by the towering rocks. As I stare at the cliffs rising into the sky, a song Mom used to sing pops into my head. It starts in my memory, but gradually I realize I'm hearing it for real. I'm humming it. The music gets louder until I finally sing the words. Before I know how I started, my voice fills the living room.

I'd like to make your golden dreams come true, dear
If I only had my way
A paradise this world would seem to you, dear
If I only had my way

The song was slow the way Mom used to sing it, but I sing it faster and add turns in the notes that sail through the rooms.

You'd never know a care, a pain, or sorrow
If I only had my way
I'd fill your cup of happiness tomorrow
If I only had my way

I hold out the last note for a long time. I feel like my voice has been shoved tight and small inside me for so long, and I never expected it would be such a relief to let it out.

A dog's barking startles me from my last note. It's coming from outside the back patio doors in the kitchen. I crouch low behind the furniture. Maybe there's someone out there with the dog. I don't want to get caught being in here without permission. I peek out from around the couch. A scruffy dog paces on the other side of the sliding glass doors. It has black fur and pointy ears and isn't wearing a collar.

It barks again. I rush to the doors. "Shh!"

The dog spins around twice and presses his nose to the base of the doors, sniffing at it and whining. He looks up at me again and wags his tail. His pink tongue hangs from his open mouth. He must be so thirsty.

I grab a cup from the dining table, which is decorated for a fancy meal. I fill the cup with water from the kitchen sink and slide the patio door open a few inches. As I slip outside with the cup, the dog jumps on me with his big front paws and licks my arm. I spill half of the water.

"Aw, look what you made me do," I say. "Do you want a drink?" His black fur is chalky from the desert's red dirt. But I don't even mind that he gets it on me.

He whines and spins in a circle. "Sit," I tell him, holding my closed fist out in front of me, like Chloe did with Sherman.

He shoves his nose into my stomach.

"Oof!" He's a big dog. "You want a drink?"

I place the cup on the ground, and he eagerly laps up the water. Then he lifts his head and starts spinning again. I pick up the cup before he can knock it over and break it. I reach for him and rub behind his ears. He pushes into my hand.

"Do you have a home?" I ask him. "It can't be good for you to run loose in the desert like this."

He wags his tail and licks my arm again. He runs down the deck stairs, turns back, and barks at me.

"Shh," I tell him.

He spins again. I think he wants me to play, but there aren't any sticks lying around in this desert backyard.

"I just have to put this cup back."

His ears perk up, and he waits by the bottom step.

"Stay." Maybe he will learn the word if I say it when he's already being still.

I slip inside the house, dry the cup with my shirt, and place it back on the dining table.

My phone rings.

It's Aunt Maggie.

"Hello?"

"Harrison, where are you? Tabitha texted and told me you left over twenty minutes ago."

"Oh, um . . ." Shoot. "I'm still at Cactus Gulch, just . . . looking around."

"Listen, I know you probably want some independence, but this is a desert and you don't have sunscreen or water. Besides, I need to take you to the school."

"Tabitha gave me water," I say, watching the dog pace at the bottom of the deck stairs. He lifts his head high in the air and sniffs toward the canyon. "But you're right about the sunscreen."

"I'm getting in the car now, and I'll meet you at the Cactus Gulch sign, okay?"

"Yep, okay." I glance around the model home to be sure I didn't leave any evidence behind, and I exit out the sliding glass door.

"Aunt Maggie? Are you still there?"

"Yes."

The dog rushes at me, all excited, but I turn sideways before he shoves his nose into my stomach again. His tail thumps against my leg.

"I found a dog, and I think he's a stray. If I can get him to come with me, can we take him back to your house? Maybe find out if he has an owner?"

"Be careful, Harrison. Does he seem friendly?"

I hurry down the steps with the dog at my heels. Then he runs forward and back, like he wants me to follow him.

"Oh, he's really friendly."

"I'm not making promises about whether or not you can have a dog," Aunt Maggie says, her car beeping in the background, "but I will help you with this if you can get the dog to come with you."

"Thank you!" I say. "See you in a minute."

"Hey, boy," I say to the dog. He's too excited and won't stay still long enough for me to get a hold on him. But without a collar and leash, I'm not sure I could hold on to him anyway. For now, he's staying with me. We walk away from the house toward the canyon. Leaving from the back of the house hides me from view for a little while.

"I need to call you something," I say to the dog. He trots ahead of me a few paces, but when I speak to him, his pointy ears turn toward my voice. "Do you have a name?"

He acts like he owns this desert and like *he's* leading *me*. He skirts around a sharp black lava clump that matches his fur, and I know what I want to call him.

"Obsidian," I say. "How do you like that?"

If the way his ears move is any sign, he's listening to me.

"Obsidian. That's your name when you're with me, okay?" He glances behind to make sure I'm still following him, but he's heading off the wrong way—through the desert brush toward the canyon instead of toward Coyote Way and the paved path.

"Obsidian!" I call to him. "Hey, boy!" I slap my leg to get his attention, and he turns. "We have to go this way." I slap my leg again. "Come!"

Obsidian rushes toward me, but he stops before I can grab hold of him. He looks at my face and then at my feet and then at my face again. I imagine him saying, *You, move your feet*.

He barks at me.

"Come with me, please," I say.

He barks again, but this time, it's a low snort. I don't know dogs very well yet, but I think he's frustrated with me. Obsidian turns and runs full speed toward the canyon. I call him, but he doesn't come back.

CHAPTER 11

TIP ELEVEN:
SILENCE IS POWERFUL

A unt Maggie pulls up to the corner of Coyote Way and Cactus Gulch Lane a few minutes later, and Obsidian is no longer in sight.

"I think you've had enough sun for one day," she says when I open the car door. "Do you feel okay?"

"Yeah." My cheeks always get red when I'm hot or when I exercise. It doesn't always mean I'm sunburned.

My aunt looks past the open door as I get inside. "What happened with the dog?"

"He ran off. I tried to get him to come with me, but he had his own ideas. He's pretty big." I wipe the sweat off my forehead with the back of my hand. "I didn't have a way to hold on to him."

"Well, if you find him again, let me know. A lot of people around here have microchipped their pets. If we

97

can get the dog to a vet, they can check and see if he has an owner."

"Okay," I say, leaning close to the air-conditioning vent as Aunt Maggie puts the car in drive.

I watch out the window for Chloe. But she's probably got all the dogs back to their owners by now.

My phone buzzes.

> **Dad:** Hi there. I'm on a break from my production meetings. How is your second day in Muse going?
>
> **Me:** Pretty good. I met Chloe and Mr. Taylor again. Do you remember them?
>
> **Dad:** I do remember them. They're a great family.
>
> **Me:** Chloe took a cool picture of me in the art village with the dogs she was walking. I'm sending it to you.

I send Dad the picture of me and the levitating dogs. A typing bubble shows up as Dad types something, but then it disappears.

The land near the road rises and falls with the sharp lumps of black rock between occasional buildings.

"Chloe says those are lava rocks," I say.

"Yes. These are lava fields," Aunt Maggie says, "from an extinct volcano."

"Is this where the lava tubes are? The caves you told me about?" I stretch tall in the seat to see around the cars next to us. Red Cliffs Middle School isn't actually located in the town of Muse, which Aunt Maggie says is too small to have its own middle school. The school is in Ivins, a nearby town.

"The lava tubes are at the Lava Flow Overlook in Snow Canyon. Do you want to go sometime?"

"Yeah," I say. "But I'd like it better if we went when Dad comes back."

"That's a good plan," Aunt Maggie says.

> **Dad:** That's a great picture! It's amazing what artists
> can do to create an illusion. Also, that's a lot of dogs!
> **Me:** Yeah.

I kind of want to tell Dad that helping Chloe with the dogs made me want a dog. I want to tell him about the stray I found and lost today. But I remember how Mom said that we should get a dog, and we never did, so I decide not to bring it up.

> **Me:** Did you find out if you have a break before
> October to come back to Muse?
> **Dad:** I checked it out in our meeting today. I really
> think the first week of October is the soonest I can
> take some time off. I'll be in Arizona, heading out to
> California, so I can visit you for a few days on the way.
> **Me:** That's a long time from now.
> **Dad:** I know, Harrison. I'm sorry.

"Who are you talking to?" Aunt Maggie says, startling me.

"It's Dad."

"Oh?"

"He says he can't come visit until October." My voice sounds more disappointed than I want it to. I clear my throat and show her my Harrison the Magnificent smile. "But the weather will still be good for hiking then, right?"

"Yes. People hike here in October all the time." She smiles back at me and exits out of a traffic circle. The school is straight ahead. The sign in front says RED CLIFFS MIDDLE SCHOOL—A CHARTER SCHOOL FOR THE ARTS.

"And the art contest is in October, right?" I ask.

"Yes, it is!"

I go back to texting Dad.

> **Me:** Do you know anything about the art contest they have here?
>
> **Dad:** Yes, I know a little.
>
> **Me:** People here say that magic used to happen at the contest.

A typing bubble shows up, then disappears, and shows up again. It's weird how a typing bubble is like watching someone think.

> **Dad:** Your mom sometimes talked about that.

Even in a text, I can feel the heaviness when Dad mentions Mom. I can feel it all the way from Las Vegas.

CHAPTER 12

TIP TWELVE: NOT EVERYTHING IS WHAT IT SEEMS

Aunt Maggie turns into the parking lot and parks far from the school entrance, where a small tree provides a little shade.

"Will you tell me more about the art contest?" I ask, rubbing the polished edges of the obsidian rock with my thumb. "Chloe says you won a wish. Is that true?"

"It's true," she says.

"No way!"

"Yes." She laughs. "I wouldn't be living here, running my own art gallery, if it weren't true."

"Did my mom know about this?"

"Yes, she did."

I can't believe this. "Was she here when it happened?"

"No. She was living in New York. It was before she had you and you all moved to Virginia."

"What was the muse like? What was your winning art entry like? What did you wish for?"

"Whoa there." Aunt Maggie laughs again and motions for me to get out of the hot car. We sit on the curb, in the tree's shade.

"You'll have a hard time finding two people who can answer your first question the same way. I think the canyon muse is unique for everyone. It may even look different to different people. And it does what muses do—it inspires. The answer to someone's wish is personal, because it comes in the form of an idea, and that will depend on the person."

"An *idea*?" That sounds like a lot of work. It takes ideas to come up with something to enter in an art contest in the first place. And then the magical wish is only another idea? It's like you have to work for the wish part, too. "Why can't the muse just give someone what they want? I mean, how is an idea *magic*?"

"Aw, now"—my aunt pats my shoulder—"it's still magic. It hasn't happened for a few years, but it was definitely magic when it did."

"Chloe said it's been a lot of years."

Aunt Maggie looks up at the tree branches like she's doing the math. "I suppose she's right. But it doesn't seem that long ago to me."

"What did you enter in the contest, and what was your wish? Can you tell me?"

She nods.

"I was driving through here, on my way to visit your mom in New York—before you were born. I'd had some disappointments in my life and was feeling pretty lost. I saw the signs for Muse and the art festival. They had music, good food, and the art contest. I didn't know anything about magic or the prize for the winner, but I had some pottery packed up in my car, and I thought, 'Why not?' I pulled into Muse on the afternoon of the festival, selected one of my pottery pieces, and took it to the sign-in desk."

"You didn't even live here when you entered?"

"Nope." Aunt Maggie brushes away some ants crawling between us on the curb and flicks some off my shoe.

"Did it bother people that you were a stranger, some-one new to the town, and you won a wish?"

"I don't know, but I don't think the muse cares where someone is from. Besides, I wasn't the only one who won a wish that year. Sometimes, multiple people win."

I like those odds.

"And what did you wish for?"

"I think I actually made my wish when I pulled out that piece of pottery from my car, more than at the mo-ment of the contest. I wished for a way to share my love of art with others. Not just my own work, but in a community of artists. I wanted to find a place I felt at home. I'd been moving from job to job and never felt settled. I wished to belong somewhere."

"That's a big wish."

"You're right," Aunt Maggie says. "And when I saw that strange light over my entry and followed it into the desert, I got the idea for Gallery 29. And I got the ideas for how to make it happen."

I inhale deeply. I need an idea that big.

"I think people are brought to this place when they need it," she says. "Or maybe, the muse needs them. Unfortunately, we don't know why the muse hasn't shown up for a while. I still think it could return." She glances at her watch and stands up. "Well . . . you ready?"

"To start a new school year at an arts school in a new town?" I give her my look of mystery. "Never."

✛   ✛

Red Cliffs Middle School is a lot smaller than my school in Virginia. A few students are wandering around with slips of paper that tell them where their classes are. They seem younger than me, and I'll bet they're the new sixth graders. I'm going into seventh, but since I'm new, I'm going to look like a clueless sixth grader, too.

Aunt Maggie acts like she's been here before. She strides past the front office to a big commons room with music playing. She motions for me to follow her and approaches a man sitting behind one of the tables. He has wavy blond hair and wears glasses. His T-shirt sleeves are rolled up, and it shows a sharp tan line and part of a tattoo peeking out on one arm. I can't tell what the tattoo is supposed to be exactly, but I think it's cursive.

"Hi, Maggie," he says with a smile.

"Hi, Sam," she says. "So they've got you working orientation, huh? How have you been?"

"Can't complain," he says. "And who is this?"

"This is my nephew, Harrison Boone. He should be all registered, except we were told he needs to choose one elective."

"Hi, Harrison," the guy says. "I'm Mr. Bradley. I'm one of the art teachers here."

"Hi."

"Let me just pull up your information." Mr. Bradley types on a laptop. "Your last name is Boone?"

"Yes."

He types that in and says, "Maggie, if you're up for it, I'd love to have you come back and do another pottery unit with my class. The students really enjoyed it last year."

"I'd be happy to." My aunt tucks a bit of her loose hair behind her ear, and I can see why a guy like Mr. Bradley might think she's pretty.

"Great!" Mr. Bradley smiles at Aunt Maggie. "I'll be

in touch soon about that." He glances back at his laptop screen.

I pull my cards from my pocket and shuffle them.

"Here we are. Harrison Boone. You're going into seventh grade?"

"Yes."

"Your schedule is all set, except for your arts elective. We focus a lot on the arts here, so we have several options for you to choose from."

"They have a really good choir," Aunt Maggie says to me, a little louder than I would've liked. "Does that count as an elective?"

Mr. Bradley nods. "Yes, it does. The choir class meets fifth period. But Harrison has PE fifth period. We'd have to move some things around."

"Oh, what about jazz band?" My aunt is reading a list of classes on the table. "I don't think many middle schools have their own jazz band."

"I don't play an instrument," I say. She knows that.

"But the jazz band always needs singers. That's what I meant. You could sing." Aunt Maggie heard me sing with Mom when she came to visit us in Virginia. I was ten.

"Our jazz band director teaches a great class where you'll learn about jazz musicians and theory, but you'll have to commit to some after-school rehearsals, too," Mr. Bradley says. "You know, if you like performing, we have an excellent theater program, too."

I've never performed except with Mom.

I do a weave shuffle with my cards and shove down the lump in my throat. I notice Marco Swift on the other side of the room, with a girl and a dark-haired lady. They all look kind of alike, so I think maybe that's his mom and sister. He's showing the girl where the doors to the gym and the cafeteria are. I wonder how it would be to have a brother or sister. It seems like losing Mom, moving here, Dad leaving, and starting school would all be so different if I had someone going through it with me.

"Harrison?" Mr. Bradley says.

I look back at him. "Um, I'd rather not do any singing or the stage stuff." I can tell that Aunt Maggie is watching me with a sad expression. I want to tell her that I'm not a wilting houseplant.

"Got any classes for magicians?" I ask, successfully completing a one-handed cut without dropping a single card.

"Sorry, no magic classes." He smiles. "How about art?"

Now, that's a good idea.

"Do you have a class that would help me enter something in the Art Festival Contest?"

Mr. Bradley smiles and leans forward so that his bare forearms rest on the tabletop. He clasps his hands together. "Absolutely," he says. "That would be *my* class."

"Oh."

Mr. Bradley laughs. "It'll be great! We work on lots

of different styles, and your art contest entry counts as your project for the term."

"I'll take art, then," I say.

"Great choice," Mr. Bradley says. He types it into the computer, and my schedule spits out from the printer on a table a few feet behind him. Instead of standing to get the paper off the printer, Mr. Bradley steers away in a motorized chair. His legs are slightly smaller than the rest of him, and they don't seem to be able to move at all. He steers his chair to the printer, spins around, and hands the paper to me. As he reaches his arm out, I can read two of the cursive letters on the tattoo going up his arm: FE.

"Now, all your classes are there in your schedule. Teacher names and room numbers are on the right. Your locker number and combination are at the top."

"Thanks."

"Most of the teachers are in their rooms meeting students today. So pop in and say hello. Except for art class." He pulls his glasses down a little and peers over the top of them. "You've met your art teacher."

I smile. "Nice to meet you."

"Likewise. See you in class on Monday, Harrison," Mr. Bradley says. Then he turns to Aunt Maggie and says he'll call her about that pottery unit, and I realize that I'm taking a class where my aunt will be a guest teacher. I wonder if this is going to get weird.

I find my locker. I try the combination twice, but it doesn't work for me.

Aunt Maggie tries to help. "Did you go right first, and then pass zero to the left before stopping at the second number?"

"What?" I had a locker last year, but I avoided using it. So I'm out of practice with combination locks.

"Here, let me show you. What are the numbers?"

I hand her the paper.

Other kids are walking past the lockers and notice my aunt helping me. And then I find a familiar face.

"Marco!" I call to him. He's with the same dark-haired woman and girl.

He glances in my direction and nods a hello. He's showing the girl where one of her classrooms is.

The woman calls back to me, "He says hello."

That's weird. Marco runs his hand through his hair and says something quietly to her. It looks like a serious conversation, but then a group of students and their parents approaches the same classroom, and the crowd hides Marco from view.

As people file into the classroom, Marco emerges alone and joins me at my locker.

"I thought you were just visiting," he says. "You're going to school here?"

"Yeah. I'm staying with my aunt while my dad is traveling."

"Got it!" says Aunt Maggie as she celebrates opening my locker. "Do you want to try it?"

I take the paper from her and exchange a glance with Marco that says we both understand this embarrassment of moms and aunts treating us like little kids.

Marco notices my schedule. "Do you want to see if we have any classes together?"

I turn the paper to show him, and he skims my list.

"PE with M—Ms. Camacho and art with M—Mr. Bradley," he says. He prolongs the *m*, and then it comes out a little explosive. I try not to seem startled when he does it. I've never known someone who speaks this way before. I remember a girl in second grade who stuttered, but unlike Marco, she repeated sounds.

"You're in those classes at the same time as me?"

"Yep."

"Cool."

"Maaarco." The girl he was with before calls him from down the hall. "I need you to show me where my science class is."

Marco glances over at her and back to me. "M—My sister, Adrienne. She's starting sixth grade, and she's . . . nervous about changing rooms for each class." He gets stuck on the *n* in *nervous,* but his face relaxes when he gets past it. "I've been showing her around."

"That's nice of you," I say. Aunt Maggie leans against the lockers, waiting to show me how to manage my combination. I appreciate her, but I still wish I had a brother or sister to do this with.

"So I guess I'll see you," Marco says.

"Yeah. See you."

"Bye, Marco," Aunt Maggie says. Then, as he walks away, she leans in and tells me quietly, "If you have more questions about the muse or the art contest, Marco is the one to ask. He knows more about it than any other kid around."

CHAPTER 13

TIP THIRTEEN: MUSIC CAN SET THE MOOD

The diffuser in the kitchen is spouting a mist that smells like oranges and grapefruits. The dining room ceiling fan clicks as it spins overhead. We ate a vegetarian dinner that Aunt Maggie made, and then, because she could tell I gave it my best shot and was still hungry, she ordered pizza, too. Then she suggested we have some fun with clay.

"Here you go," she says, slapping a large reddish-brown chunk on a tray at the table. She places a small dish of water next to it. "The water is to keep the clay damp and to soften it as you work. Don't use too much or it'll get really muddy and sloppy. Dip your fingers in the water, and then slide them over the surface when you want a sleek texture."

I press my fingers into the lump. It's cool and stiff at

first. "What should I make?" I thought this was going to be kind of a lesson. Since Aunt Maggie makes pottery, I thought she'd show me something at her pottery wheel. But this is okay.

"Create anything you like," she says. "Personally, I like to put on music, close my eyes, and let my mind wander. Usually, something will come into my head. A design, an object, even a feeling. Then I'll open my eyes and start."

"Okaaay," I say.

"What?" Aunt Maggie goes to the counter and turns on her Bluetooth speaker. "You can do it. There's no right or wrong answer here. You aren't going to be graded on what you make. Enjoy it!"

She finds a song on her phone, and folk music with drums and rainsticks starts playing. I pull apart a section of the clay mound and hold it between my palms. It warms up quickly, and I think of how I warmed Sylvania's cold hands this way. My aunt sits across the table from me with her own mound of clay and closes her eyes, listening to the music. I close my eyes, too.

With the lump softening between my palms and the memory of warming Sylvania's cold hands, the image in my head is of the people living on the Mall in the cold. And I think of James, who knitted scarves and mittens to give away, and how he played guitar. I think of James's Art Collective and Mom's painted sunset and the green and blue light that leaped between the art panels. But I don't know how this will help me know what to create. It just makes me sad.

I push into the clay with my fingers, pull on it, and then roll it into a ball. Aunt Maggie's instructions weren't specific enough for me. At least with karate, our instructor gave us steps to follow and we did them. Step back, block, right kick, chop. Done.

I try focusing on the music. The drums seem to be calling something here, or maybe sending something away. The rainsticks and the drums get louder and faster and remind me too much of rain on the car window and the thump of frantic windshield wipers trying to keep up. My heart pounds with an ache I don't want to feel. My toes dig into the thick rug beneath the dining table, and I'm done trying this exercise.

I open my eyes, set the clay back on the tray, and get up from the table.

"I don't want to do this," I say, my voice stiff.

Aunt Maggie calls after me as I take the stairs to my bedroom, but then leaves me alone.

I'd kind of thought that with all the excitement today with the birds in the orchard and meeting Marco and Chloe and finding the model home and the stray dog, that I would avoid this. But the sick feeling has come back anyway. It's a feeling of watching myself. Like this isn't real, that it shouldn't be real. That Mom should still be here, and Dad shouldn't have left, and we should all still be together. I shut the bedroom door to mute the rainstick-and-drum music that reminds me of cars driving in the rain.

+ +

Me: Can you talk?
Dad: What's up?
Me: Can you call me?
Dad: I'm setting up for the show and a film shoot for the news. I can text, though.

I start typing about Mom and the rainstorm and then erase it. Then I start typing about the Cactus Gulch house. I erase that, too.

Me: Aunt Maggie tried to teach me to sculpt something with clay.
Dad: What did you make?
Me: It didn't go well.
Dad: You may not be immediately good at everything you try. You know from your card tricks and karate that you have to practice.

I want to type, "We're not good at getting along without Mom. Maybe we'll get better if we practice together." But I don't.

Me: Yeah.

Dad: I'm sorry I can't talk more right now. But I can call you tomorrow, okay?

Me: Ok

I type "Tess Winterrose" into YouTube and watch Mom's performance at the Kennedy Center, because Dad isn't here to ask me to turn it off.

I glance over at Mom's clay sculpture of us, on the dresser. It's one of the few things I've unpacked since I got here. Next to it is the framed picture of Mom and Dad and me at the red-carpet opening of Mom's show at the Kennedy Center Opera House. Dad and I wore tuxedos with bright-green ties to match Mom's dress.

I fall asleep to Mom's singing for the first time since she died.

CHAPTER 14

TIP FOURTEEN: KNOW WHEN TO STOP A TRICK

L unchtime on the first day of school at Red Cliffs
Middle School is pandemonium. I go with the flow
of traffic, and it takes me ten minutes of standing
in one line before I realize I don't want the hot meal.
The grab-and-go lunch line with fruit, sandwiches, and
chips is at the other end of the cafeteria. I leave the hot
meal line and get in the grab-and-go line behind two
girls wearing cheer uniforms.

Suddenly, speakers overhead play music, and a screen
on the back wall of the cafeteria shows a video of the
student council officers. The video is pretty impressive.
Special effects zoom in on the student council members
one by one, and they welcome everyone to a new school
year. They act out skits to explain the school rules.

The grab-and-go line moves forward, and one kid hollers, "They're already out of chocolate milk!"

Now, the student in the video is talking about the Muse Art Festival.

Mysterious epic fantasy music plays as the student body president looks straight into the camera and says in an attempted movie trailer voice, "Is the wish real, or is it a myth? Any art is accepted, so get working on your projects and get an entry form from Mr. Bradley. Forms are due by September thirtieth!"

The video ends. People cheer for the student council, and the grab-and-go line moves again. I'm almost to the lady who takes the lunch account numbers when I realize someone is waving at me. It's Chloe. She's holding two lunch trays.

I wave back, and she walks over to me.

"Do you want one of these?" She holds out one of the trays with a ham-and-cheese sandwich, barbecue chips, and apple slices. She even has a chocolate milk on there.

"Why do you have two?" I ask.

"I saw you way back there in the hot lunch line. By the time you got your food, you'd only have five minutes to eat it. I just punched in my ID number twice and got two lunches." She practically shoves the tray into my hand.

I take it. "Thank you. How much are the lunches?"

Chloe waves her hand like it's no big deal. "My parents add to my lunch account whenever I ask. Don't worry about it."

"Thanks," I say again. "Maybe I can get you lunch next time."

Chloe smiles. "If you want. But I take the media arts class and help run the sound for these lunchtime presentations, so I'm usually in here early to set up."

At Red Cliffs Middle School, we're allowed to eat lunch outside. Even though it's hot, I could use a break after three hours of class. "Do you want to sit outside?" I ask Chloe.

"Sure," she says.

We leave the building through the lunchroom doors. The desert heat is like an invisible force field radiating off the rocks. There's something about the orange-red cliffs around us that feels alive when I'm near them.

We head toward the soccer field, where some kids are playing games, and find a patch of shade beneath some trees at the corner. Chloe and I sit near some kids who've spread out their drawings to show each other. The kids are talking about making a graphic novel.

"What did you do at your old school?" Chloe asks.

"What do you mean?" I bite into an apple slice.

"I mean, what did you do for fun?"

"My friends and I used to shoot hoops, but then they grew. And I didn't." I pass my hand up and down the length of myself to illustrate my height.

Chloe laughs. "Yeah, but that shouldn't really matter."

"I don't know." I shrug. "I kind of stopped doing fun things for a while."

"Oh." Chloe nods and takes another bite of her sandwich.

Suddenly, I notice Marco sitting on the other side of the graphic novel designers. At first, I think he's watching the kids on the soccer field, but he's actually concentrating on something in the desert, just beyond the grass.

"Hey, Marco," I call to him.

He smiles, but he points at the desert like he doesn't want to move at the moment. I try to follow his gaze, but I can't tell what he's looking at.

Some kids Chloe knows join us in the shade.

"This is Harrison," Chloe says. "He just moved here, but we've known each other for a long time." It seems like Chloe is proud to tell them that.

"I'm Marisol," says a tall girl with a streak of deep purple in her brown hair.

I repeat her name carefully, trying to roll the *r* like she did. I'm not sure I did it right.

"Yeah, you got it." Marisol smiles.

"And I'm Simone," says a blond girl. "You and I are in the same math class."

"Nice to meet you," I say.

There's a boy with them. His pale skin is pink in the outdoors, and he's even shorter than I am. He seems more interested in the games at the soccer field than in talking to me.

"This is Leon," Simone says.

Leon hears his name and says hello, but he looks at me like he's trying to figure out which one of us is better.

"Harrison is really good at card tricks," Chloe says.

"You haven't even seen me do any card tricks." I take a drink of my chocolate milk.

"Yeah, but you said you did them."

I shrug. "How do you know I'm good at it?" I'd really like to show off an illusion, maybe impress these kids, but it doesn't always work that way. Sometimes all kids want to do is find a mistake and tell everyone how you did it.

"Maggie said you're really good."

"You talked to my aunt about my card tricks?"

"Do you have your cards?" Chloe asks, ignoring my question.

"Yeah, I have them."

"Great! Show us some magic."

"Yeah, I love magic tricks," says Marisol.

They seem interested enough, so I take the cards from my pocket.

Leon says, "Card tricks are lame. I'm going to play soccer. Who's coming?" Now, I recognize this kid— from the student council video. He was in the skits about school rules and anti-bullying.

"You go if you want, Leon," Simone says. "I want to watch this."

Leon saunters off, toward the field. As he passes the graphic novel designers with their drawings spread across the grass, he says to them, "Hey, if you want some awesome inspiration, I'll show you the comic book I made. I could give you some pointers."

To Marco he says, "Hey, Marco Polo."

"Hi, Leon." Marco glances over at the rest of us. He picks up his lunch like he's going to come join us, but he moves closer to the edge of the grass, still watching something.

"Okay, show us a trick," Simone says. She and Marisol and Chloe are watching me eagerly, so I show them the deck and let them shuffle the cards.

I turn an empty lunch tray upside down for a work surface and divide the cards into three piles. I do the same trick I did for Tabitha at Cactus Gulch. I ask Chloe to move the top two cards to the new piles and take the third card and study it. She's the one who asked about my card tricks first, so I want to let her do it. She shows her card to the other girls, and they all nod.

I really use Harrison the Magnificent as I pretend to keep getting her card wrong.

Simone says, "I thought you were good at this."

"Just wait," Marisol says. "He's not finished yet."

I place the small final stack between the first two knuckles of Chloe's hand and tell her to squeeze them tight. I'm about to smack the cards out of her hand, leaving the one behind that should be her card, when Marco yells, "Look out!"

He's running toward us, waving his arms for us to get out of the way. The graphic novel designers grab their drawings and scramble off the grass. Chloe drops the cards and pulls me away.

"Banded Gila monster," Marco says, pointing at the grass.

A lizard with beadlike scales and alternating pinkish-orange and black stripes stalks toward my upside-down tray. The Gila monster's body wiggles from side to side as it walks. Its black feet end in five widely spread, sharp claws.

"Cool," I say, watching its fat tail swinging back and forth and its front feet stomping at the earth. The lizard heads for the cards that Chloe dropped and is only a few feet away.

"Watch it!" says one of the graphic novelists. "They can leap into the air and bite you, and if it bites you, it won't let go until it hears thunder."

"You'd have to run out to the canyon thunderstorms with it hanging from your arm," says another kid.

"That's not true," Marco says. "The leaping part *and* the thunder part are wrong. But Gila m—monster bites are painful. And they're venomous."

We all back up again. The Gila monster stops on top of my scattered cards. And then it grabs a card in its mouth, turns around, and creeps back the way it came, into the bushes beyond the grass.

"Guess you can't show us your trick now." Marisol sounds a little disappointed.

"Can you still do it with one missing card? If you start over?" asks Chloe.

Now there's a bigger crowd of kids than before, and that makes it difficult to watch all the angles. Besides, a good magician never repeats a trick. The girls might figure out the secret if I start over.

I shake my head. "Nah." With the Gila monster gone, I go back to the scattered cards on the grass and pick them up. "I'll get another deck and show you some other time."

Chloe and the girls look disappointed. And it's kind of nice to feel appreciated.

Marco is standing at the edge of the grass, where the Gila monster disappeared into the red dirt desert. Chloe and I join him.

"How do you know so much about Gila monsters?" I ask him.

"He probably knows because he spends so much time outside with his dad and their birds," Chloe says matter-of-factly.

Marco turns and looks at both of us, but mostly at Chloe. He takes a deep breath, like he's thinking of exactly what he wants to say.

"Please"—he got stuck on the *p* sound before the word *please* burst out, but it doesn't seem like he's mad—"don't speak for me."

Chloe is quiet for a minute. "I didn't mean to speak for you," she says softly. She tugs at a string on her shirt.

"You aren't the only one," Marco says. "It happens a lot. I wish people would just have m—more patience and wait."

"I'm sorry," Chloe says.

I'm glad I'm not the one who jumped in and spoke for Marco.

Everyone is gathering their backpacks and lunch garbage and heading inside. We all pick up our lunch trays. Marco finds an empty milk carton and a loose chip bag that someone left behind, and he picks those up, too. The three of us walk back to the cafeteria doors together.

"Marco and I have art next," I say, trying to lighten the mood. "How about you, Chloe?"

"I have history," Chloe says, looking relieved that I changed the subject. "And then I have PE."

"So do we," Marco says. "M—maybe we can all choose each other for teams, if you want."

"Yeah," Chloe says. "That would be great."

"Being forced into groups is the worst, and everyone says M—Ms. Camacho still m—makes you do it." He smiles at Chloe.

I don't think I've ever met a kid like Marco before. He stands up for himself, and he gets over things kind of quickly. I remember what Aunt Maggie said about Marco knowing more than any other kid about the muse and the art contest. And I wonder whether he'll talk about it if I ask him.

Part Two

TIPS
FOR ARTISTS

Find what speaks to you and take time
to understand. Then you've found your art.

—ELI TAYLOR, VISUAL ARTIST

CHAPTER 15

TIP ONE: NOTICE THE LITTLE THINGS

Mr. Bradley is moving through the art room in his motorized chair and placing art contest forms on the tables. The room smells like paint and the clay Aunt Maggie uses.

"Harrison and Marco! How's the first day going?" Mr. Bradley has a strong, booming voice.

"Fine, thanks," I say.

Marco marches right up to Mr. Bradley. Without thinking about it, I just kind of go along. Marco glances around at the crowd filing into class and asks him, "Do I have to enter the art contest if I'm in this class?"

Mr. Bradley leans forward in his chair and says quietly, "If you'd rather not enter, I can let you submit a different project for the term. But are you sure?"

"I don't like how the arts council m—makes a big

deal out of m—me," Marco says. "I went to the contest last year. To go with my family. I didn't even enter, and . . . people still talk about, you know, what they think should have happened."

Mr. Bradley nods and rubs his hand over his jaw while he thinks. The rolled shirtsleeve over his forearm moves enough that I glimpse more of his tattoo: FEAR. "And they ask you why *you* think the muse has gone missing?"

"Yeah." Marco folds his arms.

"I'm sorry you get that kind of attention and that it bothers you," Mr. Bradley says.

I feel like I'm not supposed to be part of this conversation, but I think it would be even more awkward to walk away now.

"I could work on something for class but just n—not submit it to the contest," Marco offers.

Mr. Bradley looks around the room at all the students who've come in and motions for everyone to sit down. Then he says to Marco, "How about the Walk and Chalk? Invite a few friends with you, claim a spot, and create your chalk art. Take a picture of what you draw and write two paragraphs about it. Does that sound fair?"

"Yeah, I can do that." Marco sighs like he's relieved.

"Great," Mr. Bradley says. "Now, go pick a seat."

I think the first sign of a cool teacher is that kind of understanding. The second sign is when they let you choose your own seat. Marco and I find two open spots at the table next to a long counter with small buckets of paintbrushes and a sink. The opposite wall is covered in a large mosaic made up of broken tile pieces. The design is low enough that someone short like me could have done it without a ladder. The center of the design is like an outstretched hand with colorful swirling patterns rising from the open palm. I don't think it's finished, though.

I wonder why the art contest is such a big deal to Marco. If he doesn't like talking about the muse and the contest, maybe I'll have to ask Aunt Maggie to tell me what Marco knows.

"Have you taken art with Mr. Bradley before?" I ask him as we sit at the table.

Marco shakes his head no. "I haven't. But I heard he's an awesome teacher."

"Yeah, he seems cool. How do you know him?"

Before Marco can answer, Mr. Bradley tells everyone to be quiet. He has a way of raising his eyebrows at one kid who is whispering, so no one else says a word. Mr. Bradley steers his motorized chair around the tables. Everything in the room is positioned the right distance apart to allow space for his chair. As he moves past the tile design on the wall, I notice it's just the right height for him to work on. Maybe he made it.

Mr. Bradley tells us about how art is a way to share our experiences and point of view. I try to pay attention, but my mind keeps wandering to the contest and the entry forms on the table.

"Your job in my class this year," Mr. Bradley says, "is to be artists. Artists are storytellers, messengers, and inventors. I'll guide you through different techniques, and you'll complete one major project each term. Your first term project is to submit a piece of original artwork to the Muse Art Festival Contest. The entry forms are due September thirtieth."

Murmurs rise from every table. Two girls across from us start whispering about the muse. I hear the word *wish* a few times, and some of the kids look in our direction. I don't know why.

"Now," Mr. Bradley says, "you aren't expected to whip out that major project without some foundations and some practice. So everyone pick up a book from the cart. We're reading the first chapter, 'Art: A Personal Journey.' And then we'll get out the supplies."

He goes through the first chapter with us, and when we finish, he tells us to draw something we like. I try sketching the stray dog from Cactus Gulch. It looks like kindergarten work. My dog is flat, and his head is shaped more like a mouse's. I hide it with my arm as I erase lines and try again. How does Mr. Bradley expect me to make any sort of art if I can't even take what's in my head and draw it?

People whisper a little while they work, but Mr. Bradley doesn't mind.

"Marco," I say.

Marco is drawing a brown-and-reddish-orange bird

with outstretched wings that spread the whole length of his paper. He's using a sort of chalk to color the wings.

"Wow, that's good," I say. "Is that Pepper?"

"Yep."

"I've never seen chalk that bright before." The colors and textures of Marco's hawk are so real I imagine I could stick my hand into the paper and there would be feathers.

"They're oil pastels."

I wonder whether oil pastels would make my dog sketch better. Probably not.

"How did you learn to do that?"

Marco shrugs. "I've been drawing a long time. A lot of practice, I guess."

"Oh." My voice drops, along with any hopes I had of victory in the art contest. Even if the muse hadn't disappeared, what made me think I could create a winning entry?

Marco looks up and smiles. "Also YouTube tutorials." He laughs. "How did you learn your m—magic tricks?"

"Same way, mostly. YouTube tutorials."

"It takes"—Marco's face squinches as he gets stuck—"practice. Same as your card tricks."

I wonder if speaking smoothly takes practice for Marco. I think certain sounds give him more trouble than others. Or at least, he's careful about the words he chooses.

"I can help you if you like," Marco offers, indicating the drawing that I've mostly covered with my arm.

I don't really want to show him my kindergarten art. "Oh, um . . ."

"Come on."

I move my arm and slide it in front of Marco. He tilts his head a little. "First, you might want to try having a live example, or at least a photograph, in front of you. That will help you find details you've missed."

"Or details I got totally wrong," I say, laughing. "It looks like a mouse-dog."

"But it's a start."

"Thanks. You probably have the details of your hawk memorized."

"Yep."

"Is it a lot of work—taking care of a hawk?" I ask, thinking I'd like a hawk to fly to my hand as it did for Marco.

Marco pauses like he's thinking of the best way to start his answer when Mr. Bradley's booming voice startles me from behind. "Time to put your materials away and choose a cubby that will be yours for the semester."

Then, in a lower voice, Mr. Bradley says, "Sorry I surprised you there, Harrison."

"No problem," I say, attempting to keep my dog drawing covered. He notices.

"I'm not going to grade you on mastery of techniques at this point," he says. "Only that you make an effort."

I nod. "Um, drawing and painting are new for me."

Mr. Bradley smiles. "Hey, I admire anyone willing to try something new. That's my motto. Observe the art around this room and around Muse. Maybe you can ask your aunt to show you what she has in the gallery, and search different art online. Then choose a style you like and let me know what you want to try for the contest. Not every style is for beginners, but I'm sure we can find something that fits."

Marco has gathered up his oil pastels and hesitates a minute. He and Mr. Bradley glance at each other like they both know something.

"You don't have to be an expert to win the contest, if the m—muse is the judge," Marco says quietly. "You don't even have to be the best." Then he leaves the table to put his supplies away.

Mr. Bradley nods. "He's right."

The bell rings. I make sure to pick up the entry form before I leave. Marco and I walk down the hall together, since we both have PE next.

"You seem to know a lot about the art contest and the muse," I say. "If you don't want to talk about it, that's okay. But since I'm new here, I'm just wondering what the story is." I figure he can just say nothing, so there's no harm in asking.

Marco thinks for a minute as we head down the

135

science-and-math wing. A couple kids get stopped by one of the teachers for throwing a ball in the hallway.

When we get to the gym doors, Marco says, "People talk about it enough that you'll probably find out anyway. . . ."

A few kids pass us and say hi to Marco. He says hi back and waits for them to go into the gym before he finishes.

"I won the art contest when I was a little kid."

"Oh," I say. This is big. I want to ask what he wished for, but I don't think I should.

"The thing is, I was the *last* person to m—meet the m—muse and get a wish. It hasn't been back since."

+ +

"I can't believe Ms. Camacho is making us actually work out today," Chloe says when I sit next to her and Marco on the gym bleachers. Ms. Camacho gave us our Red Cliffs Middle School T-shirts and shorts, and we had to dress for PE on the first day. I don't really mind it, but Chloe is annoyed. She says she wishes we didn't have to take PE, that she does yoga at home with her mom and doesn't need this.

Ms. Camacho is a small lady with long brown hair and a lot of energy. She leads us through some warm-ups and tells us to jog around the gym five times. She says it's too hot to send us outside to run.

Leon, the kid from lunchtime who said card tricks were lame, catches up to Marco and Chloe and me on our first lap around the gym. "We totally could have gone outside for this," Leon says as he passes us. "Inside or outside, running is so easy."

Marco shakes his head as Leon leaves us behind, running way too fast for some simple PE laps. It's like he's running a race but no one is racing him.

"Do you both take the bus after school?" I ask Marco and Chloe. "My aunt has a pool, and you could come over."

"I usually take the bus," Chloe says, "but today, I have a meeting with the audiovisual club."

"Oh. How about after that?"

"After that, I have four dogs to walk."

"Four? What happened to six?"

"Matisse's owners went on vacation for a week, and Pearl has a vet appointment."

Marco laughs. "It's funny that you have to know the schedules of six dogs."

"Funny maybe, but I'm making good money," Chloe says, passing Marco and me to cut the corner on our second lap.

"Besides," Chloe says when she slows down and we're next to her again, "it's funny to *me* that you can't go on vacation because of your birds."

"You can't?" I ask Marco.

"N—not really. You can't leave three raptors alone

for days, and not many people know how to care for them."

"I would do it," Chloe says between breaths. "If you taught me."

We finish our laps. Leon is standing with one leg up on the gym bleachers in a stretch. "Beat ya," he says.

"It wasn't a race, Leon," Chloe says.

"I'll teach you sometime, Chloe," Marco says. "About the hawks and falcons, I mean."

I want to learn about the hawks and falcons, too, but I feel weird asking about it after Chloe did.

"Stretches," Ms. Camacho calls out to us, and we follow along in some lunges and hamstring exercises. We did this in karate all the time, so it doesn't really feel like work. Leon moves to a spot near the front and tells a group of girls that their form is wrong.

"Do you take the bus after school?" I ask Marco.

"Usually," Marco says. "But today my dad is picking me up for a bird abatement job we have at the Rawson . . . Peach Farm."

"Oh," I say. "Maybe you can come over a different day."

"Yeah," he says.

Ms. Camacho divides us into teams for an indoor game of kickball, and we don't get to choose who we're with, but Marco and I end up on the same team anyway.

"You know, we can talk more about the contest sometime. If you want," Marco says as we line up.

"Sure," I say, surprised.

"It seems like you're interested in it."

"Yeah," I say. "I am."

It's my turn to kick the ball, and Chloe is waiting at first base to tag me out. I'll bet she doesn't know how well karate teaches you to kick. I step up to the plate.

"M—maybe we can figure out what happened with the m—muse," Marco says just before the pitcher on the other team tosses the kickball toward me.

And just like that, I think I might have a friend who also wants to solve this muse mystery—maybe as much as I do.

CHAPTER 16

TIP TWO: LOOK FOR IDEAS IN NATURE

I send Dad a text while Aunt Maggie and I eat grilled portobello mushroom caps with vegetables on wheat buns, instead of hamburgers. It tastes okay, but the big mushroom is gray and slimy and looks like an enormous slug.

Me: Can you talk now?

While I watch for a typing bubble, I pick off the rest of the mushroom and finish eating my veggie-burger thing.

Me: If you have a show tonight, can you call me later?

"What do you hear from your dad?" Aunt Maggie asks.

I set my phone down on the table. "Nothing yet. I guess he's busy."

My aunt stabs too forcefully at a piece of avocado, and it breaks apart on her plate. She sets her fork down. "I'm sure he'll call you. He said he would, right?"

"Yeah, he did." Talking about Dad reminds me of the contest. "Oh, Mr. Bradley gave us the contest entry forms today. We need to have a parent or guardian signature. Will you sign mine?"

"Of course! I can help you get the supplies you need, too. Do you know yet what style you're leaning toward?"

"No. But I'm supposed to study some of the art around Muse."

"That's a great idea. Do you want to go tonight?"

"Sure," I say. "And is there a store where I can get playing cards? A Gila monster took off with one of my cards, and now I don't have a full deck."

"Harrison! How close did you get to a Gila monster for *that* to happen?"

"Not that close. I was showing Chloe a trick, and Marco spotted the Gila monster coming toward us in the grass. Chloe dropped the cards she was holding, and the Gila monster grabbed one."

Aunt Maggie laughs. "Well, that's quite a story." She takes some dishes to the sink, and I help her. She doesn't mention my giant leftover mushroom.

"So you hung out with Chloe and Marco, huh?"

"Yeah. I invited them to come here and go swimming sometime. Is that okay?"

"They're welcome anytime," Aunt Maggie says.

141

"Help me do these dishes, will you? I promised your dad that I'd give you some chores."

I groan, but she can tell I'm joking around.

"In art today, Marco asked Mr. Bradley if he could get out of entering the art contest," I say. "And Mr. Bradley let him out of it."

"Hmm. Did Marco tell you why he didn't want to enter the contest?" She hands me a rinsed plate and tilts her head toward the dishwasher. I take the plate and set it in the lower rack.

"I wasn't sure if I should bring it up. I waited until after class and asked him what he knew about the contest. And then he told me he won when he was a little kid."

"Yep." She nods, handing me a rinsed pan. "Marco won the October after you and your parents lived here. He was probably five or six years old."

"He told me that the muse hasn't been back since."

Aunt Maggie turns the water off and dries her hands, leaning against the fridge. "I wonder if he thinks it's his fault. Because it's certainly not."

"He said something about people making a big deal out of him and talking about what they think should have happened."

"Mmm." My aunt presses her lips together. "That's not surprising."

"He said he'd talk about it more sometime."

"Well, it sounds like he trusts you." She pours herself some coffee, and the smell rises from her mug. She takes a sip. "Small towns excel at a few things, Harrison. Celebrations, home-baked goods, and gossip. So I've told you that Marco knows a bit about magic, but I'm going to let him tell you the rest."

"Okay."

I check my phone for messages. Kennedy sent me a funny video of a dog in a pirate costume, with the text, *Have you walked any more dogs?* No text from Dad yet. He only left a few days ago, but him being gone makes me feel like Mom is farther away than ever.

"Aunt Maggie?" I pocket my phone. "I was wondering if you'd take me to the amphitheater in the canyon."

She puts down her mug. "Of course."

+ +

The days are long, and although it's past seven, the sun is still out. But over the canyon, the sky is dark with clouds. Not long after we turn onto the canyon road, lightning streaks from the clouds down to the cliffs.

"Ooh," Aunt Maggie says, turning on the headlights and the windshield wipers. Rain begins falling and pelts the glass. "This is a big one. We probably shouldn't go in too close."

"Is it like this a lot?" I watch the canyon alternate between clear and blurry as the windshield wipers try to keep up.

"At night, yes. The canyon storms have happened almost every night for several years. Although usually it's lightning with no rain."

Thunder cracks, and the rain falls harder. It bounces off the road in front of us and forms little rivers in the gutters. I don't like driving in the rain. Not since Mom's accident. The tune of "Lavender's Blue" enters my head and I can't stop it.

"Can we pull over?" My voice comes out tight and stiff.

Aunt Maggie pulls over to the side and turns on the hazard lights. They're like red spotlights flashing on and off the rocks where the road curves ahead. It's darker here, but I can still make out a waterfall of rainwater pouring off a cliff to jagged rocks below.

My aunt takes in a sharp breath. "It doesn't mean anything, you know."

I think I know where she's going with this. I wish she wouldn't.

"The rain," she says. "It's just rain. It's not the rain's fault. And it's not your fault."

I want to open the car door and run away. But that's what Dad does.

I stay.

"I could be wrong, Harrison, but I think I know the signs." Aunt Maggie turns off the car. Lightning streaks down where the cliffs open up in the distance. A bolt illuminates the clouds from the inside. Another one branches out and stretches across the canyon. I count five separate bolts in the pause before my aunt speaks again. "I know your mom was on her way home to see you that night."

I feel the weight of my phone in my pocket.

"How do you know that?" I ask, trying not to feel any of this. Trying not to hear Mom singing in my head.

"I know that's what she did. I know she liked to visit with her fans, but she also wanted to tuck you in before you went to sleep."

I nod, wishing to be anywhere else. I close my eyes and listen to the rain and thunder.

"What if she'd stayed with them a little longer?" I whisper. "What if she hadn't rushed home?"

"Oh, Harry. No one ever wins at the what-if game unless it's used to create or to inspire. If you want to ask what-if, ask it differently."

I open my eyes. Aunt Maggie's skin is usually bright and rosy, but her face is in shadow right now.

"What if you could do real magic?" *She's* asking what-if questions now. "You know, your card tricks make people feel a sense of wonder. What if it was real?"

"No magic can change what happened. Every movie and book about magic will tell you that," I say.

"No. You're absolutely right. That isn't what I meant."

A lightning bolt spikes from a cloud on the left and

across the canyon to the other side, just as another bolt meets it in the middle from above and splits into two. It makes a triangle of light.

"If I had *real* magic," I say, "I'd find a way to get my dad back. He should be here, watching this light show with me . . . instead of running away."

Aunt Maggie smiles. "You're wise, like your mom." She rolls her window down a little and holds her hand outside, letting the rain soak it. "You can't control what your dad will do, though. All you can do is figure out *you*."

I nod, but I'm not really sure what she means.

"If you do that, I think your dad will come around."

I pull my phone from my pocket. No messages.

"And if he takes a while"—she tilts her head—"you've always got me."

"I know," I say, trying not to focus on how much she looks like Mom. "Thanks."

My aunt brings her hand back inside and rolls the window up. "You're welcome."

The storm over the canyon lights up like a mad scientist just threw the switch to bring his new creation to life.

"Can we come back when it isn't storming?" I ask.

"Yes. Let's try during the day sometime. The lightning storms only happen in the evening."

"That's weird."

"Oh, it gets weirder." Aunt Maggie leans forward

onto the steering wheel to get a better view of the sky. "The evening storms are the reason the amphitheater closed in the first place and hasn't reopened. It's normal to have a few summer storms in the desert, but suddenly, they happened more and more, until a storm hit almost every night. The theater can't plan a season or sell tickets when they know they'll probably have to cancel the shows all the time."

"When did the theater close?"

"The storms got bad the summer after your mom performed here."

"That's weird," I say again. The lightning over the amphitheater reminds me of the storm I feel inside me, the one that I hide with Harrison the Magnificent.

CHAPTER 17

TIP THREE: A MISTAKE CAN TURN INTO SOMETHING GOOD

*T*he smoke detectors were going off again.

I bolted out of my room and into the upstairs hallway to the smell of spiced chicken and burning oil. Mom must've been attempting to make one of her fancy dinners again. She had a service called Fresh Table send her boxes of ingredients with instructions and recipe cards.

"What is it this time?" I call, running down the stairs.

"Cheesy chicken skillet with black beans and peppers," Mom called back.

"I said I'd help you," Dad said, laughing and opening all the windows in the living room.

"But I want to prove to myself I can do this," Mom hollered over the sharp pitch of the smoke detectors.

"Harry, will you get the windows?"

I opened the windows to the backyard and the front yard, letting in a rush of humid, tree-smelling air.

"Have you got it all under control?" Dad asked. I could tell he was trying to let Mom do it, but he also didn't want her to burn down the house. "Is there something in the oven that needs attention?"

"I got it. I got it," Mom said.

Dad waved a magazine beneath the detector in the kitchen, creating a breeze. With the outside air pouring in and the smoking skillet cooling beneath the oven hood, the alarms turned off.

I think sometimes Mom felt bad about being gone in the evenings a lot. It was part of the performing life; I understood that. Still, Mom signed up for Fresh Table and tried these complicated dinners. The trouble was, Mom was best at burning the oil. Sometimes the recipes had Mom doing too many things at once, and she almost always refused Dad's help.

Mom stood in front of the stove with one hand on her hip and another hand holding the instruction card. She scratched her head and grumbled. "Forty minutes, ha! This says the prep and cooking time together is forty minutes. I've been working on this for over an hour."

She made sure all the burners and the oven were

turned off, set down the recipe card with the colorful, perfect picture of the meal she was supposed to make, and asked, "Who wants to play a game?"

"I . . . kinda wanted to eat first," I said, and Dad shook his head to tell me I shouldn't have said that.

"This game is dinner," Mom said.

And she drove us all to Food Lion. Everyone could pick two things from the freezer section, and then we would meet in the ice cream aisle to learn what our dinner would be for the night. It was so fun, and it was the first time I remember Mom letting me roam free in the grocery store without having me in her sight.

I showed up in the ice cream aisle holding frozen lasagna and frozen French fries. Dad came holding a box of orange chicken and frozen prepared rice, and Mom had one bag each of frozen broccoli and peas. She laughed and said she knew Dad and I wouldn't show up with green vegetables. We threw it all in the cart, and Mom let me choose the ice cream. Chocolate Mudslide.

Mr. Bradley said that sometimes we can turn a mistake into art.

Mom knew how to do that.

CHAPTER 18

TIP FOUR: BE WILLING TO SHARE YOUR WORK

The only playing cards at the Muse Market have ZION NATIONAL PARK printed on the back. But that's actually great, because the pictures show different hikes in the park, and that gives me ideas of things to talk to Dad about. Inside Gallery 29, the art is so professional that I can't imagine doing anything like it myself, let alone entering it in a contest. But Mr. Bradley said he'd help me, and so did Mr. Taylor and Aunt Maggie. I just need to find some ideas.

There are so many ideas in the gallery: photography of old bicycles, watercolor paintings of a horse and a purple prickly pear, animal statues, and pottery. One corner is full of sculptures made from old bike chains, plastic pieces, and rubber tires. It's labeled RUBBISH REVIVAL.

I notice a table with a sign that says ELECTRIFIED WOOD. The blocks of wood there have blackened tree-like branches spreading across them.

"Electrified wood? The artist did this with electricity?"

"Yep," Aunt Maggie says. "Those are called Lichtenberg figures, or fractal burning. It's incredibly dangerous to do, and you have to be very knowledgeable to stay safe, so I don't want you to ever try it."

"I won't," I say.

"But I'll show you another cool feature of the electrified wood. This artist painted the burned fissures. Watch this." She flips a switch on the wall and turns out the gallery lights. The tree-branch-shaped burns in the wood glow electric green and blue.

"Wow! Glow-in-the-dark paint!"

"Nearly every customer who is interested in this electrified wood buys a piece after I show them this."

Just then, my phone rings in my pocket.

It's Dad!

Aunt Maggie goes to another part of the gallery to let me talk.

"Hi, Dad!"

"Harrison, I'm sorry to call so late. We needed to have a put-in rehearsal this afternoon for the backup bass guitarist. He had to go on tonight and needed the extra practice. Can you talk now?"

"Yeah, I can talk," I say.

"How was your first day of school?"

"It was pretty good. I made a few friends and won a game of kickball."

"That's nice for a first day. How were your classes?"

"Fine. The teachers mostly talked about rules and what we're going to learn. No homework yet except for art."

"You have art homework?"

I examine the edges of the electrified wood. "Our term project is to enter the annual art contest, and I'm supposed to get some ideas for what I want to make."

"Ah," Dad says, his voice dropping a little. "The Muse Art Festival, huh?"

"Yeah."

He's quiet for a moment. Voices mumble in the background. I can tell he's in the greenroom—the backstage area for performers and crew. I hear pieces of conversations about lights and cues, and the assistant stage managers' instructions from their headsets.

"Don't get your hopes up about that contest, okay?" Dad says. "I mean, it's great if you want to make something artistic—I'd love for you to show it to me—but do it because you like creating things, not because of some wish. Maggie told you the wish stopped working, right?"

"Yeah, she told me." I trace the fiery pattern on the wood, even though I'm probably not supposed to touch the art. "It feels different here, Dad. The canyon, and the sun on the rocks, and all the art. And there are these lightning storms every night. Did you know that's why the amphitheater shut down?"

"I didn't know that."

"And I met a kid who won the last wish before the muse stopped showing up. I think he knows more, because he wants to tell me about it. I just want to find out what the contest is like—give it a try."

"Hmm." Dad seems distracted. Maybe it was my mention of the theater. But also, I don't think he believes in the muse. I don't think Dad believes in much anymore—except maybe Dorian Striker. More conversation from the greenroom buzzes through the phone.

"Sorry, Harrison, there's a lot going on here. I think I missed the last thing you said. Is there anything else you want to tell me?"

Suddenly, I know exactly what I would wish for if the muse appeared and gave me a wish. It's all I can think about when I hear Dad's voice on the phone.

"I found a house for us, Dad. We could live here and hike Zion National Park and explore the lava tubes in Snow Canyon."

"You found a house, huh?" Dad says. But it doesn't sound like he thinks I'm serious about it.

"We could start over. The two of us."

Dad doesn't say anything.

"I like this place," I say. "I think it would be good for us. To be here together."

"I'm going to come when I can," Dad says.

I listen to the voices and noises of the stage-managing life he chose rather than to be with me. I wonder if Dad has memories of Muse with Mom, just like we both have memories of Virginia with Mom. Maybe Dad feels about Muse the way I felt when I returned to the ice cream aisle at Food Lion after Mom died. It was hard to be there without her. Still, if Dad won't let me be on tour with him, then he needs to be here with me.

"I'll show you everything when you visit in October. You'll see."

CHAPTER 19

TIP FIVE:
STOP COMPARING
YOURSELF TO OTHERS

The rest of the week, I sit on the bus with Marco and Chloe. I bring my new Zion National Park deck every day. But I don't show them card tricks when other kids lean over the seats to try and figure out how I do it.

On Friday, Chloe knocks on Aunt Maggie's door before I leave for the bus stop.

"Want to walk to the stop together?" she asks. She's wearing a purple shirt that says WALK AND CHALK: BRING BACK THE MUSE.

"Sure. Just a second." I grab my backpack and phone and holler a goodbye down the stairs toward my aunt's studio. She started on her pottery wheel early this morning.

She calls back from the basement, "Fox Art Supply will have your order ready for you after school, if you want to walk there from the art village bus stop!"

"Thanks! I will!"

"What did you order from the art supply store?" Chloe asks as we head down the street.

"Stuff for my contest entry. I think my aunt bought me a mix of things, since I don't know what I want to make."

"My dad will help you if you want," Chloe says.

"Yeah, he told me he would, but would that be weird? I mean, he's *your* dad. Is he helping *you* with the contest?"

Chloe looks at me like I'm ridiculous. "I'm not entering the contest. Well, not the way you are."

"Oh. What are you doing?"

"I had this idea to show the arts council that just because my dad is a famous painter doesn't mean I like the same things."

"Uh, Chloe? You're not planning to ruin the contest, are you?"

"No." She laughs. "It won't ruin it. I think it'll make it better, though."

"Do you think it'll bring back the muse?" I'm joking, sort of.

"That's not a bad idea," Chloe says. "Hey, did you ever talk to Marco about his wish?"

"No. Not yet. He's been busy with his falconry all week."

"Hmm. I want to know."

"Maybe you should ask him, too," I suggest. "I mean, the muse is a mystery we could all work on together."

"Yeah. Maybe we can find out what happened the first year the muse didn't show up."

As we turn onto Coyote Way, I glimpse something running in the desert across the street. The scruffy black dog from the model home is weaving his way through the lava field. His pointy ears stick up over the top of the rocks as he goes behind them.

"Obsidian," I say.

"What?"

"There!" I point at the dog. "It's the stray I found last week. I tried to get him to come home with me, but he took off."

"Do you want to try to catch him now?" Chloe asks. "I'll help you. I think I can get him to come with us."

"We'll miss the bus," I say, not sure what Aunt Maggie would think about that.

"Yeah, but it's a good cause. Maybe Maggie would drive us to school."

I pull out my phone and call my aunt's number. While it rings, Chloe and I cross the street.

"Do you recognize the dog? I mean, does he belong to anyone you know?" I ask Chloe as the phone continues to ring.

She squints and holds her hand above her eyes to shade them from the sun. "I don't think so."

Aunt Maggie's voicemail picks up. She must still be working at her pottery wheel. I leave her a message: "Aunt Maggie, I found the stray dog I was telling you about. He's in the desert across Coyote Way, and it's so hot out here. Can you help Chloe and me try to catch him?"

But before Chloe and I can even get close, Obsidian runs away from the road, farther into the desert. The hills and clumps of lava hide where he went.

"Aw," Chloe says. "If we didn't have school, I'll bet we could find him."

"Out there?" I hold my arm out at the desert. "You'd go wandering *out there*?"

"No worries, Harrison. There's another road hidden behind all that. And running trails, and more houses. Plus, we'd take water. I know my way around."

"Oh."

"You're right, though—it's good to be careful in the desert. The dog is probably hanging out at the construction sites, and workers are probably giving him food and water. He'll be okay."

The school bus approaches where a few other kids are waiting at the stop.

"We're going to miss the bus if we don't run," I say.

Chloe waves her hand at me. "No, we won't. The bus driver waits when she can see us coming."

I give her a sly smile. "Bet I can beat you there."

"Bet you can't." Chloe takes off fast down the sidewalk, and I'm right behind her. I pull ahead, and then she does. We run faster and faster, trying not to let the other one win. Sweat beads on my forehead and dampens my shirt.

Marisol with the purple-streaked hair and Marco are in the crowd of kids waiting.

"What are you two doing?" Marco asks. "It's ninety degrees already."

"We"—I'm out of breath and trying not to show it—"didn't want to miss the bus."

"Looks like you didn't want to miss a chance to compete or something," Marisol says. She's wearing a colorful, woven bracelet and eating what looks like a homemade doughnut. "I think Chloe's faster. What do you think, Marco?"

"Don't put m—me in the m—middle," Marco says.

"I think we're equally fast," Chloe says. She's out of breath, too, and smiling.

"Hey, did you see that stray dog out there just now?" Marco asks.

"Yeah, I was hoping I could catch him and bring him home with me," I say. "Do you know if he has an owner?"

"I don't know, but I doubt it," Marco says. "M—my dad and I have run into him a few times in the canyon when we take the hawks out. I think he lives out there."

Just then, Aunt Maggie sends me a text asking if we can still see the dog and if I made it to the bus on time. I tell her *no* and *yes*. She says she'll keep an eye out for the dog when she heads to the gallery.

We all climb onto the bus. Chloe and Marisol share one seat, and Marco and I take the one across the aisle.

"I have one of these for you," Marisol says, handing me a woven bracelet like the one she's wearing. "I get these when I visit my grandparents in Peru. It's a friendship bracelet."

"Thank you," I say, not sure what this means. But Chloe has one, too, so I think it just means Marisol is nice.

All three of them ask me to show them some card tricks. Luckily, I learned enough new ones on YouTube last night to last us all the way to school.

CHAPTER 20

TIP SIX: LEARN ABOUT LIGHT AND SHADOW

MUSE ART FESTIVAL
Contest Entry Form

Return to Mr. Bradley by September 30th

NAME: _Harrison Boone_

AGE: _12_

GRADE: _7_

ENTRY TITLE: _Desert Dog_

MEDIUM: _Colored pencil_

+   +

I filled out my contest entry form, but I'll probably want to change it. So I grab a few more in art class and stuff them into my backpack.

Mr. Bradley is teaching us about grisaille painting. It means to paint in different shades of gray, using layers. But first, we're supposed to sketch the subject on our canvas. Mr. Bradley shines special lights on a ceramic pear and a sculpture of a face. He says we're supposed to notice how three-fourths of the object is in light and one-fourth is in shadow.

Shadows make drawings more realistic. But it's hard for me to take the shadow shapes in front of me and draw them. Marco is busy sketching next to me like this is easy.

"My dad and I are taking the hawks jackrabbit hunting tomorrow," Marco says quietly.

I look up from my drawing of the face.

"I wondered if you'd want to come."

Jackrabbit hunting? With hawks?

"Yeah, I wanna come!" I can hardly keep my voice down. "You *hunt* with your hawks? I mean, besides pest bird control?"

Marco nods. "The hunting is the real fun part."

"When do you go?"

Marco shades his shadow outlines. "We go pretty early. We'd have to . . ."

I can tell he's stuck on his next word. I hardly pay attention to his stutter anymore, but it stands out most when it seems to bother him.

"... pick you up around six-thirty. Are you up for it?"

"Yes, definitely," I say. "Is it okay with your dad?"

"Yeah, I already asked him."

"Cool," I say. "Thanks! I'll ask my aunt if I can go, but I'm pretty sure she'll say yes."

Mr. Bradley's chair makes a soft whir as he drives it around. It's a calming sound, like the overhead fans that cool the room. He adds some tiles to the mosaic on the wall, in between answering people's questions about their drawings.

"Hey," I say to Marco. Mr. Bradley doesn't mind if we talk quietly when we're working on a project. "Can you tell me more about the contest? I'm kinda wondering about the muse."

Marco looks up from his sketch.

"I mean, I'm entering the contest, and I was hoping we could figure out how to get the muse to show up again."

"The arts council tried to make it bigger and better the year after I won," Marco says, watching Mr. Bradley add tiles to the wall mosaic. "But I think they got it all wrong."

"Like how?"

"They advertised and m—made it an event to bring in tourists. But that's not what the muse wants."

A girl at the other end of our table, Savannah, leans toward us. "What did you wish for, Marco? Maybe it was too much for the muse. Maybe you drained its energy."

Marco ignores her and keeps working on his drawing. He doesn't seem angry, or even sad. It's almost like he's protecting something. I remember what Aunt Maggie said about wishes being very personal. She also said the muse might be different for every person. I decide that no matter what I want to know about the muse and the art contest, I won't ask Marco what he wished for.

+   +

On the bus ride home, I show Marco and Chloe another card trick I learned this week. I found the instructions in an article called "10 Easy Card Tricks That Will Make You Look Like a Wizard." The tricks *are* easy, but it still takes some skill to present them in a believable way. The mind reader ones are my favorites for the bus. Chloe and I share a seat, and Marco sits across from us. Leon is in the seat in front of Marco.

Leon watches as I do the trick. I identify Marco's card as the ten of spades.

"Right!" Marco says.

Leon turns all the way around in his seat to jump in. "Okay, but what if I shuffle the cards, choose a card myself, and hold it up so you can't see it? How about you read my mind that way?"

I square up the card stack in my hands and shrug. "I can't."

Leon's just going to ruin it for everyone else. I'll save my tricks for another time.

"He can't do it," Leon says to Marco. "Must not be that good, then. Right?"

"I liked it," Marco says.

"Here. Let me have the cards," Leon says. "I can show you a better trick."

Leon's *not* my favorite person, and I *don't* want him using my cards. These aren't even the ones that Mom's friend gave me at her funeral, but it feels like Leon is taking something from me just the same. I shake my head and put the cards in my backpack.

"Come on," Leon says.

I don't know what to say or how to say it without being Harrison the Magnificent. "I don't loan out my cards," I say.

"'Cause you know my trick will be better."

"Leon . . . ," Chloe starts, but then Marco stands up and moves to an empty bench at the front of the bus.

Chloe and I look at each other, pick up our backpacks, and follow him.

"Geez," Leon says as we pass.

Chloe and I squeeze in next to Marco—three to a seat.

"I like your card tricks," Marco says. "Sorry Leon does that stuff."

"He's always been like that," Chloe says. "We're all just kind of used to him, I guess."

"Does anyone ever say anything to him about it?" I ask.

Chloe shrugs. "It doesn't really work."

From a magician's perspective, silence is sometimes better.

But sometimes it isn't.

All this makes me think about things and people differently. About how everyone has things they need to say and reasons they keep quiet. And something about it feels like the silence in the canyon, the way the red rocks rise into the sky and don't make a sound, and the way the sky erupts at night with lightning bursts and cracks of thunder. Almost like the sky can't take all the silence.

Some of the kids at the front of the bus are in the school choir. They have been singing songs from their medleys all week, and today Marisol is joining in with them. Now, they sing at the top of their lungs, and Marco, Chloe, and I couldn't have a conversation if we wanted to. The singing kids seem to think that loud means good and yelling means musical theater. They're trying to outsing each other. Mom would've coached them to not open their mouths so wide and not push so hard to fill all the available space. They're singing Broadway songs that she used to sing around the house.

I pull my phone from my pocket and check for new

texts. I haven't heard from Dad yet today. He's been taking longer to text me back sometimes. I know he's busy with his job, but it still feels weird.

> **Me:** Have you ever heard of grisaye . . .

I check the internet for the spelling and fix it.

> **Me:** Have you ever heard of grisaille painting?
> **Me:** Text me when you have time
> **Me:** Please

I watch my phone for the typing bubble as the choir kids scream-sing the songs that Mom used to sing. I wish they wouldn't sing so loud. I wish Dad would text me back, because I want to tell him about the three-fourths light and the one-fourths shadow on the pear and the face sculpture. I wonder if sadness makes a shadow on people. I think of Dad the day we arrived in Muse—like someone moved the light and made shadows where there weren't any before.

CHAPTER 21

TIP SEVEN: DON'T BE AFRAID TO JUST GET STARTED

I say goodbye to Marco and Chloe when the bus reaches our regular stop, near Joshua Circle. I'm staying on until I reach the art village today.

"You wanna walk the dogs with me later?" Chloe asks before she steps off.

I shake my head. "Thanks, but maybe another time."

"Okay," Chloe says. She tilts her head at me. I think maybe she knows I'm doing that thing I do of suddenly wanting to be alone.

I get off at the next stop. All of Oasis Lane is decorated with signs and banners advertising the first fall festival: WALK AND CHALK, SEPTEMBER 15TH. Strings of outdoor lights and colorful flags zigzag overhead between the shops.

I find Fox Art Supply next to a photography studio. I pick up my order and sit outside on a large orange rock. The sun feels so much closer to the earth in this desert than anywhere else I've been. It tingles my skin like the tiny needles that brush against you in an evergreen forest. I look through the art supply bag. Three prepared canvases, watercolors, oil pastels, paintbrushes, a wood block, a pad of drawing paper, and drawing pencils.

"Wow." I pull out my phone. Still no reply from Dad yet. I text Aunt Maggie.

> **Me:** Thanks for all the great supplies!
>
> **Maggie:** You're welcome! Do you want to stop by 29?
> I'll be here for another hour.

The warm, tingling feeling from the rocks and the sun hasn't changed the fact that I still want to be alone for a little while. As usual, it doesn't make sense.

> **Me:** No, I'd rather go home.
>
> **Maggie:** Do you have water?
>
> **Me:** Yes.
>
> **Maggie:** Okay. Stay on the paved paths along Coyote
> Way, and I'll see you in an hour.

With my backpack pressing against my shirt, making me sweat even more, I cross Coyote Way to the paved path. In the evening and early mornings, the paths in Muse are full of joggers and bikers, but it's too hot for that right now. Even though Marco said it isn't very common to spot a Gila monster, I watch the brush for any sign of one. I'm not scared of them, really. I just think they're cool. I take several drinks from the water flask Aunt Maggie has me take to school.

At the Cactus Gulch sign, I look down the street for the Mulberry Silk front door on the model home. Tabitha's SUV is parked at the sales office. I know I told Aunt Maggie I was going home, but at this moment, I feel like the model home counts. I cross the road, and when the construction workers several houses down are facing the other way, I try the door. It's unlocked. The house is completely quiet, so I slip inside.

I know I shouldn't be here without permission, but I head to the kitchen for a big, cold drink from the faucet anyway. Then I take a glass from the dining table and fill it half-full with water. I find paper towels under the kitchen sink and take everything to the art studio down the hall.

I move the sample artwork off the easel and set it on the long counter. I don't want to use up any of my newly prepared canvas until I've experimented a little first, so I tear a sheet of drawing paper from my new pad.

I stare at the cliffs outside the windows for a minute and then begin by lightly sketching an outline. When

I'm finished with that, I add the shaded areas on the rocks.

The house is quiet. I pull out my phone and type *Tess Winterrose* in a YouTube search. Mom's official page is full of live videos and studio recordings. I start with "You Are." It's a song that was written just for Mom to perform. She's the one who made it famous.

As she sings, I begin painting over my sketch with the watercolors. I mix orange with white and then more orange with brown and red in the paint lid, creating different combinations for the light and dark shades of the cliffs. The paintbrush on the paper makes a satisfying swish. Soon, I'm humming with the brushstrokes, and then I'm singing along with Mom—something I haven't done in what feels like forever. That song ends, and another begins. I keep singing and dipping my paintbrush and mixing more colors.

Suddenly, I'm startled out of my trance.

A dog is barking.

Just like before.

It's Obsidian, the scruffy stray. And he's right outside, staring at me.

"Oh my gosh! It's you!"

He barks again.

"Shh," I say, waving my hands at him to be quiet, even though he can't possibly hear me or understand.

If his barking gets someone's attention, I might be caught in here. I hurry down the hall to the kitchen.

Obsidian appears on the back deck next to the sliding glass doors. He comes right up to the glass. I grab a bowl from the dining table display and fill it at the sink.

I slide the door open, just enough to squeeze myself through the opening.

"Hey, boy. Do you need a drink?"

He rushes at me, burying his nose in my stomach and making me spill water on him and down my shirt.

"Oof! Look what you made me do, silly dog!" He wags his tail so fast it thumps the railing on the deck. He whimpers again, backs up, and wags his tail some more. His black fur is still covered with red dust. It comes off him in a cloud when I pet him.

"Do you live out here, hanging around these houses?" There's a little water left in the bowl, so I set it down on the deck. Obsidian doesn't want it.

He whimpers like he'd speak if he could and backs up again. Like the first time we met, I think he wants me to follow him. I reach for him and brush more dust from his fur. He wriggles from my grasp, backs up more, and barks. He's now wagging his tail like he flipped on a maximum-power switch. He spins in a circle.

"I don't have anything for you to play with," I say. I scoot the bowl closer to him. "Come on. You want a drink?"

He sniffs at the bowl and then turns away, leaping to the bottom of the steps. He spins in a circle two more times and stares at me. He looks from my feet to my face and back to my feet again. I imagine his words: *You, move your feet.*

"I can't follow you," I tell him. "I have to get my art supplies and clean up."

He tilts his head.

"Please be quiet. I'm gonna get caught, and they'll lock the door from now on."

He barks once.

"Obsidian." I lower my voice and use a firm tone. I hold my hand out to him like Chloe does with the neighborhood dogs. "Sit."

His round brown eyes stare deep, like he's peering inside me. But he doesn't sit.

"Stay," I say. I figured it was worth a try.

I take the bowl, slip inside the house, and close the sliding glass door. Obsidian stays. "Please don't run off," I whisper as I back away, watching him.

Just then, voices sound from behind the front door. People are coming up the front porch steps. I think Tabitha is bringing some customers to tour the model home. Tabitha's voice carries through the front door as she opens it.

"The designer was truly inspired by the natural shapes and colors of the Mojave Desert."

Footsteps shuffle on the entrance tiles.

Tabitha continues. "His goal was to maintain the

integrity of the desert scenery with designs that blend into the natural environment."

"That's the first thing we noticed about the homes," says a man's voice. "You can't even distinguish them from the rocks at a distance."

The hallway to the art studio is at the back of the kitchen, so if I go that way before the people enter the living room, they won't see me. I'd be seen for sure from the dining room, so I hang on to Obsidian's bowl. With my heart racing, I give the dog a pleading expression and hold my palm toward him, begging him to stay. He barks as I leave the kitchen. *Perfect.*

I quietly open the studio closet door and set the paints, water glass, and bowl inside. I grab my backpack and the Fox Art Supply bag and close myself in the closet. The voices are in the kitchen now. I breathe as softly as I can as I set the bags on the closet floor. My mixtures of desert rock colors spread into each other in the tray lid. It isn't until I hear Tabitha's voice outside the studio door that I remember I've left my painting on the easel.

"As you've noticed, the culture of Muse is an artistic one." Tabitha enters the room. I can see her and a man and another woman through the thin space between the closet doors. "So this model includes an art studio for those who find Muse creatively inspiring."

"Ooh," exclaims the woman. She walks around the

room, inspecting the counter and the drawers. "I could do so much with a room like this."

The man agrees. They like the art studio. The man turns straight toward the closet.

"Lots of storage space," he mutters.

Tabitha has stopped in front of the easel and is looking at my half-finished watercolor of the cliffs. The man is reaching for the closet door. I hold my breath, thinking frantically of how I could be Harrison the Magnificent and act like I meant for them to find me in here.

"Let me show you the other side of the house and the study," Tabitha says to the man. "You mentioned you work from home. I know you'll love the work-space options."

The man drops his hand and turns away. As Tabitha leads the couple out of the room, she glances in my direction—at the closet doors.

I wait quietly until Tabitha and the others leave the house and their voices disappear down the street. Obsidian isn't barking anymore, and I wonder if he's still waiting for me outside. I slowly open the closet.

I rush to put everything back the way it was. I wipe the watercolor tray with the paper towels and wrap it all up inside my Fox Art Supply bag. With my nearly dry painting tucked inside the drawing pad, I take everything to the kitchen.

I peer out the sliding glass doors, but Obsidian isn't on the deck or in the backyard. Still, maybe I can catch up with him. I rinse the glass, wipe it out, and return it and Obsidian's bowl to the dining table. I leave out the back, and as I shut the sliding glass door, I peek into the house from the outside. It feels like the house is mine, even though I know it isn't.

I'm angling away from the model home toward Coyote Way when, suddenly, Obsidian comes bounding toward me. He leaps over a boulder and slams into my legs. I lift my arm in the air to keep the art supply bag from getting smashed and almost fall into a cactus. Obsidian is panting with his mouth spread so wide that it looks like he's smiling. He barks and stomps his front feet with excitement.

"Good dog," I tell him. He smells my hands and arms. Then he sniffs at my art supply bag. Maybe he's smelling the paint.

"Will you come home with me, boy?" Trying not to drop anything in the red dirt, I start typing a text to Aunt Maggie. Obsidian walks in a circle around me, and I think he may have finally calmed down enough to stay put. I type: *I'm by Cactus Gulch and I found the stray.* And then Obsidian knocks my arm, and my phone goes flying.

"Aah!" I watch it catch the sunlight and land in a prickly desert bush. At least it didn't land on the rocks. I run to the bush to get my phone, keeping an eye on the crack in the nearby boulder. I'm a little worried about the Gila monsters and rattlesnakes out here. A tiny green lizard scampers across the boulder and makes me jump.

Obsidian runs toward me and rams into my stomach again.

"You gotta stop doing that."

He barks and looks down at my feet and back at my face. *You, move your feet.*

I just want to get him safely back to Aunt Maggie's house. I touch my phone screen to call her. Luckily, the phone still works. It starts ringing just as Obsidian sits in the gravel and howls toward the canyon.

Then he takes off, running away from me. He's going too fast and leaping over boulders, and I really hope he doesn't land on a rattlesnake. And I wonder, even if I ever do get Obsidian back to Aunt Maggie's house, if maybe he'll never stop trying to escape into the canyon.

CHAPTER 22

TIP EIGHT: IMAGINE YOUR FEELINGS IN COLORS AND SHAPES

MUSE ART FESTIVAL
Contest Entry Form

Return to Mr. Bradley by September 30th

NAME: Harrison Boone

AGE: 12

GRADE: 7

ENTRY TITLE: Canyon Light

MEDIUM: Watercolor

+ +

I was able to snap a picture with my phone of Obsidian as he ran away. It's not clear enough to show much, but I try using it as a reference for drawing him, like Marco suggested. It's definitely better than my first try, but it still isn't very good. I add watercolors to the sketch anyway. It looks like a little kid did it. I leave it on the dresser in my room.

"I'm sorry about the stray dog," Aunt Maggie says over dinner.

I pull the sprouts out of the veggie wrap on my plate. I can handle the peppers, avocado, onion, and carrots, but the sprouts are too much.

"Thanks," I say.

"I know you really want to bring him home, but it's hard to tell if that arrangement would work well for us or for the dog." Aunt Maggie sips her kombucha. "I want him to be okay, though. Does he seem hungry or dehydrated?"

"I've given him water," I say, careful not to give away anything about the model home. "He sometimes drinks it, but not always. And he definitely has enough slobber and his nose is wet."

"Well, that's good, I guess." She smiles. "Please don't go following him around the desert, though, okay? Call me just like you've been doing, and I'll come as soon as I can."

"Okay."

"How's the artwork coming?" she asks, as though she knows I have two watercolor paintings in my room that I wouldn't dream of entering into a contest.

"Um . . . I was thinking of asking Mr. Taylor for help. Chloe said I should."

"That's a great idea." She nods as she notices a text come in on her phone. "Also, how about Mr. Bradley? Isn't he helping you prepare for the contest in class?"

"Yeah, he is." Mr. Bradley gives us stuff to work on, but I don't want to make my contest entry with so many people around.

"Well, let me know how I can help if you need anything else."

"I will, thanks."

My phone buzzes with a text.

Marco: Can you come tomorrow at 6:30?

I almost forgot!

"Can I go hunting with Marco and his dad tomorrow morning with their hawks? They invited me to go, and they have to pick me up at six-thirty."

"In the morning?" Aunt Maggie's eyes go wide. "You sure you can get up and get going that early?"

"Marco says that's the best time to take the hawks out."

"Well, that's exciting! You can totally go. Wear sunscreen, and I'll pack you some snacks and water."

"Thank you!"

"Will you help me water the trees in the orchard when you get home?"

"Sure," I say.

I text Marco back.

Me: I can come! Should I bring anything?

Marco: Probably should wear long pants. We'll be hiking through prickly spots.

Me: Okay

Marco: And bring a water bottle

Me: Got it

Marco: See you tomorrow

Me: See ya. And thanks for inviting me.

Aunt Maggie has finished eating her wrap. "What do the hawks hunt?"

"He said jackrabbits," I say, stuffing the rest of my wrap into my mouth.

"Ooh. I was thinking birds, since that's what they hunt in my orchard. Are they taking their falcon tomorrow or just the hawks?"

"I think he said just the hawks."

"Hmm." Aunt Maggie's forehead wrinkles up. She stands from the table with her plate, pauses next to my chair, and touches my shoulder gently. Her hand is warm through my T-shirt. "It sounds like this will be different from what you saw here. Do you think it might be hard to watch a hawk take down a jackrabbit?"

I hadn't thought about that, but it didn't really bother me to see Pepper take down a starling. "It's just hawks doing what they do in the wild, right? No guns or anything."

"Definitely no guns. Falconry lets the birds catch their natural prey. And in this desert, I imagine it'll be pretty amazing to witness. I just want to be sure you're okay with it."

I don't understand why she's concerned. I just want to see what Marco gets to do with his hawks. "I'm excited about it," I say.

"Okay."

But something's a little strange in my stomach now. It's all fluttery, and it feels hollow, even though I just ate dinner. I check my phone. I finally have a text from Dad.

Dad: Hey! Sorry I took so long to get back to you. Do you want to talk on the phone for a minute?

Me: Yes

Dad calls right away. I go into the backyard and mosey along the edge of Aunt Maggie's pool as we talk. I tell Dad about art class, and Chloe and me trying to catch the stray dog before school, and about going hunting with Marco in the morning.

"You have a lot of great things happening," Dad says. I hear what I think is a lobby full of people—maybe at a theater, maybe at a hotel.

"Yeah. It's pretty good." I want to tell Dad about the

shadow sadness, and how art made me think of it. How I can sit in the sun with the buzz of the desert vibrating off the rocks and still feel like I'm in a shadow. I'm not sure how to say these things to him. "I wish you were here, though."

Dad clears his throat. "I know you do."

I sit on the edge of the pool and stick my bare legs in. A tiny toad has found its way into the water, and I watch it swim around near the steps. "I went to the house again," I say. "The one we can live in when you come back."

"Harrison . . ." Dad sighs. "I'm . . . I'm not sure you should get attached to a house right now."

"Why?"

"I don't know what you can plan on, and I'd hate for you to be disappointed."

Too late for that.

Dad asks me if I want Aunt Maggie to help me find a karate studio nearby. I might've said, "Maybe later," but I don't know, because all I can think about is that Dad doesn't want me to be disappointed. And he's the one disappointing me.

Dad says something about jackrabbits and a sound they make, but I don't really pay attention.

"We're flying to Houston tomorrow," Dad says. "But I'll call you on Sunday, okay?"

"Okay."

We hang up, and Dad is on his way to somewhere

else—not wanting me to plan on anything like a house or a family that stays together. I keep my legs in the water for a minute while I turn the smooth obsidian over in my fingers and watch the little toad. He can't get out of the pool on his own.

Aunt Maggie has a net on the end of a long pole that she uses to remove leaves and insects from the pool. I get the net and carefully scoop up the toad. I lower the net to the ground and let the toad out in the bushes by the fence.

When I go back inside, my aunt is nearly done with the dishes. I help her finish loading them.

"You okay?" she asks.

"Yeah."

"Harrison?"

I look at her.

"It's okay to have a lot of strong feelings. Especially right now. If you want to talk, I'm a good listener."

I take a deep breath. "Actually, can I have a small bit of clay in my room if I'm careful?"

She's surprised by my question, but she says okay. She gives me a tray with some of the mud-colored clay, a small dish of water, and a few rags.

And in my room, I form the shape of a man without a face. I don't worry about making it realistic. I can tell what it is. His shoulders are hunched, and his head is down. I turn him around, so his back is to me. I grab a new contest entry paper from my backpack.

MUSE ART FESTIVAL
Contest Entry Form

Return to Mr. Bradley by September 30th

NAME: ___Harrison Boone___

AGE: ___12___

GRADE: ___7___

ENTRY TITLE: ___Dad's Disappearing Act___

MEDIUM: ___Clay___

I place my faceless man on the dresser next to Mom's sculpture of her and me. His back is turned away from both of us.

+ +

I went to visit Sylvania two more times. Once more with Mom.

"Is your name really Sylvania?" I asked, holding the large umbrella over her knitting so it wouldn't get any wetter than it already was. Mom had given Sylvania three umbrellas before, but Sylvania kept giving them to other people.

"It's my name now," she said.

"How did you get it?" I thought it was so interesting to have a different name than the one you were born with.

"A friend gave me the idea."

"Will you tell us the story?" Mom asked.

"Well," Sylvania began, smiling. "This friend of mine told me I was a light in a dark world. It made me think of the millions of lights all over the Mall at Christmastime. And that same year, the light show in front of the National Gallery of Art was sponsored by . . ." She leaned closer and her eyes got wide. "You wanna guess?"

"Sylvania?"

"Sylvania Electric Products." Sylvania laughed. I think the rain stopped at that moment. "I thought it was destined to be."

James had been teaching Sylvania to knit, and she knitted me a pair of socks that looked like they had taken hours and hours to make. The socks were a little damp when she handed them to me, but I thanked her and held on to them.

That day, Sylvania asked Mom and me to sing "This Little Light of Mine." It's a simple song that repeats a lot, and many people know it. So if you sing it in public, strangers join in like they just can't help it. By the second verse, at least ten people were singing with us, including Sylvania. By the last verse, James joined us with his guitar, and the sidewalk in front of the National Gallery was full of voices.

After Mom died, Kennedy and I took the Metro to the Mall to visit Sylvania. I wanted Sylvania to know that Mom didn't just stop coming to visit her—but that she couldn't *visit anymore.*

Kennedy and I searched the trees near the pond. We searched in front of the National Gallery and at James's Art Collective, which had grown by several panels and had some signs with sponsor names. We asked people if they'd seen Sylvania. No one knew where the smiley, wrinkled lady with the bright-green eyes was. Finally, I found James on the corner, playing his guitar for tips. Kennedy and I waited until James finished a song, and we placed some money in his hat. Some other people dropped money in the hat, too.

"Hi, James," I said. "You probably don't remember me, but my mom and I—"

"Harrison!" James said. He did remember me. "How's your mom?"

And then I had to tell James the words I didn't want to say.

He listened, nodded, and picked up his guitar. "Come with me," he said.

Kennedy and I followed James to the art panels. He led us right to the panel where Mom had painted a sunset and signed her name. He began to play and sing "Amazing Grace."

He invited me to join him, but I couldn't do it. I couldn't sing there in that place, without Mom.

"It's okay," he said when the song was finished. "You sing for her when you're ready."

I didn't think I would ever be ready.

"Do you know where Sylvania is?" I asked James. "I've been looking all over for her."

And then James did the strangest thing. First, he tapped the side of his head with his finger. He said, "She's here." Next, he tapped his chest, over his heart. "And she's here."

"What do you mean?"

"Sylvania doesn't stay in one place for too long. She likes to wander. She said something about Chicago, and then maybe Sacramento?"

"Oh," I said.

"Now that you're here, though, and knowing about what happened to your mom, I think maybe Sylvania knew. She has a sense of things that's different than other folks."

And then he picked up his guitar, closed his eyes, and played the most beautiful music.

CHAPTER 23

TIP NINE: OBSERVE ANIMALS UP CLOSE

Marco and his dad pull up in front of the house in the Swift Bird Abatement van. Marco gets out the passenger side.

"They're here," I call toward the kitchen.

Aunt Maggie brings me a reusable lunch sack. The side says it's made of recycled water bottles. "I packed you some snacks, in case you get hungry," she says.

"Thanks."

She pulls me into a side hug, giving my arm a squeeze. "Have lots of fun."

"I'm sure I will."

"And put on your sunscreen *twice*."

I pull the travel-sized sunscreen tube from the cargo pocket of my long pants. I'm going to be so hot and sweaty from wearing these in this heat.

"And watch out for rattlesnakes, Gila monsters, and scorpions."

"I'm leaving now," I say, shaking my head.

"Have fun!" Aunt Maggie calls down the sidewalk. I wave back at her.

Marco opens the back door, and we climb in.

"Thanks for letting me come with you, Mr. Swift," I say.

"Always glad to have a fellow wildlife enthusiast join us, Harrison. Marco said you've been interested in the birds. And you can call me Byron."

A large crate with a handle on top sits in the back of the van. It's like a dog kennel, but it's completely enclosed except for small holes at the top.

"How many birds have you got in there?" I ask Marco.

"Two," he says. "Pepper is the one you m—met last week. And we've brought his mate. Her name is Spice."

"Pepper and Spice. That's cool."

"Yeah, we try to name the birds as pairs, but it doesn't always work out. We used to have two falcons—two females named Cherry and Blossom—but we lost Cherry on a hunt a few years ago."

"Oh no! What happened?"

"It's okay," Marco says. "We think she's alive and happy in the wild. Raptors are never really tamed. People watch us working with them and think they're like pets. But that isn't how it is. We train them, but if they came from the wild, they go back to the wild really easily."

When Marco talks about his birds, he doesn't stutter as much. At least, I haven't noticed it.

"Did you get another falcon after that?"

"Yeah. Since my dad has his master falconer's license, we're allowed to trap and keep wild raptors."

"You trap them?" I ask. "Can't you just breed the birds you have?"

"That takes a special breeding license," Byron says from the front. "Some falconers are also breeders, but master falconers can trap and train wild birds, too. We often release them back into the wild after a time."

"Is it hard to let them go?"

"Yeah, it's tough when you have to say goodbye," Marco says.

"Do you think you'll ever let Pepper go?"

"No," he says. "Pepper is different than the other birds we've had."

I twist in my seat to look at the large crate. I can't see the birds at all. "They're being so quiet," I say. "Are they used to driving around?"

"They have a perch in there. And we put hoods on them to help. They stay calm if their eyes are covered."

We've left Muse behind, and the curving road heads into open desert with cliffs on either side. We pass a sign for Snow Canyon State Park, and another one up ahead says ZION NATIONAL PARK: 30 MILES.

"Are we going to Zion?" I ask, thinking of all the hiking trails on the back of my new deck of cards. Maybe I could take pictures and text them to Dad.

"Hunting isn't allowed on federal land, so we don't go to Zion," Byron says. "But Marco and I have an agreement with some private property owners who allow us to bring the birds onto their land."

"They like letting the hawks hunt there because they catch rodents," Marco says.

"That's cool."

I take a few pictures out the window with my phone. It has a pretty good camera, but none of the shots come close to showing what it's like to be near these orange-and-red rock formations beneath the bright morning sky.

I send one of the pictures to Kennedy with the caption *The reason artists come here to paint the scenery.*

Kennedy: !!

Kennedy: Reason number 10 why I need to come out
there and visit you!

Me: That would be awesome!

Kennedy: I have my fall break in October. I'll check with
your dad and ask if it's okay.

Me: He won't care

Kennedy: I'll check with him anyway. And probably
your aunt.

Me: Ok

"Who are you talking to?" Marco asks.

"A friend from Virginia. Her name's Kennedy." I pull up a picture of her and show it to Marco.

He smiles.

"She used to hang out with me a lot . . . when my mom died."

Marco nods. "Sorry about your m—mom."

"Thank you."

Byron looks at me in the rearview mirror. His eyes are kind. I think if Dad lived here, he and Byron maybe could be friends. I think we could do stuff like this all together.

I open the snacks Aunt Maggie packed and offer them to Marco. We eat the plantain chips and veggie straws, and save the trail mix for later. The birds rustle inside their transport box, which Marco calls a "giant hood."

Byron turns the van onto a dirt road, and the cliffs are suddenly all around us. This place is familiar.

"I think I've been here before. Is the outdoor theater around here?"

Marco points to the right. I shade my eyes against the sun and find a roof in the distance.

"The stage is on the other side of that building over there," Marco says. "That hasn't been open for years, though."

"My mom performed there."

"Your mom was a performer at the Red Cliffs Amphitheater?" Byron asks in surprise.

"Yeah. She was a singer," I say. "A really good one."

"You lived here then, didn't you?" Marco asks.

"Yeah, we lived here for that summer. I was five."

"Have you been back to the theater since then?" Byron sounds worried.

"I tried to come with my aunt a few nights ago, but it began storming."

"It does that a lot," Marco says.

Byron pulls the van to the side of the gravel road so he can turn around in his seat. "I'm really sorry, Harrison. I didn't remember that your mom performed here."

I shrug. "I didn't expect you to know."

"It's just that we're hunting on the amphitheater land today. But if it's hard for you to be here, we can find another spot."

I don't think this will be the same as the flood of memories at Food Lion or the National Theatre or the Mall in DC. "It's okay. Really."

"You sure?"

"Definitely," I say. "I *want* to be here—in this place."

Byron nods and starts driving again, and rocks ping against the van's underside. The towering cliffs appear much larger when you get this close. They seem to be moving around *us* instead of us moving around *them*. I feel like a bug.

Byron steers between rocks and desert plants before finally parking. "You guys ready for this?"

"Yes!" Marco and I say together.

We climb out into the sunshine. Marco gets a pole from the back and leans it against the van. He and his dad put on gloves, and his dad hands me one. It's made of thick leather, darkened and worn. "Here you go, Harrison. Put that on. You can get one of the birds."

"Really?" I stand next to Byron, who opens the giant hood and reaches inside.

"If your glove is slightly higher than the perch," he says, "and you place your hand near their feet, just in front of them, the hawk will step onto your glove."

"Okay." I'm getting jittery with nerves. This is so cool.

"Once the bird is on your hand, you can pull it out like this." Byron is holding a beautiful red-and-brown hawk with white-tipped tail feathers. "This is Spice."

On Spice's head is a sleek brown leather hood that completely covers her eyes. Byron moves aside some feathers on the hawk's back, revealing a small device in the center, just above her wings. It's a metal plate, strapped on like a backpack, with thin straps going under each wing and then crossing like a figure eight over her chest.

"And *this* is a radio transmitter." He points out the antenna. It's clipped to the metal plate and hangs down Spice's back between her wings. "Marco has the receiver. This allows us to track the birds. That way, they can fly higher, and we're less likely to lose them."

"A tracker for your hawk," I say. "I didn't know you could do that."

"Yep. Falconry is pretty high-tech these days. We turn it on with a magnet"—he holds a small tool near the transmitter—"and then . . ." He loosens Spice's hood and lifts it off.

Marco whistles, and Spice flies to the top of the pole.

"Does she stay there?" I ask.

"Usually," Marco says. "If she doesn't, we track her. That's one reason we go hunting so early in the morning. If she decides to fly away, then we have all day to find her."

I'm amazed that this wild bird can take off at any moment but Marco and Byron don't seem worried.

"Spice stays because she knows we're going to flush out some game for her," Marco says. "The bond between a raptor and a falconer is mostly about food."

"Really?"

"Yeah," Marco says. "Except it's a little different with Pepper. You ready to get him out now?" he asks me.

I put the glove on.

I reach into the giant hood and rest my hand near Pepper's talons. He steps onto the glove. His grip is strong, but he weighs less than I expected.

"Have you got him?" Byron asks.

"Yeah, he's on my hand."

"Okay, bring him out carefully. Give him space so he doesn't hit his head."

"Got it." I slowly bring Pepper out into the sun. He's much smaller than Spice and has more brown in his feathers.

"What do you think?" Marco asks eagerly.

"Wow," I whisper. I have a bird of prey on my hand. It's closer to magic than anything I've ever felt.

Byron moves closer, turns on the transmitter, and removes Pepper's hood. Then the hawk presses against my glove, spreads his wings, and lifts off.

He circles Marco and the T-perch for a moment. Marco smiles like someone who has never had a problem in the world. He lifts the pole high, and Pepper lands softly next to Spice on the top.

"And . . . that's how it's done," Marco says.

Byron takes a garden hoe from the truck and slings a gear bag over his shoulder. I grab the water bottles.

"We've already scouted out a spot that has plenty of game," Marco says, leading the way with the hawks. I run to catch up with him, and Byron follows behind. We hike along the base of the cliffs, where the ground slants and the brush grows heavy in the red, sandy soil.

"This is called slope-soaring," Marco says. "The hawks soar on updrafts created by the cliffs while we flush out the game down here."

Spice rustles above us, and something wet drops onto Marco's shoulder with a giant splat.

I bust out laughing at the big white spot on Marco's shirt.

Marco glances at his shoulder and laughs. "It'll probably happen again, to be honest. They poop a lot."

"Gross," I say, still laughing.

"You wanna hold the pole?" Marco asks.

"No, thanks. I don't want to get pooped on."

Byron moves on ahead of us with the garden hoe, using it to shake up the bushes and tap the ground.

"What is he doing?"

"We have to scare the rabbits and mice out of hiding. They'll make a run for it, and then the birds will come for them."

Spice is the first to go. Pepper waits a bit longer, and when he takes off, he circles over Marco and me before joining Spice in the air. They fly close to each other, rising higher and higher up the cliffs, the power of their wings stronger than gravity. They perch on a ledge so high above us that they're only tiny specks.

"That's so cool," I say.

"Not everyone understands why I like falconry so much," Marco says. "I think sometimes you just have to experience it."

"You said that Pepper is different than Spice—before, when you were talking about why the birds don't escape. What did you mean?"

"We got our birds different ways." Marco watches the hawks on the cliff. "Spice is a bird we trapped in the wild, and we'll eventually release her back to the wild. "

He points at a cluster of rocks. "Don't step over any rocks without first checking on the other side. And listen for rattling."

We listen and check. It appears to be rattlesnake-free, so we keep walking.

"So how did you get Pepper?" I ask.

"He showed up by my window the morning after I made my wish."

I'd promised myself I would never ask Marco what he wished for, but maybe he's just told me. I'm not sure.

"Wow."

"You said you were wondering about the art contest and the muse. I have a couple theories."

"Really? Like what?"

"The muse seemed happy when I made my wish. Everything felt good. I was only six years old, but I remember that. Then, when the muse came back the next year, something happened."

"Wait, I thought people said the muse didn't come back the next year."

"Oh, it came back." Marco raises his eyebrows. "But it left again, very upset. I recognized the feeling of having the m—muse around, but then it changed. I don't know what was different, except that the contest was bigger than the year before and that the arts council wanted me there."

"Why?"

Marco shrugs. "So everyone at the contest could m—meet the kid who won a wish, I guess."

"Oh."

We pause at another heap of rocks. "If you come across a rattlesnake, give it at least five feet of space, if you can." I take in a sharp breath, but we don't find any snakes. "Don't worry. Usually they're just sunning themselves or searching for a place to hide. They won't attack unless they feel threatened."

"Okay." When I'm sure we aren't about to step on an unsuspecting snake, I ask, "Is there more to your theories?"

"Well, the contest was a lot more crowded the year after I won. My dad said the arts council advertised and brought in art judges."

"I thought the muse was the judge. Isn't that the point?"

Marco nods. "Yeah, I think it should be."

"Have you told anyone else that you think the muse was unhappy?"

"I don't think they'd believe me. But I thought *you* might."

"I do."

Here is something I know: I know how it is to go

from happy to unhappy, and what it feels like to suddenly not want to be around anyone. Maybe that's what happened to the muse.

"I think we should talk to Chloe about it, too," I say. "She told me she's planning something unusual for the contest this year. Maybe she has some ideas about all of this. I mean, her dad is an artist, and he talks about bringing back the muse."

"That's a good idea," Marco says. "I want to find out what happened, you know? I feel like I didn't get to thank it. And I want . . . people to stop asking if my wish made the m—muse leave."

Suddenly, his dad shouts, "Pepper's onto something!"

I shield my eyes from the sun in time to see the hawk fold his wings and dive from the sky, just as he did in Aunt Maggie's orchard.

CHAPTER 24

TIP TEN: FIND THE VANISHING POINT

Something darts out of the bushes and takes off across the slope. It's gray and brown, and blends in with the rocks.

"It's a field mouse," Marco says.

"He's on it!" Byron calls.

Spice leaves her perch on the cliff, diving fast. Pepper heads straight for the quickly moving target. He levels out and spreads his wings, gliding over the slope. Spice turns in the air, giving us a perfect side view of her wings angled back, her legs straight in front of her, and her talons outstretched, reaching for her food. The hawks are working together. Pepper sent that mouse running so that Spice could attack it.

Pepper turns in the air. Spice lands for half a second and is up again.

"They missed it," Marco says. "Come on."

I follow him, sending pebbles sliding down the slope as we scramble over the ground.

"There!" Marco points to where two rabbits are bounding across the slope. He lets out a short whistle, and the hawks are on the move, diving again.

Pepper turns first and sails to the ground, with his legs and talons outstretched. Then Spice joins him. It's a coordinated attack from the sky, and it's the coolest thing I've ever seen. Suddenly, there's a high-pitched scream. The cry steals my breath away.

The startling noise came from the rabbit. I didn't know they did that. My heart races in a strange way, like I'm a rabbit myself, running scared. I try to take deep breaths.

Marco is running to the spot where the hawks landed, and Byron follows with his shoulder bag. But everything around me seems to be going in slow motion.

I'm aware that my feet are moving to follow, but I don't really want to go. I don't want to see what the hawks have done. But even though I try to stop them, my feet keep moving.

The hawks are standing on top of a motionless gray rabbit. Spice is already pulling at the meat with her sharp hooked beak. Standing here and watching this— it's not what I expected when we started out. I don't know why, but even when Aunt Maggie asked me if I was okay with it, I didn't think about the death part.

I turn away for a few seconds, like I'm rubbing my nose. I don't want Marco and Byron to know this bothers me. It seems stupid to be sad about a jackrabbit when these hawks are so amazing to watch. Especially when this is what birds of prey are supposed to do.

"Harrison," Marco says, "I'll show you how we keep Spice coming back to us."

I don't want them to know how this has made my heart pound and my stomach feel strange. I'm so embarrassed, but I pull out my Harrison the Magnificent smile.

"We can't let them eat all of what they catch. If they're full, they're more likely to leave. . . . Well, Spice is."

Marco pauses. I don't think he's actually stuck on his words this time—it looks like he's just thinking about how Pepper is different—but Byron kind of jumps in. "And they'll have no reason to return when we offer them a tidbit of food to lure them back."

Marco focuses on the birds on the ground.

His dad continues. "But we also have to let them eat a little of what they catch, because it's very motivating to them. They need the reward of the hunt. So after they eat some of their catch, we use the game bag to conceal the catch and replace it with a tidbit of food."

"Don't they still smell it?"

"They rely a lot m—more on their sight than smell," Marco says. "Besides, we're giving them a bit of jackrabbit meat anyway."

Byron demonstrates, kneeling on part of the dead rabbit, keeping the hawks from pulling it away while they grip it tightly. Marco offers a piece of meat to each of the hawks, and when they let go of the rabbit, Byron slips it into his game bag. Pretty slick.

As the hawks tear at the food, Marco raises the T-perch above his head again. Pepper and Spice finish their snack, eye their surroundings for a few seconds, and fly to the top of the pole.

I'm expecting the birds to lift off toward the cliffs again at any moment, but they stay with Marco for now.

Byron heads up the slope, using the garden hoe and stomping with his boots to flush out more game. We follow after him.

I watch the hawks on the perch and notice the pattern of the tracker, which is mostly hidden beneath their feathers. I observe everything about them, to get my mind off the screaming rabbit.

"I noticed that your dad does that thing you don't like," I say to Marco quietly. "He talks for you."

Marco nods. "That's probably the reason I don't like it."

"I mean, you told Chloe not to do it. Have you told *him*?"

"I tell him," Marco says. "He just forgets sometimes. M—my whole family forgets, and I have to remind them. Do you tell *your* dad every time something bothers you?"

"No."

"Like what?" Marco asks.

"What do you mean?"

"Like what kinds of things bother you?"

Marco is waiting for me to answer. Why did I even bring this up?

"Like singing," I say.

"Your dad's singing bothers you?"

"Haha, no. He doesn't want *me* to sing. At least not with him around."

"That's weird."

I nod. "It's complicated."

"What's complicated about singing?" Marco asks. "Singing is actually one of the easiest things. I n—never get stuck on sounds when I sing."

"Really?"

"Yeah." Marco shrugs. "I don't know why."

I'm thinking of what to say to that when Marco begins singing. It's a funny song, but he's right. He doesn't stutter one bit.

Give me a sky
With the sun in my eye
And a serpentine road that's free

The hawks take off from the T-perch, wings beating fast, on the hunt. Byron calls out that he can't see the game they're after. We run through the desert brush, following Pepper and Spice. Then they do something I think might be a problem. Instead of angling toward something on the ground like a hunt, they rise higher and higher and head straight into the open canyon.

CHAPTER 25

TIP ELEVEN: MUSIC CAN INSPIRE YOU

Pepper and Spice have disappeared. They're too fast, and they fly too high for us to see where they went.

"Their transmitters and the receiver are paired to each other and linked to the satellite," Marco says, showing me the tablet with the GPS map. "We can track them."

Byron approaches us from the slope. "Where'd they go, Marco?" he calls.

"Over that ridge there." Marco points. I follow the path of the hawks on the map, past where Marco is pointing. They're headed toward the amphitheater.

"I think they're diving down," I say, watching the screen.

"Must've found something," Byron says. "We have to hurry. If they eat until they're full, they'll take off again."

"I don't think Pepper will leave," Marco says to me. His voice quavers a little, though, and I think he's worried. We start running.

"Let's get back to the road," Byron calls. "They've gone just past the plaza."

I carry the T-perch so Marco can keep an eye on the tablet screen as we run. I feel like this is my fault somehow. Maybe I shouldn't have gotten Marco talking about other things. Maybe I distracted him from the hawks, and that's why this happened.

It's a lot of zigzagging to get back to the road. The desert plants are sharp, and leaping over things isn't safe in rattlesnake territory. Rocks get in my shoes. It can't be much past eight in the morning, and already the heat pours off the red rocks. Something prickly is lodged in my sock, but I keep running.

We reach a parking lot full of sand and desert debris. Trees in planter boxes are scattered across the large cement lot, and weeds grow in old flower beds between the parking rows. A long walkway divides the lot in half, and we jog up it toward the theater plaza.

I remember this spot. I remember holding Mom's hand as we walked toward the theater and a splashing water feature in the center of it all.

"Keep going that way," Marco calls to Byron, who takes the stairs to the outdoor plaza two at a time.

Marco watches the GPS track. "Dad," he shouts, "they've taken off again! They're at four hundred feet!"

"Is that high for them?" I ask, my mouth dry from running in the heat. I've left the water bottles somewhere in the desert.

"If they soar in thermals, it can be up to three thousand feet. We really don't want them to go up there, though." He stops running for a second and studies his tablet screen. "They're rising." Then he yells up the stairs, "Five hundred fifty feet!"

Oh shoot. The hawks probably caught something, ate it, and now they're going to fly into the canyon with no motivation to return. I think that's what Marco is thinking, too. We look at each other and take off up the stairs.

On the right is a brick building with closed ticket windows and empty frames on the walls, which probably used to hold show posters. It's so eerie to be in an abandoned theater where Mom once performed. It's ghostly. Like another world.

Marco and I run through the center of the plaza, past empty concession carts and a closed gift shop, with red dirt clouding the windows. Beyond the shop is a giant metal arch. It leads from the plaza into the theater itself. At the top of the arch is a sign with muddied lettering that says WELCOME TO RED CLIFFS AMPHITHEATER.

The theater is even larger than the Opera House at the Kennedy Center. The stage is wider, and it has more seats. There's no ceiling overhead, and the backdrop behind the stage is actually the canyon cliffs. The theater is in complete open air. Not much of the natural setting has been changed, other than the stage and its wings, the concrete floor in the audience area, and the stadium-style seats.

Byron stops in front of the lighting booth at the back of the theater and watches the sky.

"They've come down to two hundred feet," Marco says. "There!"

The hawks are soaring high above, directly over some buildings beyond the stage-left wing. They are dark specks moving together against the bright-blue sky.

"Well, we found them," Byron says. "Do you know what happened?" he asks Marco. It doesn't seem like he's accusing him of anything, only that he's trying to figure this out.

Marco shakes his head. "They were on the perch one minute, and then they were off. I thought they'd gone after some game you flushed from the slope."

I try to remember what else was going on right before the hawks flew off. Marco was singing. But that can't be the reason. Can it?

Byron opens his game bag and holds out a long rope with something big and furry on the end. Marco grabs it, and we run down the long set of stairs to the bottom of the amphitheater.

"What is that?" I call to Marco on the steps.

"It's a lure. The birds are trained to come to it. They know I'll give them a larger piece of food when they do."

"Be careful back here, guys," Byron says.

A chill overtakes me when I get close to the stage. It's a new feeling of being where Mom once was—a different connection to her. I recognize equipment and parts of the setup from going to work with Dad and watching Mom from the wings at the Opera House. The scaffold bars overhead are still in place, but the lights have been taken down. Since the cliffs are a natural backdrop, there aren't any ropes and pulleys for large curtains. We're in the stage-left wing. Beyond that is a concrete pad with wheeled carts and old set pieces.

We come to a few trailers and small buildings. Pepper and Spice are circling high above the small building on the end. Marco rushes to get directly under them. I want to find out how he uses the lure to bring the birds back, but I pause to get a closer look at the first brick building.

Tall weeds crowd the walls. I peek in the grimy windows. Inside is a small kitchen, tables and chairs, couches, and shelves with books and games. I think this was the greenroom for the performers. I wipe the red dust from the glass and imagine Mom in there with the cast and crew of her show, having meetings and waiting to go onstage.

Marco and Byron have gone down a slope to the next building. The hawks still soar far overhead. Marco holds the rope end of the lure and swings it like a giant lasso as the large furry piece on the other end circles in the sky. I stay out of the way, near the door of the smaller building.

Suddenly, a shadow crosses the door. I turn around, and Spice swoops toward me. I duck and shield my head with my hands. She flies directly over my head, and so close that I feel the breeze from her broad wings. But she doesn't touch me. She snags the furry end of the lure with her talons and slams it to the ground.

"Yes," Byron says in an enthusiastic whisper.

Marco moves in quickly, rewarding her with a large piece of meat. As she pulls at the feast with her sharp beak, Marco holds the strap from her anklet and gets her to step onto his glove.

Suddenly, Pepper lands right next to me. I still have the leather glove on my hand, but I don't have anything to feed him. Pepper moves closer, his head jerking in fast, little movements. I hold really still.

Byron places a piece of raw meat in my glove. "Hold your arm out," he says.

Pepper flaps his wings and flies to my outstretched hand, gripping the glove with his talons and eating the meat.

"Great job, Harrison," says Byron softly. "Do you see the leashes hanging from Pepper's anklets?"

I look for the straps I saw dangling from the hawks' legs as they flew. They're threaded through a hole in Pepper's leather anklets.

"Carefully, so you don't startle him, grab hold of the leash," Byron says.

I do. "Got it."

"Here, Dad," Marco says, handing Spice off to Byron.

Marco moves closer to Pepper. He takes the leash, threads it through a metal ring on the glove's cuff, and quickly ties a knot.

"We're also going to hood him, to keep him calm." He slips the hood over Pepper's head, covering his eyes. Immediately, the hawk's wings settle against his body.

"Well," Byron says, sounding relieved. "I guess we're done for today."

Marco nods. "Yeah. I don't know what got into Pepper."

"Marco," Byron says, "I think the longer you have him, the more he's going to act like a wild bird with instincts. I think you have to start thinking of Pepper as the wild hawk he is, instead of as something magic." His eyes look kind of sad as he gathers up the scattered T-perch, lure, and garden hoe.

Marco says to me, "I don't think that's it. Pepper has flown over here before. We didn't have to chase him down that time, because he flew back."

"What could it be if he's not actually catching food when he comes here?" I ask.

"I don't know," Marco says. "Besides food, the only thing here is the theater."

"And the storms," I say. I wonder if birds sense the weather when they soar hundreds of feet up in the sky.

"All ready, boys?" Byron asks.

"Can you take a picture of me holding Pepper before

we go?" I ask Marco. "I'd like to show this to my dad and Kennedy."

"Sure," he says.

I pull my phone from my pocket with my free hand and hold it out to him. He takes a few shots of me posing with the hooded hawk. All of a sudden, my phone starts playing audio from YouTube. The last video I had open was Mom's performance of "You Are" with the National Symphony Orchestra. Her voice sails out of my phone speaker right at the big key change.

"Oops," Marco says. "Not sure what happened there." He holds the phone out to me. "I think I got some good shots."

I take the phone in my free hand as Mom's notes go higher and higher, sending goose bumps all over my arms. Instead of stopping the music, I let Mom finish the phrase.

A bigger world
A heart of gold
You are the breath, the light that makes me whole

Then I tap the screen with my thumb and turn it off.

Marco steps away from the abandoned building with a confused expression. "That's weird," he says.

"What's weird?"

Marco looks at the building and then shakes his head. "I don't know how to explain it. I thought I saw

216

something. M—must've been the sun in my eyes. Was that your mom singing?"

"Yeah."

"I didn't know she sang that song."

As we carry the hawks back through the theater and along the road to Byron's van, I can't shake how it felt to hear Mom's voice so unexpectedly in this place— even if it was just from a phone speaker. Her voice rang through this canyon once before. It's strange to think that all these ancient rocks that rise in walls around the theater were the same when she was here. They were here for her the same as they are for me. And they were here for people before us. They've heard it all.

CHAPTER 26

TIP TWELVE: THINK ABOUT WHAT PEOPLE NEED TO SEE

I dream all night about hawks flying away and a stray black dog barking at me. I also dream that the dog I named Obsidian actually turns into a giant lump of obsidian. It's so shiny that I can see myself in it.

I wake up to the feeling that my face is on fire. The sunlight shines through the bedroom curtains. I touch my cheek with the back of my hand. It's burning up. I'm tired, but I don't feel sick.

I slide out of bed and stumble to the dresser to check my face in the mirror, just as Aunt Maggie pokes her head in the doorway.

"Oh, kiddo! Look at that sunburn! Didn't I tell you to apply the sunscreen twice?"

My skin is bright red and shiny. It feels tight, like it will split if I move a muscle. And it really hurts.

"Come on," she says, waving me to the door. "Let's put some aloe on that."

I've been sunburned before, but never like this. I follow her downstairs.

"We should have done this last night," she says. "I didn't realize how bad it was."

"Why is it so bad? I was only outside for the morning, and then a little in the orchard." I sit on the stool at the kitchen counter as Aunt Maggie pulls a spiny-looking potted plant down from the windowsill. She cuts a large leaf from the plant and lets liquid from the end drip into a dish.

"We're three thousand feet above sea level in Muse," she says. "That's almost three thousand feet closer to the sun than what you're used to. You're gonna burn here unless you wear your sunscreen." She holds my chin and tilts my face up. "I think you should also wear a hat when you go out. Do you have one?"

"Yes."

Aunt Maggie uses the knife to slice the sides and top of the leaf and remove the gel inside. She soaks a cotton ball in it and then touches the cotton ball to my cheek.

"Yow!" I exclaim as the cold hits my skin. "That's so cold. It kind of hurts."

"It's room temperature. That just shows you how hot your skin is."

I get used to the cold as she covers my face with the aloe vera gel. It leaves a sticky feeling behind.

"After this, you need to drink a lot of water all day. You can also put a cold washcloth on your face and then reapply the gel."

"Okay."

She finishes with the cotton ball and sets a few clean ones by the dish.

I notice she's wearing a skirt and a nice white T-shirt tied in a knot on the side. "Why are you dressed up?"

"Oh, Sam invited me to go to church with him and then to his church picnic. I was going to ask if you wanted to come along, but maybe you shouldn't be in the sun today. Give your skin a rest, you know?"

"Sam?"

"Mr. Bradley."

"Oh." My aunt is going to church with my art teacher?

"Have you been to church with *Sam* before?" I raise my eyebrows at her.

"Nope. This is a first. How do I look?"

Aunt Maggie's hair is always a little out of place—with strands falling loose from a ponytail or a bun—but it's kind of sporty and fun. Like she doesn't mind the outdoors.

"Great," I say.

"Do you want to come? Or . . . I mean, I'm not going to make you come. But you *can* if you don't want to be here by yourself. Do you feel sick from your sunburn or anything? Maybe I shouldn't leave you."

I laugh. She's all flustered, and that's not like her. "No, you can leave. I'm fine. And I don't want to come on your church date."

"Hey." She points at me. "Watch the teasing. I know where you sleep."

I laugh harder, but it hurts my cheeks. "Ow."

"It's all fun and games until you remember you have a sunburn, isn't it?"

"If I wear a hat, can I hang out with Marco and Chloe today?"

Aunt Maggie smiles. "Yes. I'm meeting Sa—Mr. Bradley at his house, and I can drop you off at Chloe's on the way if you want."

"Okay. Thanks."

"Call and make sure it's okay with Mr. and Mrs. Taylor first."

I call Chloe's number, but her mom answers. Her voice jumps to a higher pitch when I tell her who I am.

"Harrison! You get yourself over here and let me see you!"

✢   ✢

Chloe lives only one block over from Joshua Circle. I don't remember the house when we pull into the driveway, but I remember the tall palm trees out front.

Chloe's dad answers the door. Aunt Maggie calls out of the open car window, "Thanks for letting him visit, Eli!"

Mr. Taylor waves at her. He takes one look at my face, and whistles. "Boy, you got a lot of sun."

"Yeah. I went hunting with Marco Swift yesterday and didn't understand about the elevation here."

"I'm sorry, Harrison," he says, inviting me in. "Do you need anything for it?"

"My aunt Maggie gave me aloe vera." I hold up the small container of gel.

He chuckles. "Well, you keep putting that on. Mrs. Taylor will probably remind you."

I walk into the Taylors' house, which smells familiar, like fresh laundry soap. Mrs. Taylor is sitting in a living room chair, reading a book. Her black hair is pulled back sleek against her head and tied back in a puff. Where Chloe's skin is bronze brown, Mrs. Taylor's is lighter brown and golden.

"Hi, Mrs. Taylor."

She glances up from her book. "Ooh," she exclaims. "How you've grown!" She sets her book on the coffee table and stands up. "You were *this big* last time I saw you."

Mrs. Taylor demonstrates my five-year-old height with her hand near her waist.

"I'm glad you called, because I was about to march

over to Maggie's and insist you come for a visit. It's so good to see you!"

"It's nice to see you, too." I remember Mrs. Taylor a little. Mostly, I remember how I felt at home here.

"Mmm. That face. You have something to put on that sunburn?"

"Yeah." I show her the container of aloe.

"Well, Maggie's taking good care of things. You want anything to drink? Chloe can show you where everything is."

"Okay," I say just as Chloe comes inside from the backyard and lets Sherman in the house. He's a bit wet, like he ran through some sprinklers.

"Hey, Harrison," Chloe says. Her eyes get wide when she looks at me. "Whoa."

"I know. It's really red."

Mrs. Taylor grabs a towel from a basket by the door and dries Sherman off. "It's good to have you back in Muse, Harrison. It's been too long. And we didn't have Sherman when you were here before."

She laughs at Sherman's enthusiasm. "Are you okay with dogs?" she asks, holding him back.

"I love dogs," I say.

She lets him loose. He sniffs at my hands and wags his tail. I remember how he tangled up the leashes that day in the art village. But he's pretty calm in comparison to Obsidian the stray.

"Sorry you got burned," Chloe says.

"It was worth it," I say. "I went hunting with Marco and his hawks."

"Hunting? What do they hunt?"

"Jackrabbits."

"Oh," Chloe says, wrinkling her nose. "I'll help Marco take care of his birds if he wants to teach me, but I'm not going to watch them kill a rabbit."

"I think you might have to *feed* them rabbit," I say.

"You don't need to take care of any more animals, Chloe," Mrs. Taylor says. "You've got enough on your hands as it is."

Chloe shrugs, rubs Sherman's fur, and says, "Well, I'm glad this guy eats dog food from a bowl."

"Among other things," Mr. Taylor says, chuckling.

Chloe and I head downstairs to their family room. I remember it being a huge space to run around and play in when it was too hot outside, but it isn't actually as big as I remember. Plus, they have a pool table down here now.

Chloe racks up the balls with a plastic triangle form. "You wanna play a game?"

"Sure. I'll give it a try."

She hands me a stick, which she calls a *cue,* and we take turns trying to hit the balls into the pockets. Chloe is solids, and I'm stripes.

I tell Chloe what Marco said about the contest and the muse.

"If something made the muse sad enough"—Chloe angles her cue on the pool table, lining it up toward a corner pocket—"maybe that's why it decided to stay away. If that's true, maybe we can get it to come back if we get its attention in a new way."

"That's what I was thinking. Marco wants it to return so people will stop asking if his wish made the muse leave. I told him we should ask you for help."

"And *you* want the muse to show up, too, huh?"

"I mean, if I can have a chance at a magical wish . . ."

"Let's invite Marco over," Chloe says.

We both text him. Dad and Kennedy each responded to my picture of Pepper on my glove.

"I'll go get us some snacks," Chloe says, noticing I have some messages. "Be right back." She heads up the stairs.

> **Kennedy:** Wow! You're holding a real live hawk!
>
> **Kennedy:** Hey, guess what? I asked your dad, and he said it's fine for me to come for a visit, if I check with your aunt. I have a break from class the last week of October, and my parents said they'd pay for a plane ticket.
>
> **Me:** Really? That's great news! I'm glad you want to come!

That will be after the Art Festival Contest is over. No matter what happens with the contest, having Kennedy come for a visit would be awesome. I send her some happy emojis and Aunt Maggie's phone number.

Dad: That is amazing, Harrison! Looks like fun.

Me: It was. I can't wait for you to come so we can go hiking.

Dad: Did you find some good hikes?

Me: Yeah, Zion and Snow Canyon are full of them.

Dad: Good. So, the tour schedule may be changing, but I'll let you know as soon as it's certain.

Me: But you're still coming for the festival and the contest, right?

A typing bubble appears and then disappears.

Dad: What is the date again?

I send a screenshot of the Muse Art Festival flyer.

Me: October 3rd

Dad: I'm going to do my best, buddy.

Chloe returns with apple slices and chips. Her dad comes down the stairs a few minutes later, singing "Don't You Worry 'Bout a Thing." Mr. Taylor's a great singer. He gets to the bottom of the stairs, rounds the corner into the family room with some sodas, and serenades Chloe and me with, "Don't you worry 'bout a tha-a-a-a-a-a-a-a-a-ang."

Chloe laughs, and it makes her dimple show.

"Dad, I invited Marco Swift over. Is that okay?"

Mr. Taylor stops singing. "Sure."

Chloe checks her phone. "Good. 'Cause he's on his way."

"Great!" Mr. Taylor says. "I came down to tell you that you can use the movie projector if you'd like." He turns to me. "Chloe uses it for things besides movies. Maybe she'll show you her latest project."

Mr. Taylor winks at Chloe, and she smiles back.

"I'd like that," I say. I reach into my pocket for the obsidian. "Mr. Taylor, can I ask you an art question?"

"You bet."

"I want to make something for the art contest that has to do with this." I hold out the smooth stone to show him. "My aunt Maggie told me that rocks and crystals have qualities that help people. This is obsidian. Some websites I found say it's also called the mirror stone."

"Oh, yes, obsidian," Mr. Taylor says. "May I?"

I hand the stone over, and he rolls it around in his fingers. The websites said that obsidian can give a person knowledge and wisdom from other realms. The knowledge I'm hoping for has got to come from another realm. Perhaps a muse's realm.

"I'm wondering how I could use black paint with other colors coming from it without having the black paint take over all the other colors," I say.

Mr. Taylor nods. "That's a cool idea, Harrison. You could manage it pretty well with something called

Dutch pour. You use acrylic paints and pour them onto your surface one color at a time, and then use a blow-dryer to move the paint into patterns. I can help you with that if you want to give it a try."

"You use a blow-dryer on the paint? That sounds fun."

"It is. I think you'd enjoy it." Mr. Taylor hands the stone back to me. "Honestly, I think these are the sort of ideas that make great art. You've thought of something meaningful to build your art around."

"Dad," Chloe says, "why do you think the muse stopped coming to the contest and granting wishes?"

Mr. Taylor wrinkles up his forehead and rubs his goatee. "I don't know."

"Marco thinks it's because something made the muse sad," Chloe says.

"He does, huh?"

"Yeah," I say.

"Well, that's very interesting," he says. "I'll have to think back about what happened that first year the muse didn't show."

"Marco says it *did* show," I say. "It came to the contest that year, but then it left."

"Hmm." Mr. Taylor leans back against the wall and folds his arms. "It's hard to know how a being like that thinks—*if* it thinks or feels the way we do. It's possible that muses hold grudges. Or get . . . bored." He shakes his head. "I'll think about this some more. Maybe Mrs.

Taylor has some ideas. You two have fun, and I'll send Marco down when he gets here."

"Thanks, Dad," Chloe says.

Mr. Taylor leaves, looking like he has a lot on his mind.

When Marco arrives, Chloe and I tell him about her idea to get the muse's attention with something new. I tell him Mr. Taylor's suggestion that the muse could just be bored.

Marco joins our game of pool, and he and I trade off trying to hit the striped balls into the pockets. "But if the entries at the contest every year don't get the m— muse's attention," Marco says, "what do you think will?"

Chloe smiles. She strikes the white ball, and it hits a solid ball, but it doesn't go in. "Your turn," she says to me. I hand the cue to Marco for him to take this one.

"You said you were working on something special for the contest this year," I say to Chloe. "Do you think your idea would encourage the muse to come back?"

"It might." Chloe eats an apple slice while she thinks.

Marco takes a shot, and the white ball bumps a striped ball that's already close to a pocket. It goes in.

"Yes!" I cheer.

"Good job! You get to go again," Chloe says. "So I've been taking media arts since last year. I love making big spectacles with special effects for the theater department. It's kind of what I was thinking of doing for my contest entry. You know, something colorful and big, but not a painting—so maybe people in the town will finally stop asking when I'm going to paint like my dad. There isn't even a category for what I'm thinking of doing, but I don't care about winning in a category."

"Hey, special effects!" I say. "That's a good idea. Are you thinking of using lights, then?"

"Yeah, and music," Chloe says. "A whole big production."

"Well, m—maybe that would work," Marco says. "It's worth a try."

I hesitate a minute and then add, "You know, I think I saw a muse once."

Marco stops aiming for his next shot, pulls the cue off the table, and gives me his full attention.

"I saw it in Washington, DC. It was near something called the Art Collective, where people gathered to paint and draw on big panels next to the National Gallery of Art. Have you ever seen pictures of the northern lights?"

"Yeah," Chloe says, her eyes wide. Marco leans against the pool table and spins the cue in his hand.

"People were painting on the panels, and this guy James was playing his guitar, and something made of blue and green light sort of—I don't know—*flowed* over the art panels. I think it showed up because of the art but also because of the music."

"I wonder if there's more than one," Marco says.

"My aunt says she thinks there are powerful beings like that in many parts of the world."

"Maybe that's it, then," Chloe says. "Maybe the muse wants art *and* music. And maybe we need to do something *before* the Art Festival Contest, to help bring the muse back. There's the Walk and Chalk coming up."

"Yeah," Marco says. "I have to do the chalk festival for my term project."

"It's a perfect place for us to start," Chloe says. "I'll show you what I have in mind." She goes to the other side of the room, where a projector sits on a shelf mounted from the ceiling. She turns it on and opens a laptop on the nearby table. "I bet my dad will help us set this up at the Walk and Chalk. Maybe Maggie will let us use the front of her gallery."

"I bet she will," I say.

"I learned how to use this program to create a light show with music." Chloe connects the laptop to the projector with a cable. "Can you guys close the curtains?"

We cover all the basement windows, and it gets pretty dark in the room except for the white projector light.

"I'll just choose some music here . . ." Chloe searches a list on the laptop. "And link the projector to the program . . ."

Marco and I exchange glances.

"Now, this will look even better with fog, but we can save that for the actual art contest."

"What the heck?" Marco whispers. "Fog?"

We asked Chloe for something amazing, and I don't think she's going to disappoint us.

"Now, I just need to connect to the Bluetooth. . . ."

Upbeat music with a good drum rhythm starts playing from the surround speakers in the Taylors' basement. The projector sends arrays of colored light beaming across the darkened room. Chloe changes the patterns with her computer program, and the lights spin, flash, and angle off in different directions—all to the beat of the music.

Marco and I jump around and dance as the lights streak across the ceiling. I holler to be heard over the speakers, "If this doesn't get the muse's attention, I don't know what will!"

CHAPTER 27

TIP THIRTEEN: MAKE ART A CELEBRATION

September might be heading into fall, but it's just as hot as ever in Muse. Marco and Chloe and I arrive in the art village early on the morning of Walk and Chalk. I remembered to apply sunscreen, as I've done ever since the big bad sunburn.

Colorful flags are strung above Oasis Lane and between the buildings. Music plays over the outdoor speakers, and I can't help thinking that if music would bring back the muse, then the music the art village always has should have already made a difference. I push the thought down for now, though, because Chloe's music-and-light idea to go with all the chalk art is all we have going for us right now.

The air smells of waffles and syrup mixed with hot oil. Sections of the street are roped off as shop owners set up tables with things for sale. Most of the street is divided into a grid, with large rectangles drawn in thin white chalk. Some artists have already claimed their spaces and have begun drawing.

"I'm going to save our spots," Marco says. "And then I'll be there to help you set up." Marco grabs three RESERVED cards from the registration table and takes off toward one of the desert gardens.

"Hurry back," Chloe calls after him. She and I are carrying a bag of cables and a box with the projector in it. Mr. and Mrs. Taylor follow behind us with the laptop and some tools. Chloe is planning to mount the projector high on the outdoor wall of Gallery 29. Aunt Maggie has been setting up displays since before sunrise, and she's expecting us.

"I'm excited to see this," Mrs. Taylor says. "I'm glad you're working on a project together again—except this time it doesn't involve a mess of flour, peppermint extract, and blue food coloring all over my kitchen."

"Mom," Chloe says. "Please don't remind us."

I had forgotten about that until now. I remember the biting peppermint smell and stirring thick wet flour we took from the pantry. "Haha, didn't we think we were making cookies?" I ask Chloe.

She gives me a sideways glance. "I always thought it was going to be muffins."

Marco joins us, a little out of breath. "I saved us three squares together by the Meditation Labyrinth."

The *what*?

"Oh, that's a good spot." Chloe nods. "Away from the main path. Not so crowded."

I'm the only one who's new at these festivals, so I'm glad they know what they're doing.

Aunt Maggie comes outside to help us with Chloe's setup. She brings a ladder from inside the gallery. Marco is taller than both me and Chloe, so he volunteers to help Mr. Taylor, and they take turns on the ladder. Mostly, I hold the cables and wait for Chloe to tell me what she needs. The art village swarms with people as we work.

"What are you doing?" asks a nasal voice.

It's Leon.

"Helping Chloe with a project for tonight," I say, leaving out the important details.

"If you want to know the best way to angle those speakers, I know how to do it," Leon says, walking closer to the ladder and looking up at one of the speakers Mr. Taylor just mounted to the wall.

"I think Chloe knows what she wants to do," I say.

"Okaaay," Leon says. "Just trying to help you get the best sound for this corner—that's all." He swaggers away.

Mrs. Taylor and Chloe are setting up a small table for the laptop. Chloe watches Leon with narrowed eyes and puts her hands on her hips. She takes in a deep breath and goes back to connecting cables.

"He's a helpful kid," Mrs. Taylor says of Leon.

Chloe shakes her head.

When everything is set up the way Chloe wants it, Aunt Maggie lets us store the laptop behind the front counter in the gallery.

"You can come back in here and let me know when you're ready," she says.

"What time are you planning to do all this?" Mrs. Taylor asks us.

"After sundown," Chloe says. "We need it to be dark, or we won't get the effect."

"Then we should be sure the village lights go out," says Mr. Bradley. He's approached our group and stops his chair next to my aunt. He hands her a cup of coffee from the café. "Maggie told me you're working on a surprise presentation. If you need it to be dark, I can speak with the store owners and the arts council and ask them to dim the lights when you're ready."

"Thank you, Mr. Bradley," Chloe says.

"I'm happy to help."

Aunt Maggie smiles at him and sips her coffee. After their "church date" and the picnic, Mr. Bradley has come over a few times to see her. Mostly, they hang around outside in the orchard and water the trees and talk.

"Hey, Marco," Mr. Bradley says. "When I said you could do Walk and Chalk for a term project, I didn't expect you'd go above and beyond on another project." He looks up at the projector and the mounted speakers and cables.

"It was Chloe's idea. It's for the m—muse," Marco says. "We want to . . . get its attention."

Mr. Bradley doesn't seem surprised, and I think maybe Aunt Maggie has told him the whole story. "Well, I hope it works. This town needs the muse, don't you think?"

Marco nods.

"Amen to that," Mr. Taylor says, rubbing the back of his neck where the sun is shining.

Chloe, Marco, and I thank everyone for helping.

"Meet you here at sundown," Chloe says to the grown-ups, and we take off for the drawing spots Marco saved for us.

He leads us to a small desert garden full of wind spinners and chimes on stakes in the landscaping. Beyond that is a giant circle of small rocks with benches lining it. More rock circles get progressively smaller and go all the way to the center, where a big orange boulder sits. It's like an invitation to rest after exploring the paths. A small sign staked in the ground says MEDITA-TION LABYRINTH. Marco's reserved three rectangles on the pavement at the labyrinth's edge.

We buy our chalk from the nearest vendor, and Chloe hands me a rag. "Some people use their fingers to smudge and blend the chalk, but it tears up your skin after a while."

"Thanks," I say.

"I brought a couple of them. We can all share."

Chloe takes the rectangle farthest to the right, I take the middle, and Marco takes the left.

"What are you going to draw?" I ask Marco as I lift a few colors from my box of chalk.

Marco opens a folded sheet of paper from his pocket. It's a drawing of a Gila monster, and he's drawn a grid of squares in light pencil over the top.

"That's really good. What are the squares for?"

Chloe leans in to have a look.

"I'll show you." Marco pulls out a long piece of string. "Chloe, you know how to do this, right?"

"Yep."

Together, they rub white chalk over the string. Then Chloe takes one end of the string to the top of Marco's rectangle space while Marco holds the other end tight. They make a straight line of white chalk by tapping the string on the pavement.

"You make a grid of equal-sized boxes," Marco says as they make a second straight line a few inches away from the first. He uses a ruler to measure the distance between lines. "Then all you have to do is draw what's inside each box, one at a time. But since the boxes on the pavement are bigger than what I've drawn on my paper, this enlarges the whole picture."

Chloe and I help Marco finish making the grid over his drawing space.

"Have either of you seen that stray black dog anywhere lately?" I ask.

"I haven't," Marco says.

"Me neither," Chloe adds. "And I've been keeping an eye out for him, too." She settles in front of her pavement space and begins drawing circles and swirly designs.

Even though I didn't plan in advance like Marco, I try drawing Obsidian the stray. It feels good to sit in the sun and color on the ground. I smudge a chalk line with my finger.

"Where do you think a muse goes when it disappears?" I ask. "Do you think it's still around, waiting for something spectacular, or do you think it could be somewhere else?"

"Maybe up in the sky," Chloe suggests. "It could be the reason for those lightning storms."

Marco smudges some yellow and orange chalk on his drawing. "Interesting idea," he says. "Those storms have been around for almost as long as the muse has been missing."

"I've heard people call it the canyon muse," I say. "Maybe it goes into the canyon, and it's far from the village."

"Well, that's another good reason for our light show and the loud music," Chloe says.

I do my best on the dog drawing, but a black dog with a desert background isn't very colorful for chalk art. So I begin making a sunset sky—like Mom's sunset painting at the Art Collective. I use pink and orange, with hints of blue and purple. My knees and hands ache from the hard pavement, so I sit back and rub them.

Chloe works on a section of her swirls in shades of green and purple. She has purple chalk all over her hands and some on her cheek. Marco is about half-finished with his Gila monster.

"Do you want to get waffles from the food truck?" I ask them.

"Good idea," Chloe says.

"If we wait too long, they m—might run out."

We each get "The Works." It's a waffle with a crunchy cookie spread along with berries and whipped cream. It's the biggest waffle I've ever had.

After we eat, we finish our chalk drawings. Marco's Gila monster is so good I imagine it could come crawling out of the pavement with its tail swinging.

"That's awesome," I tell him. "The shading makes it look so real."

"Thanks," he says. "I'm supposed to take a . . . picture of it to show Mr. Bradley. Will you take one with me in it?"

"No problem." I take his phone and get a few shots of Marco next to his Gila monster, which is a little larger than life-sized.

Then Chloe says, "Let's get one of all three of us."

We sit smashed together, and she holds her phone up to take a selfie, but her arm doesn't reach long enough to get the three of us plus our art. That's fine with me, because my chalk dog is cut out of the frame, but you can see some of my sunset, some of Chloe's green and purple swirls, and the head of Marco's Gila monster. Chloe shares it with all of us. And that's how I got a picture to send to Kennedy of me almost getting swallowed by a Gila monster.

The rest of the day, we try the free samples from Rocky Mountain Chocolate Factory and listen to the bands playing by the Prickly Pear café, and I reapply my sunscreen. Listening to the musicians makes me think of James in Washington, DC, and singing for Sylvania. But if *that* music made a muse happy, why shouldn't this? I don't tell Marco and Chloe my concerns, though. We have a plan, and I don't want to jinx it.

We also check out the other chalk drawings. Some of the artists are *really* good. The ones that trick you into thinking you're on the edge of a cliff or a shark is coming out of a sewer grate are my favorite.

When the daylight turns golden and the sky goes from blue to orange and pink, Marco's family shows up. Mrs. Swift wears a wide-brimmed hat that shades her entire face and neck even though the sun is going down. She has pale skin, which probably burns like mine. Byron is wearing his Swift Bird Abatement T-shirt and says hello to a lot of people as they stroll down Oasis Lane. Marco's sister, Adrienne, is here, too. She comes right up to me and stands really close. Marco pantomimes something behind her back. He points at her and at me and draws something in the air with his finger. I don't know what he means, and I shake my head at him.

"We want to see what you all drew," says Mrs. Swift.

While everyone else checks out our chalk art, Adrienne says to me, "Can you show me one of your magic tricks, Harrison?"

She's really eager, so I pull out my cards and do a mind-reading trick. She pays close attention to everything I say. When I finish the trick and I've told her which card she was thinking of, she smiles big and giggles.

The sun is fading fast, so Marco tells his parents and his sister that we have to set up for our big event. His family follows us over to Gallery 29. The Taylors are already waiting there, and Aunt Maggie waves at us through the gallery windows. It's a bit like magic to me that all these families are here to be a part of what we're doing. Like they want to help. It makes me believe this is going to work. Like it's a real-life magic trick and Chloe, Marco, and I are all the magicians. I appreciate the Taylors and the Swifts and my aunt, but something inside me begins to ache.

I miss Dad.

And Mom.

Can she see me from wherever she is? Does she know what I'm doing here, trying to summon a muse and enter an art contest and bring Dad back here so we can be a family? As I'm thinking about Mom, the sun disappears below the desert horizon, and the streetlamps come on. The lights strung over Oasis Lane make the whole village glow yellow.

While Marco and Chloe get the laptop from Aunt Maggie and connect it to the projector, Mr. Bradley comes down the street with someone else I know. It's Tabitha from the Cactus Gulch sales office. They're talking about past winning contest entries and where they are displayed.

Tabitha stops midsentence.

"Harrison! How is Muse's very own magician?"

"Hi," I say. "I'm fine."

"Have you rescued any more tortoises?" She smiles. Her lipstick is very pink, and she has a pair of gold sunglasses on top of her head, holding her hair back. She's dressed more like she's been to the Opera House for an evening performance instead of at a chalk festival with food trucks.

"I rescued a toad from my aunt's pool," I say.

"Good enough." Tabitha winks.

"We're putting on something special here," I say, "if you'd like to stay and watch."

"I wouldn't miss it."

Mr. Bradley kept his word, because all the main lights in the art village suddenly go out. The only lights left are small ones near the ground and the blue glow coming from Chloe's laptop.

I move closer to Marco and Chloe as the crowd chatters and people ask what's going on. Chloe clicks a few things on the laptop. The music begins with the wail of a saxophone followed by a jazz drumbeat. In the dim flicker from the computer screen, I notice Mr. Taylor swaying in rhythm.

More instruments slide into the song, and the tempo gets faster. In perfect timing, the projector sends blue and red light beams dancing through the air. The colors change and spin, and the people gathering in front of the gallery get louder. They like it. The crowd grows quickly.

Marisol and Simone show up with a group of kids from school and begin dancing in the streets to the jazz music and Chloe's spectacular show.

"Did you guys do this?" Marisol calls to me as their dance party grows.

I nod but point at Chloe. She should get the credit.

Chloe is busy with the pattern changes, but Marco and I watch the sky. The vibrant display actually changes the look of the nearby cliffs. I'm not sure if all of this can reach deep into the canyon, but I'm hoping the muse feels it. Can it feel the efforts of everyone's chalk drawings? Can it hover over the art village and see it all?

I watch the moving lights and reach for my obsidian, the mirror stone that is supposed to show me something new. The flashing colors reflect off its surface.

I have to talk loud for Marco to hear me. "Do you see it anywhere?"

Marco mouths, *Not yet,* as he watches the sky and the chalk art around Oasis Lane. We both look for the muse while people dance and laugh and enjoy the party. Aunt Maggie is searching the sky above the village like we are. She catches my eye and motions me toward her.

"This is amazing," she says. "Your hearts are in the right place, and honestly, I think that matters more than anything."

"Do you think this will bring back the muse?"

"I don't know," she says. "But all these people are happy because of what the three of you have done. That's got to count for something."

Chloe keeps the music and lights going for three more songs. The crowd stays and cheers for each one. Mr. Bradley tells her this should be part of Walk and Chalk every year. Her smiling cheeks glow when he says that.

But when it's time to put it all away and go home, there hasn't been any sign of green and blue light that could possibly be the muse.

"I'm not sure it worked," I say quietly as we carry Chloe's supplies back to the Taylors' car.

"You can't always tell what your efforts might do," Mrs. Taylor says. "You can work and work at something and never notice the results, and then one day . . . things begin to happen."

"Yes," Mr. Taylor agrees. "It takes time to accomplish something big. So don't give up."

"We didn't expect to have a muse appearance to-night anyway," Chloe says.

"We didn't?" Marco and I say together.

"This was to give it a boost. I think of it like giving the dogs a training treat. They get a taste or a smell of something they like, and they'll come back again and again for it. All I have to do is say 'Come,' and they do. Now, we just need to make another show for the art contest."

Marco nods. "I'll help."

The grown-ups are talking in the parking lot, so the three of us load Chloe's supplies inside the Taylors' car. Then we climb up a large rock at the art village entrance and sit. The rock is still warm from the heat of the day. Streetlamps shine overhead, and large moths flutter around the bulbs. And as we watch the fireflies flicker across the desert in the dark, an owl hoots in the distance.

"I'll keep watching for that stray dog," Chloe says. "I told my mom about him, too, and she says she'll look for him when she goes on her morning runs."

"I'll ask my sister and my parents to watch for the dog," Marco says. "Adrienne will probably try extra-hard to find him for you. She likes you."

"She does?" I feel my face getting warm, and I don't think I got sunburned today.

Adrienne is standing by Mrs. Swift in the parking lot. She's watching us, perched up here on this rock, and she seems kind of sad that we didn't invite her. She tugs on a section of her long brown hair like she's nervous.

"Marco! She probably doesn't want you to tell him that," Chloe says, giving him a look that might as well be a punch in the arm.

I try not to laugh, because Adrienne is watching.

"Well, I don't know how he couldn't have already n—noticed. She follows him around at school . . . practically every day." He turns to me. "I was trying to tell you earlier. Before she asked you to show her a m—magic trick. She thinks your card tricks are so cool."

I remember Marco pantomiming stuff behind Adrienne's back.

"Don't say anything to her. I don't want her to be embarrassed," he says, his voice a little softer.

I wonder again what it would be like to have a brother or a sister. I'll probably never know. But for now, I'm just glad I have Marco and Chloe. I don't feel so much shadow sadness when they're around. They help it fade.

It would be the greatest magic trick of all to have Dad be part of everything going on here—to have him helping us as we try to get the muse's attention. And that's when I know how I need to make my contest entry.

CHAPTER 28

TIP FOURTEEN: CREATE WHAT COMES FROM YOUR HEART

MUSE ART FESTIVAL
Contest Entry Form

Return to Mr. Bradley by September 30th

NAME: _Harrison Boone_

AGE: _12_

GRADE: _7_

ENTRY TITLE: _Inside the Mirror Stone_

MEDIUM: _Acrylic on canvas / Dutch pour_

+   +

"Are you sure you don't want to make your project here in the classroom?" Mr. Bradley asks. He's letting me borrow a hair dryer for my Dutch pour painting, one from the art room, which is lumpy from several layers of dried paint. I stayed after class to get it.

"No," I say. "I'd like to give it a try by myself. You and Mr. Taylor explained it well enough. And I watched those YouTube artists you suggested."

"Okay," Mr. Bradley says. "But if you aren't happy with your results, I'm here to help."

"Thanks." I tuck the dryer into my backpack along with the bottles of acrylic paints he let me take. Aunt Maggie already bought me so many supplies that I felt bad to ask for more. "Bye, Mr. Bradley."

I take off down the hallway. Ms. Camacho says she's showing us some kickboxing techniques today, and I don't want to be late. Marco already went on ahead. As I round the corner to the math-and-science hallway, someone calls my name. It's Adrienne. She runs to catch up to me.

"I think I saw the dog you've been searching for," she says.

"Really? Where?"

"My mom wouldn't let me catch him, and he got away before my dad could get him. He was hanging around the backyard near the birds' enclosures."

"Oh no," I say. "Did he do anything to the birds?"

"No. He was just sniffing around. He wasn't even

barking until my mom came onto the deck to water her plants. She was singing with her headphones on, and the dog barked at her like crazy. That's why she wouldn't let me try to catch him. She thought he wasn't safe."

That's weird. Both times Obsidian barked at me inside the model home, I was singing.

"Thanks for telling me, Adrienne."

She pauses at the sixth-grade science room, waiting to go inside.

"Did you notice where he went when he ran off?"

She shakes her head. "Sorry."

I say goodbye and hurry to PE. The bell rings before I have time to change, and my backpack is too full to fit in the locker. By the time I get into the gym, everyone has lined up in groups to practice kicks with blocking pads. I did karate almost every day this summer. Even if it *is* different in kickboxing, I think I can pick this up easily.

Chloe and Marco are in a group with two other kids, and they wave me over. Ms. Camacho demonstrates how to do a front kick and a side kick and how to hold the kick shield. I volunteer to hold it for the group first. If you don't know how to brace yourself, you'll get knocked over.

When Marco is up for his turn, I ask him, "Hey, did you know Adrienne saw the stray dog in your yard sniffing around the bird enclosures?"

"Uh . . . yeah." Marco gives a nice front kick to the pad, and I press forward with my back leg so he won't push me backward.

"She saw the dog?" Chloe asks. "Were you home, Marco?" Chloe comes in for a front kick, and I hold the kick shield close to my body and brace for it. Just as I thought, Chloe kicks hard. She gets competitive.

The next kid misses the shield and has to try again.

"I was home," Marco says from the back of the line.

"Why didn't you say anything about it at lunch?" Chloe asks.

Marco whispers something to Chloe, and when he gets to the front of the line again, he tells me quietly, "I knew Adrienne saw the dog, but I didn't say anything because she wanted a reason to talk to you."

I chuckle a little. I've never had an admirer before. I'm not sure I want one. But I like how Marco helps his sister and cares about her like that.

"That's not how you hold the pad," says Leon, coming over to our group. "Ms. Camacho said I should come help you guys."

"No, she didn't, Leon," says Chloe. "I just heard her tell you to find a new group."

"Come on," Leon says to me. "Let me show you how to hold this thing the right way."

I offer the kick shield to him. We should switch off anyway. I move to the back of the line, and Leon sets up with the shield in front of him and his legs spread wide.

"Uh, Leon," I call, "you're going to want to hold the shield closer to your chest and put one foot behind—"

It's too late. The kid after Marco lands a front kick to the shield, and Leon goes flying. The kid rushes to help Leon up.

"I'm fine, I'm fine," Leon says, waving his hands like it's no big deal. But he decides not to hold the kick shield anymore. As he walks away from our group, he waddles a little bit, like it hurt more than he'd let on.

After school, I say goodbye to Marco and Chloe. Marco is helping Chloe walk the dogs today, but Dad told me he had time for a video call at four. We're going to work on my contest entry together. I can hardly believe he agreed and found the time, and I have a good feeling about this.

I use the garage door keypad to get in the house. My aunt's car is still gone. She doesn't usually get home from the gallery until close to five. I text her and tell her I'm home, and she reminds me to use the roll of plastic in her art studio to cover the worktable before I start. From the videos I've watched, Dutch pour is a messy way to paint.

I take everything downstairs to Aunt Maggie's studio and set it up before Dad's call. Plastic over the worktable. A stack of books on the edge of the table to lean my phone against so I can talk to Dad while I paint. Plastic cups for the different paint colors. A pitcher of water to dilute the paint, and paintbrushes for stirring. And my piece of obsidian, where I can see it.

At four o'clock, my phone rings.

"Hey, Dad!" I say into the camera.

"Hi, buddy," Dad says. Then he gets a good look at me. "Wow! You've been outside a lot!"

I haven't gotten burned again, but my light skin *has* tanned a little and my cheeks and nose have a pink tint that isn't going away.

"Well, it *is* a desert here," I say, smiling.

I don't think Dad has been in the sun. He looks tired. And gray. Not only the bits of gray streaks in his light-brown hair, but also his face. He's sort of gray all over.

"So tell me about this art project. What are we making?"

"It's called 'Dutch pour.' We're going to mix a little water in acrylic paints and pour them over the canvas. I want it to look like obsidian with colors coming out of it."

"Okay," Dad says. He leans a little closer to the screen. "What do you want me to do?"

"I don't know," I say. "Keep me company while I do it? Maybe you can help me choose the colors, too."

"I can do that."

I show Dad how the YouTube artist mixed a little

water in the cup with the acrylic paint. "I want to start by painting the canvas black—like obsidian."

"And how did you find out about this technique in the first place?" Dad asks.

"Mr. Taylor told me about it." I keep mixing water into the black paint until it's thin enough that it runs off the brush instead of drips. "Then I watched You-Tube tutorials. Same way I learned my card tricks."

"Ah. And where did the idea for painting obsidian come from?"

"A lot of things, I guess. I've been carrying this around in my pocket since the day after you left. Aunt Maggie gave it to me." I hold up the shiny stone to the phone camera. "She says rocks and crystals can some-times help people. And when I read about it, I found out that another name for obsidian is the mirror stone."

A crowd of people start talking in the background wherever Dad is sitting. He carries the phone with him to another spot. I think he was in a hotel lobby and now he's outside. The wind makes a kind of thumping noise over the phone.

"And what does 'mirror stone' mean?"

"It means it can show you a new way to think of things or a new path when you need one. It's supposed to give you wisdom," I say. "I don't know if that's real, but I like the idea."

"Me too," Dad says.

I turn the phone to give him a good view of the table.

I pour the thinned black paint all over the canvas. Then I tilt the canvas side to side, letting the paint run over it until it's completely covered. Paint drips off the ends and runs onto the plastic table cover.

"Good job," Dad says. "Now what? We add the other colors?"

"Yeah." I lean my head over the table so Dad can see me. "I wanted you to help me choose them. We can do any of these." I show Dad all of Mr. Bradley's paint colors. "The artists I watched chose one or two really light or metallic colors for contrast. I was thinking of these." I show him the white and gold paint. "But we should put other colors in, too."

Dad chooses aqua, sky blue, and bright purple. I choose green and pink. I let Dad decide which colors go first.

He watches as I measure the paint into cups and stir in some water. I start with the diluted aqua, pouring it in a spot on the lower half of the canvas until it forms a thick, round paint puddle. The bright purple goes on top of that, in the center of the aqua circle. Then I add the rest of the colors, one at a time—some on top and some outlining the others. The colors don't mix into an ugly mess. Instead, they sit in layers.

"We should listen to music while we do this," I say.

"How about some Dorian Striker?" Dad laughs like he's trying to be funny.

"How about some of Mom's?" I immediately regret

asking that, because Dad stops laughing. He rubs his hand over his chin, and it makes a scratchy sound.

"I'm not ready for that yet," Dad says.

I stop pouring the paint. "It makes you miss her?"

"Yeah."

"I miss her whether I listen to her music or not." I pick up the gold paint and stir it. It's a little thicker than the other paints, and it sparkles in the studio light. It makes me think of Mom's shiny gowns, which helps with the shadow that tries to take over the room.

Dad clears his throat. "We can probably talk better without music playing anyway, right?" He's sitting near a water fountain outside his hotel. I can hear it splashing.

"Sure." I pour a streak of gold down the center of the thick paint layers. Then I add a few swirls of white.

"I'm so curious how this is going to work, Harrison," Dad says.

"Me too, actually." We smile at each other. "The next step is to add more black paint, like an outline, around all these colors." I carefully pour the paint on the canvas. "We need enough of the base color that the hair dryer can move it."

"I still can't believe you're going to use a hair dryer on that. Try not to mess up Maggie's studio."

I laugh nervously. "I know, right? It looked easy in the videos, but I'll be careful." I want to be sure Dad sees this part, so I hold the hair dryer in one hand and the phone in the other. "First, you're supposed to aim the dryer from the top of the canvas to the bottom, and it should blow the black paint over all the other colors."

"Let's see what happens," Dad says.

I turn on the dryer and pass it over the canvas. It does just what it was supposed to do. All that extra black paint runs right over the top of the other colors. The entire thing is black, like those other colors were never there.

"Is that what you wanted it to do?"

"So far," I say. "This next step will show us if it worked." I take a deep breath and turn on the dryer again. This time, I send the airflow straight up the center of the canvas from the bottom to the top, and it's like the darkness on the canvas breaks open. The blues and purple, green and pink, burst onto the canvas from beneath the black, spreading out in beautiful patterns, with the white and gold streaked through like glittery lightning.

"Cool!" Dad and I say together.

"That's amazing!" Dad exclaims.

I turn the phone camera toward me. "It worked! I can't believe I did it!"

Dad smiles. "You're really good at finding things you want to learn and then following through. I'm very impressed."

"Thanks for doing this with me, Dad."

"It was a good idea."

"I'm going to enter this in the art contest," I say. "And then you're going to come visit, right?"

"Yes, on the way to Los Angeles. I should have three days there with you, so find out details on those hikes. Good luck with the contest."

"Thanks," I say, feeling lighter inside than I have in a long time, with lots of good things coming. Chloe and Marco are planning to make an even bigger display for the Art Festival Contest than the one we did at the Walk and Chalk. I've got a solid entry for the contest—and it's one that means something, because Dad helped me with it. And Dad is going to come back to Muse.

When Dad and I hang up from our phone call, I text my aunt and ask if I can go to Cactus Gulch to look for the stray dog. I tell her Adrienne saw him at their house, which isn't too far from the new development. Aunt Maggie says okay, but that I have to stay on the paved paths along Coyote Way, and to say hello to Tabitha.

I take an old collar and leash of Sherman's, which Chloe let me borrow just in case I come across Obsidian. I'm not sure he'd hold still long enough for me to get a collar on him, but it's worth a try.

Cactus Gulch is pretty empty when I get there. Tabitha's car isn't at the sales office. The construction must be past the curve in the road now, because I can't even see the trucks. Chloe said that maybe the construction workers feed Obsidian, so I start down the road. I check behind the model home along the way.

At the deck stairs, I peek inside the sliding glass doors. A basket is sitting on the kitchen counter that wasn't there last time I was here. It's like one of those welcome baskets from the sales office. Did someone buy this house?

My heart pounds hard. I climb the stairs and try the door. It slides open. I shouldn't be doing this. Although this house doesn't belong to me, I still feel like someone is taking it away. I don't want anyone else to live here. I step into the air-conditioned kitchen. The basket on the counter is full of water bottles, granola bars, trail mix, chips, and some candy. And there's a note.

Harrison:

Thanks for the magic tricks. I know it can be nice sometimes to have a place all to yourself. It's okay that you're here. Just remember to keep everything looking clean and new for when I need to show the home. I placed a drop cloth in the art room closet for you to use whenever you paint.

Tabitha

P.S. Display some of your art on the easels. This place could use some more color.

Tabitha knew I was here all along. Has she been leaving the place unlocked on purpose? Heat spreads in my cheeks. Has she heard me singing? I go to the art studio and open the closet doors. Sure enough, there's a heavy cloth folded on the floor.

I walk through the house, wondering why Tabitha is letting me be in here. And then I remember her sad eyes when she asked, "Are you Tess's boy?" and that she said Aunt Maggie is a good friend of hers. I return to the basket and take a water bottle and some snacks. I'm glad to know the house isn't sold and that I'm allowed to be here. But I don't feel like I need to stay for now. I've already made an amazing piece of art with Dad, and I have a dog to find.

CHAPTER 29

TIP FIFTEEN: USE LIGHTING TO CREATE A MOOD

I didn't find Obsidian. Not that day or the next. Mrs. Taylor thought she might have seen him on one of her morning runs, but he disappeared before she could get close.

The fruit in Aunt Maggie's orchard has ripened, so Chloe, Marco, and I help her make peach jam, pick apples, and take baskets of fruit to the neighbors. The three of us swim in my aunt's pool and talk about the muse and Chloe's plan for the art contest. She's going all out—with fog machines, different styles of lights she's borrowing from the school's theater department, and surround sound. Keeping busy makes the time go by faster until Dad and Kennedy come.

And then the day of the contest arrives. It's October 3. The art village is decorated harvest-style for the Muse Art Festival. Orange and white lights are wrapped around cacti in the botanical gardens. Round glass bulbs stuffed with fall-colored leaves hang from light strands across Oasis Lane.

Dad is coming to Muse after the Striker show wraps in Phoenix. He won't be here for the contest, but if the canyon muse shows up and I win a wish, I think he'll be coming here to stay.

Mr. and Mrs. Taylor drive Chloe and me and all of Chloe's equipment to the art village in the morning. The contest isn't until sundown, but Mr. Bradley got permission from the arts council for us to set up Chloe's display before the crowds arrive. Marco meets us in front of Gallery 29 with Mr. Bradley, who has decorated his motorized chair with tiny lights. He's wearing a collared shirt and a blazer with the sleeves cuffed. It's fancier than what he wears in art class.

"I got you approved to set up your project anywhere in this section." Mr. Bradley points past the gallery, where Oasis Lane curves and a temporary arch anchored overhead says MUSE ART FESTIVAL, EST. 1991. "From Maggie's gallery to the ceramics store and across the street."

"Thank you, Mr. Bradley," Chloe says.

"Some of the council members were here the night of Walk and Chalk, and they like what you did. So it wasn't hard to convince them to let you do it again."

I give Chloe a high five.

"You still need to get store owner permission before mounting anything on the buildings," Mr. Bradley says, "and be sure to keep cords out of the walkway and tape them down so no one trips."

Chloe pulls a roll of electrical tape from one of her boxes. "No problem."

"You thought of everything," Marco says.

"You all set for the contest, Harrison?" Mr. Bradley asks. I gave him all his supplies along with my entry form for the Dutch pour, so he knows I did my painting.

"Yep. Turned in my entry by the deadline last night." I have a fluttering feeling in my stomach, but I tell myself that's because something good is going to happen.

Chloe and Marco get to work unloading the cables and extension cords, and Aunt Maggie comes out of her gallery with her ladder.

I move a little closer to Mr. Bradley. "How does this work exactly?" I ask him quietly. "I mean, if the muse shows up . . . and if it doesn't?"

"When the arts council brought in judges," Mr. Bradley begins, "everyone waited until the judges made their decisions. They announced winners in different categories. We watched for the muse, but it didn't show. Then people went home."

"Marco told me something about that. Why did they start having judges when the muse was already the judge?"

"Well, people like recognition. And I think some people wanted more. Some folks also like the power to declare what's good and what isn't. And the arts council liked the idea of advertising the contest, bringing in tourists, and inviting important judges as a way to make some money for the town."

"But the muse . . . it didn't show up when there were judges here." I say it more to myself.

"You're right. We haven't had judges announce winners for two years now, and I thought the muse would return. Maybe it needs more time to see that the contest is different again. Now we just visit as neighbors, enjoy the entries, and hope."

"When the muse used to come—how long did it usually take?"

Mr. Bradley waves at Aunt Maggie to join us. His rolled sleeve moves as his arm goes up, and I finally see the rest of his tattoo: FEARLESS. Aunt Maggie leaves the ladder with Mr. Taylor and joins us.

"How long would you say it took for the muse to show up the year you won?" Mr. Bradley asks.

"It appeared a few minutes after sundown," she says. "I've always imagined that it hovers about unnoticed during the day and shows itself at night when it finds something it likes. Remember, more than one person had a wish granted that year."

"More than one is good," I say. "I hope it likes what we've come up with this year!"

Mr. Bradley smiles. "I hope it does, too. But no matter what happens, I'm proud of all your efforts in my class, Harrison. And I can't wait to see your painting."

"Thanks!" I turn to go help Marco and Chloe, but Aunt Maggie touches my shoulder.

"Harrison, there's value in creating something, because you made it. It's even more special because you invited your dad to be part of the process. That's magic, too." She winks.

I think she's telling me not to freak out if the muse doesn't come. But I believe it's going to come this time.

It takes us thirty minutes to get the equipment laid out and in place. It takes us another thirty minutes to find all the shop owners and get permission to mount speakers, run cords, and use their electrical outlets. Mr. Taylor helps Marco mount the speakers. Chloe and I position the lights while Mrs. Taylor sets up the three fog machines.

"I'm surprised the school let you borrow all this stuff," Marco says to Chloe when he and Mr. Taylor finish with the second speaker.

"The speakers belong to us," Chloe says.

"Yeah, but what about the lights and the fog m— machines?"

"The teacher who runs our audiovisual club used to work for the Red Cliffs Amphitheater. When it closed down, he was allowed to take some of the equipment for the school. He has a lot."

It isn't as hot as summer, but before we are finished running all the cords and taping them down, I have sweat dripping from my forehead.

"Chloe, you don't do anything small, do you?" her mom says with a sigh.

"No, she doesn't," agrees Chloe's dad, laughing. "But then again, neither do I." He spreads his arms, showing us the lighting bar that he mounted on the back side of the Muse Art Festival arch. "I think we've all earned some lunch!" He holds his hand out to his wife. "Mrs. Taylor, will you join me at the café?"

"It would be my pleasure, Mr. Taylor."

She laughs and hooks her arm through his as they walk off together, leaving the three of us alone. Aunt Maggie is busy in her gallery, and Mr. Bradley probably went with her.

"Oh yeah," I say. "I almost forgot!" I pull the envelope from my pocket. "When I dropped off my painting for the contest, they gave me a bunch of coupons to use today." I hand a small stack each to Marco and Chloe.

"Cinnamon rolls at The Bun," Chloe says, holding up a coupon.

"Ice cream at Rocky M—Mountain Chocolate Factory," Marco says.

"And I've got half off the fry bread tacos at the Prickly Pear," I say. I hold up a picture of golden fry bread topped with beans, vegetables, and melted cheese.

"We should go there," Chloe says. "Those are really good."

We take a shortcut through the botanical gardens instead of walking the entire loop of Oasis Lane. The art village is pretty full of people now, so we take our tacos to go and sit on the big rock by the village entrance.

"Is your aunt dating M—Mr. Bradley?" Marco asks me between bites.

I shrug. "I don't know. They do stuff together sometimes. And he invited her to church."

"That's a definite sign he's interested in her," Chloe says.

"Why?" Marco and I both ask.

"Because why would he want her at his *church* if he didn't like her?" Chloe asks, rolling her eyes.

Marco and I look at each other.

"Harrison, I know we haven't really talked about the wish stuff that much, but I've been thinking. . . ." Chloe takes a drink of water.

"Yeah?"

"I think your painting has a chance to win a wish because of what you put into it, you know? And I was talking to my dad about what happened the year after Marco won."

Marco stares at his food.

"He thought more about it, and he remembers that it felt different around here the year they brought in judges for the contest. He said it was like everyone was trying to get on the judges' good sides. Gifts, bribing, some dishonest stuff—all to get more attention than someone else. A lot of people came for the contest from out of town, and they thought the winners the judges picked would also win a wish from the muse."

"Ha," Marco says. "As if the muse would grant a wish just because some judges decided on the winners?"

"Yeah."

Marco nods and thinks a moment. "The m—muse seemed to choose me because it liked my wish, not just my art. It wouldn't want to choose people who came to town with . . . greedy ideas."

Chloe agrees, with an "mm-hmm," and points right at me. "And *that's* why I think you have a shot at this, Harrison."

"You don't even know what I would wish for if I got a wish," I say.

"I think I know the general idea."

"A dog," Marco says, smiling.

He's kidding, but he's not totally wrong. I'd really like to find Obsidian and bring him home. But I wouldn't use my only wish on that.

"I'm just saying, maybe the muse got tired of people being greedy." Chloe glances quickly at Marco. "I mean *after* your wish, of course."

"You don't know what I wished for, either," Marco says.

"Well, I know what you *didn't* wish for." Chloe's

eyes suddenly go wide, and she covers her mouth as she realizes what she's just said. It's the thing people around town whisper about. I've been at Red Cliffs Middle School long enough to have heard what they say about Marco's stutter. And I think all that gossip is the biggest reason that he wants this muse business to get settled.

"Oh my gosh, Marco," Chloe says quietly. "I'm sorry. That just came out. . . ."

Marco nods.

"I didn't mean anything by it. People are always assuming I'll be good at drawing and painting because my dad's a famous artist, but I think we shouldn't be what other people expect. We should just be *us*. And that's all I meant. You didn't wish to be different than you are. Right?"

I shove a bite of corn and beans into my mouth and wish Chloe didn't talk so much.

But then Marco says quietly, "You're the first person I've talked to who understands that."

"Really?" Chloe asks. "The *first* person? What about your family?"

"Definitely n—not my family," he says. "I think they don't understand why I didn't wish my stutter away. They feel bad for me sometimes. That's why they finish my sentences—they don't want the waiting to get awkward or for someone to be rude to me." He laughs. "Ironic, huh?"

"Hey," Chloe says. "Wouldn't it be great if the muse

saw our amazing light-and-music display and was so happy that it granted more than one wish? We could *all* win. Let's think of what we'll wish for if we get the chance."

And we sit on the warm red rock together in the October sun, eating our fry bread tacos with the meltiest cheese and watching joggers run the paths. Flocks of birds wing in formation across the blue sky. I'm not sure what Marco and Chloe would wish for, but I know my wish. And with these two new friends making wishes with me, it feels possible.

We take a picture. The three of us on this rock with the art village behind us. I send it to Dad and Kennedy with the words *Friends with wishes.*

CHAPTER 30

TIP SIXTEEN: CREATE WITH YOUR FRIENDS

After lunch, we finish setting up Chloe's display. She checks that all the lights and speakers are working. Her fog machines sit beneath the tables where all the art contest entries will be displayed at six-thirty. The tablecloths reach the ground, and the fog machines are completely hidden. We make sure to tape down all the cords, and it takes what feels like hours.

Aunt Maggie and the Taylors are busy at the gallery showing Mr. Taylor's new series to customers, but Mr. Bradley stops by to ask how we're doing. After he leaves, a short lady carrying a clipboard comes out to see us. Her jewelry clinks when she walks, and its silver shines against her warm-brown skin.

"You're Eli Taylor's daughter, right?"

"Yes," Chloe answers.

"I'm Mrs. Flores." She rolls the *r* in her name, like Marisol. "Your dad and Sam Bradley told me that you're setting up a special contest entry. Performance art?"

"Yes, it's called Lovely Sky," Chloe says.

Mrs. Flores flips through some contest entry forms attached to her clipboard. She's wearing a large ring with a black stone in it. I wonder if it's obsidian. "Ah, here it is." She looks from Chloe to Marco and me. "It says here the artist is Chloe Taylor."

"*And* Marco Swift and Harrison Boone," Chloe adds.

Marco smiles at her. He was pretty serious about never entering the Muse Art Festival Contest again, but Chloe figured out a way to get him into it anyway. I don't think he minds.

Mrs. Flores writes down our names. "I'm not sure how to put a description card on your entry like we do for the others, but maybe we can just announce the title and your names after you show it?"

"Sure," Chloe says. "When can we present it?"

"I told Sam Bradley we could have the village lights turned out for you at seven-thirty sharp," the lady says. "We want to be sure you have a good crowd, and that will give people plenty of time to view the other entries before the lights go out."

"Great!" Chloe says. "Thanks so much, Mrs. Flores."

She smiles at each of us. "Thank you for sharing your creative ideas. I'm looking forward to this."

"Me too," I whisper after Mrs. Flores has walked away.

When we finish, we get ice cream and hang out in the back room of Aunt Maggie's gallery. I have my cards with me, so I agree to do something I never thought I'd do. Marco has been asking me to show him how to do a card trick. I show him a fairly simple one—the Ambitious Card. He practices in front of Chloe and then tries it out for real on my aunt. She's always a good sport, so even if she figured out how he did it, she didn't let on.

The day is long, and the wait is almost more than I can stand. I send Dad and Kennedy more pictures of the festival and the village. I wander around the crowded gallery and find new art pieces, hoping this day will be full of new things. The Swifts show up, and Marco has to spend time with his family for a while. Chloe goes back to check on her stuff several times. She's right. It *is* a lot of equipment and cords to leave out in the bustling art village.

Just when I think I can't stand the ticklish feeling in my stomach about the contest anymore, it's finally six-thirty. Chloe and I meet up with Marco in the botanical garden to see the displays together. We follow the red pebbled paths through the garden, past lighted cacti and colorful floodlights shining on the wind spinners. It reminds me of the Christmas displays by the Occoquan River in Virginia, except instead of Christmas trees we have cacti, and instead of snow we have red dirt. The sun has completely set behind the cliffs now, and evening lights come on in the village.

Inside the display area, all the art entries are set out on tables with category labels: PHOTOGRAPHY, SCULPTURE, WATERCOLOR. There are many more categories, but I stop when I find ACRYLIC. A lot of people are crowded in front of the acrylics table, inching close to the ropes that are supposed to keep them from touching the art. Marco and Chloe haven't seen the painting I did with Dad yet. I wanted it to be a surprise.

"Yours is an acrylic, right?" Chloe asks.

"Yeah."

"Are you . . . going to video this on your phone for your dad?" Marco asks.

"Hey, good idea!" I say. I wish Dad were here with me in person, but a video to show him would be great. Then I think a video call would be even better. He probably has a show tonight, but I'm not sure what time it is in Phoenix.

Suddenly, an announcement begins over the village speakers.

"The Muse Arts Council would like to welcome you all to the annual Muse Art Festival Contest."

Everyone cheers. It occurs to me that they still call this a contest, even though they don't have judges anymore. Without judges, or the muse, it's really just an exhibit—like what Aunt Maggie has in her gallery.

The voice continues. "We'd like to recognize the festival committee for all their hard work this year. Please enjoy the displays and remember to stop by the information booth for your Bring Back the Muse shirts, vendor coupons, and free paint sets for kids."

"Harrison!" Chloe exclaims. She's moved closer to the acrylics table. "I found it!"

Marco and I join her.

Inside the Mirror Stone sits on an easel with an information card in front of it, just like the professional art in Gallery 29. The spotlights shining on the tables catch the shimmer in the black paint. The colors Dad and I chose remind me of blue skies, green plants, the pink and purple near the end of sunset, and gold starlight. It looks like the obsidian melted open and created something new. I hope this attracts the muse's attention. It has special meaning, and that *has* to count for something.

"I love it, Harrison! It's *so* good!" Chloe says. "My dad needs to see this." She searches the crowd and finds her parents, bringing them over to the acrylics table.

I look around for Aunt Maggie. She's not hard to find because Mr. Bradley is with her, and the lights decorating his chair glow a soft white. He spots me and steers his chair through the crowd toward us. My aunt walks next to him, smiling like she knows the excitement I feel.

The Swifts join the crowd at the acrylics table. Everyone makes a big deal out of my painting. Mrs. Taylor and Aunt Maggie ask me how I came up with the idea and tell me they're proud of me.

"This is a beautiful painting style," Marco's mom says. "The patterns make me think of those agate slices in the rock shop."

Adrienne stands right next to me and smiles. "You're good at magic *and* art, Harrison."

Mr. Taylor and Mr. Bradley talk about the contrast and that they like my choice of black as the base color.

I try calling Dad. This is the biggest thing I've ever done, and although I have friends and their families around me, it doesn't seem right without him. The video call rings and rings, but he doesn't pick up. I text him.

> **Me:** Hi Dad. Are you running the show right now? Can you go in the greenroom and call me? Our painting is on display at the contest.
>
> **Me:** I want my friends to meet you and for you to see all the people looking at our art.

A rumbling in the distance echoes like drums off the sandstone cliffs. Beyond the art village, flashes over the canyon show the cloudy sky and another Red Cliffs Canyon storm. I watch lightning shoot across the desert, and my heart beats faster.

"Harrison," Chloe says. "Marco and I have an idea. Come with us."

We find a quieter spot, between the information center and the ceramics shop.

"I was thinking," Marco says, "about your card tricks."

"What about them?"

"You're really . . . good at holding people's attention with them. Like the performing part. M—maybe if we got Mrs. Flores to agree, she could announce for everyone to watch the front of the acrylics table. You could do a magic trick for the crowd right before we turn the lights off."

It's cool that Marco is thinking like a director of a show, but card tricks are tough to perform to a crowd this big.

"Isn't that a great idea?" Chloe asks. "It'll start everything off really well."

"Card tricks aren't the big sort of magic tricks, though," I say. "The best ones I know only work with a volunteer, and not everyone would have a good view of what's happening."

"Adrienne would do it!" Marco says. "She's . . . perfect for this. She'll be excited when you know which one is her card. And that'll help the crowd understand what's happening. Do the one where you knock all the cards out of her hand."

I reach into my pocket and pull out my cards, shuffling through them.

"It'll be a fun addition to the festival," Chloe says.

"I think people will love it, and then we finish things off with our big display. I'll even start the fog machines while you're doing your trick. By the time you show Adrienne her card, the whole place will be full of fog swirling around your feet. It'll be awesome!"

I haven't thought about Harrison the Magnificent in a while. I've been so focused on this art contest and how to bring back the muse. Maybe getting the crowd ready for real magic with a *feeling* of magic will help send a message to the muse. I'm ready to try anything.

"Okay," I say. "Let's do it."

"Yeah," Marco says, beaming. "I'll get Adrienne and tell her the plan."

"I'll find Mrs. Flores," Chloe says. She checks her phone. "It's seven-fifteen. We have fifteen minutes before all the lights are supposed to go out."

I stay alone in the spot between the buildings, thinking through the steps and shuffling my cards. I check my phone. Dad hasn't called or texted back. He's probably busy backstage at the Striker show right now. I don't want him to miss this, though. I have an idea and hurry back into the crowd.

"Aunt Maggie," I call, and she turns around. My voice comes out a little breathless. "Will you video this?" I hand her my phone. "But if my dad calls on video chat, will you hold the phone so he can watch what I'm doing?"

She looks confused, but she takes my phone. "I'm

happy to, Harrison. But . . . what are you doing?" She leans in closer and lowers her voice. "Do you mean the thing with Chloe and Marco? The light show?"

"Yeah," I say. "I'm also going to try starting it off with a magic trick."

"Attention, everyone." Mrs. Flores's voice comes over the loudspeakers. "We have a surprise for all of you. Will you please clear a space in front of the acrylics table and direct your attention there?"

The loud hum of the crowd lowers to whispers. People back away from the acrylics table and turn from the other displays to watch. I take a deep breath and think of my old living room and Kennedy helping me find tips for magicians.

A good magician has a style. A master magician tells a good story.

I'm Harrison the Magnificent.

I stride to the open space where everyone is staring. I turn and see Marco and Adrienne waiting in the crowd. Adrienne waves at me.

"I'm Harrison," I announce loudly to the waiting audience. I can't quite convince myself to add "the Magnificent" to the end of my name. I just keep that part in my head. "I thought since this contest has a history of magic, we could add a magic trick to the evening."

A few oohs and aahs rise from the crowd. Kids push to the front for a better view. I must be doing a good job so far, because people are paying attention.

"Can I have a volunteer?" I ask.

Hands shoot up in the air—mostly kids. Most of the grown-ups smile a little.

I add to the illusion by scanning the audience as though I'm really considering who to choose, but I finally point at Adrienne. "How about you?" I ask.

She beams and runs up to join me.

"What's your name?" I ask loudly for the crowd to hear. I know her name, but this is how magicians do things.

"Adrienne," she says.

The crowd watches silently as I go through the trick, making the steps as big as I can. I pretend to get Adrienne's card wrong over and over again, and the kids laugh. Some of the adults seem worried, but it's all part of the trick.

Adrienne is a good volunteer. She smiles a lot and acts sorry for me when I get her card "wrong." But the end is the best part. I tell her to hold out her fist, and she does. I turn her fist so her thumb is at the top and slide the small stack of cards between the knuckles of her first and second fingers.

"Now," I say, building this moment as big as I can. I notice fog swirling around the ground. The kids in the front notice it, too. They point and whisper. I have to work harder to keep their attention. "Hold those cards between your fingers as tightly as you can."

"Okay," Adrienne says. "Got it."

And then I close my eyes and wave my hand over hers, as though I'm working hard to control the cards. Goose bumps prickle over my skin as I imagine real magic appearing in the village tonight. It seems so ridiculous to believe that it will, but I saw those lights dancing over the art panels on the Mall when art and music came together. I've felt magic in this world because Mom showed it to me.

I open my eyes and smack the cards in Adrienne's hand. They all fall and disappear beneath the layer of fog swirling over the ground. All except one. And Adrienne holds up her card with the delight and enthusiasm Marco said she would.

"It's my card!" she exclaims.

And the lights go out.

CHAPTER 31

TIP SEVENTEEN: THE MEANING IS IMPORTANT

The crowd gasps in the darkness, but then music builds from the speakers and colorful lights glow over the art displays, just where Chloe planned it. Everyone's art is spotlighted, like it's calling to the muse. Other lights shine lower through the fog, and it spreads the colors, changing them and making the art seem alive. The music is just what I would imagine for a magical muse, and I'm impressed that Chloe chose it. It's airy and mystical-sounding, and it sends chills down my neck.

Whispers rise from the crowd. People are smiling and pointing at the tables. My heart pounds so hard I feel it in my throat.

"The muse," someone says.

"Maybe it's back," says another.

Voices mumble from everywhere. I find Aunt Maggie in the crowd. She's holding my phone up and recording all of this. I wonder if Dad is on the phone. And I wonder how much of my life Mom can see. Can she watch me like watching a video on a phone? Does she still notice beautiful things and love to sing? I wonder what changes when someone dies and if all that's left is what we remember. I wish my memories of Mom and her music could ring through this place like they do in my head.

Thunder rumbles from the canyon storm, and as Chloe's music keeps playing, Mrs. Flores's voice announces, "Introducing a new category for the Muse Art Festival Contest! Under the category of Performance Art, this entry is titled 'Lovely Sky.' Artists are Chloe Taylor, Marco Swift, and Harrison Boone."

The crowd applauds. Some people look to the sky. I glance up, too. They're watching for the muse, I think. I search the art for that green and blue dancing light I once saw on the Mall. I spin around, scanning every table and every display. Then I focus on *Inside the Mirror Stone* for any sign that the muse has noticed the painting Dad and I did together. But the only real spectacular things here are Chloe's music and the colorful beams moving in the thinning fog. The soundtrack builds to a satisfying end, and then everything goes silent.

Nothing else exciting happens. No aurora borealis. Nothing magical. The regular lights come back on, and people begin to move through the displays again. Some are talking about the light-and-music show. A few people tell me how much they liked my magic trick. I mumble some thank-yous. I search the crowd for Chloe and Marco.

Is it over? Is the muse not coming? My breath catches in my throat, and lightning lights up the sky.

"Harrison!" Aunt Maggie calls. She's running toward me with my phone. "That was so beautiful. You were brilliant! Chloe and Marco were amazing." She waves her hand around at all the displays. "I recorded the whole thing." She seems excited, but I can tell she's hiding something. I can tell she knows the muse didn't come and that there isn't going to be a winner this year. She feels bad about it. And that makes me feel worse. "Your dad's on the phone."

I take my phone from her and look at the screen. He's not on video chat. I hold the phone to my ear.

"Hi, Dad."

"Hi. I'm sorry I missed you. I was in the middle of calling the show."

That means he was on his headset, announcing the light cues and set changes and managing everything else that happens backstage.

"How's it going?" he asks.

"Um, it's fine. Everything's fine," I say into the phone, my voice flat. "The contest didn't go the way I wanted, but it'll be fine once you're here. When are you coming?"

"Oh, well, that's what I wanted to talk about. Something's come up."

Suddenly, the Southwestern music now playing over the village speakers is annoyingly loud. The people coming and going on Oasis Lane bump into me as I stand here, frozen to the ground and waiting for Dad to drop the news.

"There's been a change in the tour schedule," Dad says. "We received a call from *The Talk Tonight* with Oscar Higgins in Los Angeles. They had a cancellation, and they want Dorian Striker on the show on Monday night. So we're heading out to LA earlier than we planned. That won't give me time to make it to Muse between Phoenix and LA."

The names of cities blur together like gibberish. This tour . . . his schedule . . . more shows. It's a mask over what's real, and I've known it for a while. I just didn't want to believe it. Dad doesn't want to be a family anymore. If he did, he would try harder to get here.

"So you're not coming." *The Talk Tonight* with Oscar Higgins has their own stage manager, so couldn't Dad get away if he tried?

"No. Not this time, Harry."

I fume at his use of my nickname. Mom started that. It was *her* thing.

"Harrison?"

"Yeah."

"I'm sorry."

Is he sorry he isn't coming? Is he sorry I'm disappointed? Is he sorry he can't be a better dad?

"I'm doing the best I can here."

My eyes burn as tears form. I shuffle away from the contest and past Gallery 29, still holding the phone to my ear and trying to stop the shaky sound of my breath.

"I had plans for us," I say finally. It's too hard to be Harrison the Magnificent on the phone with my dad. I can't shove the feelings down. "I had things we were going to do together. I thought . . ." My voice quavers.

"I'm sorry," he says again.

I decide he means he's sorry he can't be the kind of dad who is there for his son. That's what his "I'm sorry" feels like. "Goodbye, Dad." I hang up just before hot tears fall on my cheeks and a quiet sob escapes.

I'm shrinking under some invisible pressure, and it feels like it will push me straight into the earth, like a giant mallet driving a nail into soft clay. So I run. I weave through the line of people waiting for ice cream and fudge. I follow Oasis Lane to the edge of the art village. I climb up on the rock where Marco and Chloe and I sat earlier today and thought about our wishes.

I'm so stupid for thinking any of this could actually happen. After all the videos I watched of magicians sharing their secrets, after all the tips I learned about fooling an audience so people would be amazed and entertained, I should've known better. Magic is an illusion. That's all it is.

Mom believed in magic, though. She talked about it enough. I miss her voice, and I think that's why it felt so good being inside the model home—playing her music, singing along with her like I used to, and imagining the house was ours. Now, as I sit alone on this rock and watch another flash of lightning streak over the desert, I think there's a much better place for me to listen to Mom's music and sing with her again.

And that's when Marco and Chloe show up, with Aunt Maggie behind them.

"Harrison!" Chloe yells. "We've been looking everywhere for you!"

I wipe my eyes with the back of my hand.

"You scared me, Harry," my aunt says. Her face looks extra-thin when she's worried.

Marco reaches the rock first, and he's holding my Dutch pour painting. "I picked this up for you," he says. "A lot of the artists were gathering their entries. I didn't want yours to get lost."

"I don't think I want it," I say quietly.

Marco manages to climb the rock while holding on to my painting. He sits next to me. Aunt Maggie and Chloe stay down below.

"I'm sorry the m—muse didn't show," he says. "But can I ask you a question?"

"Sure."

He hands me *Inside the Mirror Stone*. "What does this . . . painting mean? I know you said you made it with your dad, but does it mean anything else?"

I manage a grin. "What, are you the art teacher now?"

"No." He smiles. "When I drew my hawk and it won the contest, it m—meant something to me. It represented something. And even though I was only six, I still remember."

"It's about obsidian—the rock. And . . ."

Marco holds up his hands. "You don't really have to tell me. I just wondered if you've thought about it. And I wondered if you thought about it that day we were at the amphitheater with the hawks."

"Why?"

"Because when your phone started playing music—right when I was taking your picture with Pepper—I noticed something there in the amphitheater. It's hard to explain, but I kind of forgot about it until I saw your painting, and until I saw how sad you are about your dad *and* your mom."

I think this painting is about a lot of things. But it's mostly about memories. I've been avoiding the memories, just like Dad. It's like locking a creature deep down inside you, so far down that it becomes part of your bones, and if it's there for too long, it gets meaner and angrier and it threatens to break out and hurt you. I'm not going to keep it there any longer.

I thought maybe I could fix Dad with this painting and the contest. But *Inside the Mirror Stone* wasn't about Dad; it was about me. There's vibrant color beneath all the darkness, and I'm going to find it.

"Thanks, Marco," I say.

"Sure," he says.

"Aunt Maggie?" I call down to her.

She smiles sadly up at me.

"My dad isn't coming."

"I know. I'm so sorry. He called me after he hung up with you."

Chloe's expression changes as she realizes why I'm so upset.

"Will you take me to the amphitheater?" I ask. "I really want to go where Mom used to perform."

"Harrison, it's stormy again," Aunt Maggie says. But she sighs and gazes off into the canyon. "Let me give Tabitha a call, and if she says it's okay, we'll give it another try."

"Tabitha? Why do you have to call Tabitha?" I ask as Marco and I climb down off the rock with my painting.

"Because the Red Cliffs Amphitheater is"—Marco gets stuck and his face squinches up without making a sound—"private land, and her family owns it."

Aunt Maggie squints at the stormy sky as she puts her phone to her ear.

"No way," I say to Marco. "She told me that she knew my mom from the theater. I didn't know she *owned* it."

Chloe looks at me uncomfortably when Marco and I approach her. She put in a lot of work for the display this evening—we all did, but Chloe especially. She's probably disappointed, too.

"Hey," I say to her. "Thanks for everything you did to make the contest awesome. I'm sorry I took off afterward. That wasn't cool."

She elbows me in the arm. "I've noticed you need to do that sometimes."

I nod. "Yeah."

"Thanks for the apology," she says. "And you're welcome. I'm sorry about your dad and that the contest didn't turn out the way we hoped. I don't know what else we could've done."

"Me neither," I say. "But your display was amazing."

"So was your magic trick."

I shrug. "I wouldn't have thought to do it if Marco hadn't suggested it."

"We m—make a pretty good team," Marco says.

And right then, Obsidian the stray runs right past the parking lot, down Coyote Way.

"It's the dog!" I exclaim, pointing at the road.

"Let's catch up to him!" Chloe says.

And we take off, with Aunt Maggie on our heels.

Part Three

TIPS FOR
MUSICIANS

Music connects us in a way nothing else can.
It allows our souls to have a conversation.

—TESS WINTERROSE, VOCALIST

CHAPTER 32

TIP ONE:
FIND YOUR AUDIENCE

Marco, Chloe, Aunt Maggie, and I are smashed in the back of the Swift Bird Abatement van, headed onto the canyon road. Aunt Maggie called Marco's dad, and he came to help us catch the stray. Obsidian is running ahead, at the edge of the van's headlight beams.

"Chloe, did your parents answer you?" asks Aunt Maggie. Chloe was supposed to ask them if it was okay that she went with us.

"My mom says it's fine," Chloe answers. "She knows how much we've been looking for this dog."

"He's aiming right for the theater," Byron says.

"That's so weird," I say. "That's exactly where I wanted to go."

Byron pulls into the empty theater parking lot,

weaving around the landscape sections to follow Obsidian. Despite the theater being closed, the streetlamps are still working. The parking lot and the sidewalks leading to the plaza are lit, but everything else is dark.

Obsidian pauses to smell some bushes and a palm tree.

"He stopped!" Chloe says.

"Should we all go after him together? What should we do?" I'm asking all of them. Byron and Marco know about chasing runaway hawks, and Chloe knows dogs better than any of us.

"We need light, for starters," Byron says. "Marco, there are two flashlights in the emergency backpack."

Marco searches for the flashlights. Meanwhile, Chloe pulls a sandwich bag from her pocket. She hands us all some small heart-shaped dog treats.

"Put these in your pockets," she says. "We should all have some, but only one of us at a time should call him or he'll get confused."

"Chloe, you have dog treats *with you*?" Aunt Maggie asks.

"Yeah, you know, in case I run into any of the dogs around town. I like to have a little something to give them."

Byron parks the van near Obsidian, who is still sniffing the tree trunk. We get out one at a time, moving slowly to avoid startling him.

Chloe places a few training treats on the van floor and leaves the door open.

"Hey, boy," I say softly.

Obsidian stares at me and wags his tail, but he doesn't come any closer. I take another step toward him, and he stops wagging his tail.

"Try sitting down," Chloe says.

I sit on a parking bumper and keep talking. "Obsidian, do you want a treat?"

He tilts his head and stares at me.

"You call him Obsidian?" Aunt Maggie asks softly.

"Yeah."

"Hmm." She seems surprised, and she watches Obsidian like she's noticing something about him.

I hold out the treat, reaching as far as I can without moving closer. "Do you smell that? Come get it." I place the treat next to me.

Lightning streaks directly over us, flashing bright white over the parking lot and revealing the plaza roof at the top of the stairs. Obsidian flinches and ducks his head. Then he barks at the sky and runs like crazy. He runs past Byron, just out of reach, around all of us as we scramble for him, and then he slams into Chloe. She grabs hold of him with one arm over his back and the other under his chest.

"It's okay, boy," Chloe says. "I know, lightning is scary. Here you go." She tries to give him a treat, but he's whimpering, and he squirms underneath her grip. Byron gets hold of him, too.

And then, like someone turned on a faucet, rain pours down. Thunder cracks so loud that I actually feel the rumble on top of me. Obsidian wriggles away, knocking Byron over in the process. He rams into me and knocks me backward, too.

"Let's find out where he's going," Marco says, raising his voice over the roaring rain. Water streams down his forehead. "I wonder if he wants to show you something."

"I think this dog lives here," Aunt Maggie says. "Or maybe he used to. When your mom performed here, she made friends with a theater dog that the stage managers kept backstage."

"Really?" My voice spikes. "This dog could've known my mom?"

Byron takes one of the flashlights from Marco and switches it on, pointing it after Obsidian.

"It really does seem like he wants to show you something," Chloe says. "Watch. He turns around and looks at you and then runs some more."

"Harrison"—my aunt sloshes through the fast-forming puddles—"I know you've been trying to find this dog. I get it. Maybe more than you know. But this is a big storm."

"You all can wait in the van," Byron suggests. "I'll go after him."

"He's headed to the plaza," Chloe says. "It's sheltered up there."

"I'm following him," I say, wiping rain from my eyes.

Aunt Maggie is about to object. "I think your dad might prefer—"

"Dad doesn't care," I say. "If he did, he'd be here. I think Obsidian knows this place is important to me. I think he led me here for a reason."

I turn to ask Marco if I can use the flashlight, but Marco is gone. He's running up the stairs after Obsidian.

"Marco!" Byron hollers.

I take off after him, following his flashlight beam.

Rain pours from the plaza roof, forming miniature waterfalls down the stairs. I reach Marco at the halfway landing.

"Why'd you take off like that?" I ask breathlessly.

"This stuff with your dad is a big deal. You n—need this dog. I understand that, and I want to help."

"Thanks."

Lightning streaks across the sky over the amphitheater. It flashes through the empty plaza as we reach the top of the stairs. Thunder cracks soon after. Marco aims the flashlight around, and we spot Obsidian running underneath the Red Cliffs Amphitheater archway. We sprint across the plaza, skirting around empty food stands. Obsidian slows for a moment and turns his head to look right at us. He barks three times.

This time, I imagine him saying, *You, follow me.*

"Guys!" Chloe calls from the top of the stairs.

I motion for her to follow us. "Hurry!"

Byron shines his flashlight after us.

"Harrison! Please be careful!" Aunt Maggie says, reaching the top.

"I can go after him!" Byron hollers.

But I need to do this. I step out from underneath the plaza roof and tilt my face toward the dark sky with no stars. The rain pours over me and soaks my clothes. This is the first time I've not minded the rain since Mom died. I feel closer to her than I have in a long time.

The sound of rushing water builds from somewhere near the stage at the bottom of this huge basin full of seats. Marco points the flashlight toward the noise, but the beam isn't strong enough to show us where it's coming from. Obsidian is bounding through the amphitheater, toward the stage.

"Come on!" I call to Marco. We run down the steps between the center section and audience left, and the roar of rushing water grows louder. It's joined by a thick, slushy gurgle. "What *is* that?"

"Oh no . . . ," Marco says as we reach the bottom of the theater and the front row. The flashlight beam shows something thick moving toward us on the stage floor. It's traveling downstage from the open desert behind the theater. We jump back just before it glops off the stage lip into the front row.

"Mudslide," Marco says. "The rain came too fast."

"Obsidian!" I shout. Marco shines the flashlight up and down the stage. We climb into the second row to avoid the thick, moving mud. Three distant barks echo off the cliffs, and I think I see Obsidian's tail disappear in the stage-left wing.

"Over there!" I point, moving carefully along the second row after the dog. Even with Marco's flashlight, it's still so dark here except when lightning shoots across the sky.

A loud boom echoes through the amphitheater, and Chloe's voice comes over the enormous speakers. "I tried to turn on the main lights for you, but they aren't working. Sorry! The sound system is up and running, though!"

I look to the top of the theater. The lighting booth is dimly lit with a blue glow that Chloe probably switched on at the console. Chloe waves at us through the glass.

I wave back, and she speaks into the microphone again. "I can see the dog from up here. At least, I think that's him. He's headed for the buildings in back. Stay off the stage, and you'll avoid most of the mud. Also, it's hard to make it out, but a dark mass is running across the back lot. Could be a river, so be careful back there."

"Aw, Chloe! You're the best!" I call out, giving her two thumbs up, because I doubt she can hear me.

"I'm coming with you," Byron calls from about row fifteen.

The mud is rising into row two. Marco and I climb

over the seats and run along the third row and down the aisle. The mud is now spreading into the wings, but it hasn't reached all the way across, and we make it to the back lot and the greenroom building. Obsidian is waiting by the next building over, where Pepper and Spice landed the day we went hunting. He's sitting by the door, and a muddy river of rainwater flows a few feet away. Rain pelts his fur. He's much smaller with it all matted to his body.

"Hey, boy," I say quietly, hoping another bolt of lightning or crack of thunder won't send him darting into the desert. "Is this what you wanted to show me?"

"What do you think this building was used for?" Marco says.

I slog through the water to the side window. I wipe mud from the window with my sleeve, and Marco aims the flashlight at the glass. Inside is a storage space, with costumes and props, but it looks like it wasn't always for storage. There's a piano in the corner of a big room, microphones, and music stands.

"I think this was probably a rehearsal space for musicians," I say. "There's even something that might be a recording studio."

Obsidian whimpers. I hold my hand out to him, and finally he trots toward me instead of running away. He sniffs my fingers and licks the rain from my arm. Then he turns back to the building and sniffs around the door. He gives me his sad eyes and whines.

"You know how your phone played m—music over here that day?" Marco asks.

"Yeah." I remember that Marco seemed surprised. I thought it was because he didn't know my mom sang that song.

"Well, Pepper was behaving a little strange that day," Marco says.

"Yeah, that's right."

"Pepper acts differently than other wild hawks, you know? Like he doesn't seem as wild. He stays with me in a way that other hawks wouldn't, because he was what I wished for. The muse sent him to me."

"That's amazing." This is what I thought he was telling me the day we went hunting, but it's cool to have him come out and admit it.

Marco's dad and Aunt Maggie have reached the greenroom building, but they suddenly stop walking. I think they can hear what Marco is saying.

"I didn't wish for my stutter to go away, like some people think I should have. They talk about it like it's too bad. But I don't have to talk like everyone else to be okay."

"That's true," I say.

Byron and Aunt Maggie turn away, like they're uncomfortable.

"And I don't think the m—muse works like that anyway," Marco says. "I wished to have a bird of my own to train. I'd been watching my dad and wanted to be a falconer someday. I knew, and the muse knew, I needed a bird. You don't have to be a great speaker to train a hawk. Pepper and I communicate without words."

"I noticed that," I say.

I'm pretty sure Marco doesn't know his dad is close by, listening. I don't know whether I should tell him or not, but before I could, Marco continues.

"I learned from Pepper *and the muse* that my speaking isn't the problem," he says, watching Obsidian sniff at the ground. His face tightens, and the next word bursts out. "*People* need to listen better."

I glance over at Byron, who looks sadly at his son.

"You're right," I say. "They do."

Obsidian runs over to me and nuzzles my hand. He stares at me. Waiting. This is the most he's stayed in one place. What does he want me to do?

"He's much calmer than he was before," Marco's dad says, approaching us now. My aunt moves toward us, too, but slower, probably trying not to startle Obsidian.

"Yeah, he is," I say. "Aunt Maggie, do you think maybe he used to live in this building here?" I ask, pointing at the old rehearsal space. "He's sniffing around it and whining."

"I don't know," she says. "But there's something here—that's for sure."

"You feel it, too?" Marco asks her.

She nods and goes to the window to peer inside.

Marco runs his hand over the wet fur on Obsidian's back.

"Feel what?" Byron and I ask together.

"I think the muse is here," Aunt Maggie says. "And I think it's sad."

"What?" My heart beats faster. "How do you know that?"

"It's the same feeling I noticed the year the muse left without granting a wish," she adds.

"I noticed that, too," Marco says. "M—maybe Pepper was acting more skittish and stopping *here* because he still has a connection to the muse. You know, because he was my wish."

"Do you think Obsidian has a connection to the muse, too?" I ask.

"If he's the dog I think he is," Aunt Maggie says, "then he lived here at the theater when the muse was still granting wishes. Back when this theater was still open and creativity filled this place. He probably knows what it needs or wants. Dogs sense things like that."

"Do you think it needs music?" I look in the window again at the dusty piano and the music stands.

"When your phone played m—music over here, I saw a light flash near the door," Marco says. "I thought it was the sun, but m—maybe not."

A tingling on my skin sinks into my bones. It reminds me of the feeling I had when I heard my voice carry through the National Mall the day I first sang to

Sylvania. It's the feeling I get before I reveal the final piece of a card trick, when I'm sure it has worked and my audience has no idea how I did it.

"You guys okay down there?" Chloe's voice comes through the theater speakers. I wave my hand at the lighting booth and Marco waves his flashlight.

I pull my phone from my pocket. I've wanted to hear Mom's voice in this place again. And now I also want to know if that light will come back. I lean over the phone to shelter it from the downpour. The screen shows 10 percent battery. I open my music and click on one of Mom's albums. The first song is "The Most." I turn up the volume as high as it will go. I can barely hear it over the rain and the waterfalls and the mudslides. But Obsidian perks up his ears and wags his tail. He spins and runs to the building door, sniffing it again.

I follow him. "Over here, huh?"

I hold the phone near the bottom of the door and let Mom's music play. Her voice is like warm brownies and hikes in the woods and a blanket tucked around me with a whispered good night.

I've followed the side roads that promised me sun
Traveled the oceans, surprised everyone,
But this is what
I decide
When I'm done with the ride. . . .

"I'll be back," Marco says suddenly. He turns and runs for the stage and the audience seats. "Chloe!" He yells her name over and over.

Byron follows him, calling, "Marco! What are you doing?"

Aunt Maggie stays with me. Her expression says exactly what my heart does. That hearing Mom sing again in this place gives her a happy-sad feeling.

It's not the side roads or oceans I need
When you are what matters the most.

My phone screen goes dark. Either it got too wet or the battery died. With only the cliffs and Obsidian and my aunt to listen, I sing the last line again myself.

When you are what matters the most.

A flash of blue flickers near the door. Obsidian barks, but he's not barking at the flicker of light, he's barking at me. Three barks together. He nudges me and then barks three times again. *You, sing more,* I imagine him saying.

This canyon used to have music. Marco said the muse left the art contest sad and disappointed that year. I know that feeling of being sad and wanting to be alone. Maybe the muse chose this spot because this was where music was made, in this rehearsal space. And muses love art *and* music, don't they? So then, did it stay here when the theater closed? Can a muse get weak? Can it forget how to be happy?

I sing louder, as waves of light grow at the base of the building.

I'll ask for the stars that light up the sky
And for magic to find my way home
'Cause you are what matters . . . the most.

It's getting stronger. Green and blue light moves like ocean waves leaking out of the earth. Aunt Maggie moves closer to me and stands next to Obsidian, watching the light.

I remember singing with Mom and Sylvania and letting my voice carry over the trees and the traffic. I remember everything melting away except the melody and Mom's harmonies and Sylvania's hand reaching for mine. Sylvania's green eyes lit up, and the music changed her and me at the same time. Maybe muses show themselves in different ways and in different places, and some grant wishes.

Suddenly, something loud and thrilling resonates from the theater speakers—it's the orchestra playing the introduction to Mom's recording of "You Are." Marco must've told Chloe to play Mom's music from the control booth. I don't know how they did it. Maybe they found a CD in a pile of abandoned music tracks. But whatever they did, it's perfect.

Tears squeeze from my eyes as Mom's voice rings through the amphitheater and reaches us all the way back here near the cliffs—that clean, clear soprano that reviewers said would rise from the stage and take audiences to the heavens with it. The canyon itself must remember. I think the muse that chose to stay here remembers, too. The growing light has power behind it now. The building shudders, and the windows rattle like they'll come apart.

I add my voice to Mom's, singing with her outside, like we used to. It's the most alive I've felt in a year, and although I can't see her, I know I'm closer to her than I've been in a long time.

Memories rush in, but they come with a warm sort of sadness that doesn't threaten to knock me down like before. It's the sort of sadness I can handle. It means that something, or someone, really mattered. It means love is real. It's worth remembering, even if it brings tears, because it also brings the magic I've been looking for. The way to continue living without her, even if Dad doesn't know how.

Over the speakers, Marco's and Chloe's voices join mine as they sing along with Mom's famous song. I think they've also realized what the muse needs, or else they think it's what *I* need. They're here with me, even from the lighting booth.

I sing stronger and better than ever before. It's effortless—the way Mom taught me. I think if heaven is real, and that's where Mom and her music went, then she must have a way to hear this now. Maybe heaven and Earth are connected this way. I imagine a long thread of notes joining our two worlds, reaching from the top of the canyon cliffs to another place my eyes can't see but my heart can feel. In my mind, she's standing on the stage in her long, glittery gown, performing for a sold-out house but singing directly to me.

Colorful light waves sail into the night sky from the earth beneath the building. They hover over me and Aunt Maggie and Obsidian for a moment, and I feel the biggest idea I've ever had rush into my brain. It's the only thing that makes sense right now. It's the thing I need. It's what matters the most.

And I make a wish.

CHAPTER 33

TIP TWO: FIND PROFESSIONALS TO HELP

Wishes are different than you think they'll be when you get a chance to make one yourself. Aunt Maggie was right. All sorts of ideas come to you. But the first thing that happens is that I immediately know I have to talk to Tabitha about her theater.

Aunt Maggie drives me to Cactus Gulch the next morning.

"Do you want me to come inside with you?" she asks as we pull into the driveway behind Tabitha's SUV.

"You can if you want," I say. "I still don't know what I'm doing exactly, but I think it'll come to me."

"It will." Aunt Maggie smiles.

I get out of the car and open the back door for Obsidian. "Come."

Obsidian leaps out and runs up the porch steps,

barking for Tabitha. After the muse appeared, Obsidian calmed way down. And he came home with us without any struggle. Now, thanks to a bath and a good night's rest in a house instead of the desert, Obsidian already looks a hundred times better.

It's a good thing that Obsidian found Chloe, Marco, and me at the art village when he did, and that the three of us followed him. I don't think any of us could have brought the muse back on our own. It took all of us together—figuring it out and creating the music. And because of that, each of us got a wish when the muse returned. The interesting part is that all three of our wishes are turning into the same project. And while I'm here to talk with Tabitha, Chloe is meeting with her audiovisual club teacher, the one who used to work at the Red Cliffs Amphitheater. Marco is meeting with the town mayor. The mayor *and* the Muse Arts Council. He has a speech prepared. I really would have liked to see that, but Marco said he wanted his dad to go with him. Not to speak for him, but to listen.

Aunt Maggie walks to the door with me, but she lets me go in first.

"Harrison the Magnificent," Tabitha exclaims. "That was an amazing show you put on at the festival with your friends. I particularly loved the magic trick."

"Thank you," I say. "I'm glad you saw it."

"Me too," Tabitha says. Then, to Aunt Maggie, she says, "How did things go at the theater?"

Obsidian rushes to Tabitha and nuzzles her hand.

"Wait a minute! Is this Onyx?"

"Who's Onyx?" I ask.

"You're all cleaned up! Oh my goodness, his fur is so soft. Did you give him a bath? How did you get him to stay put?"

"Harrison has been calling him Obsidian," Aunt Maggie says, "and he helped us uncover a mystery at your theater last night."

"A mystery?" Tabitha says.

I'm instantly worried I can't keep Obsidian. "Is . . . is this *your* dog?"

"Heavens no," Tabitha says. "He's the theater dog, but he belongs to no one. A lot of the performers called him Onyx, after the stone. They said he was a healing dog."

"He is," I say, feeling Obsidian's warmth against my leg and hoping he will never leave.

"I tried taking him home with me when the theater closed, but he ran away to the canyon any chance he got. So I made sure to leave food and water in back of the office here. He'd come and get it every day, and then he was off roaming like he does."

Tabitha ruffles Obsidian's fur. "You should stay with these people," she says in a babyish voice to him. "Having a home looks good on you."

That's the reason he was always hanging around Cactus Gulch. "He was barking at me when I was in the model house," I say. We both know I was hanging out there, but it's weird to admit it out loud. "By the way, thanks for letting me be there. And for the note and the snacks."

"You're welcome," she says, smiling. She's wearing copper eyeshadow today, and her long eyelashes curl up and make her eyes look especially big. "Thanks for not getting paint on the carpet."

"You're welcome."

"Now, what's this about solving a mystery?" she asks.

"That's why I'm here." The ideas from the muse helped me know exactly what I needed to say and why Tabitha was the one I needed to talk to. "How would you like to reopen the Red Cliffs Amphitheater with a big concert?"

Tabitha coughs. She grabs her water bottle from her desk and takes a drink. "Are you working on your mind-reading powers as part of your magic act, Harrison?"

"Not exactly," I say. "But I *am* working with a bit of magic."

She glances at Aunt Maggie, who nods.

"I found the canyon muse that everyone talks about," I tell Tabitha. "It was below the rehearsal building in the back lot."

"Wha . . . ?" Tabitha looks as if she's trying to put something together. "What in the world was it doing there?"

"I think it was disappointed or sad. Maybe a little angry, too. It didn't like what happened at the Art Festival Contest the year after Marco Swift won. We think it was the judges the council brought in, and maybe that the tourists who came and entered the contest had greedy reasons."

Aunt Maggie and I look at each other. We've talked about this. She adds, "The contest changed that year, Tabitha. Remember? We think the muse looks for an artist, not just the artwork. I believe it wants to reward the wonder, not the wanting."

Tabitha's eyes brighten. "I remember. That definitely makes sense about the contest. But I still don't understand why it's been—did you say *below* the rehearsal building all this time?"

"Yes, beneath it. In the earth," Aunt Maggie says. "It seems connected to the earth's energy and to nature."

"We think it went to that spot," I add, "because it was a place where it knew it could find music, and it likes both art *and* music."

"Except"—Tabitha holds up a finger, thinking— "that year you're talking about, we stopped production on a new show to get some construction projects finished. There wasn't music there for several months."

I imagine a magical creature of blue and green light that feels a shadow overwhelm it when things change. It might also lose hope and forget that it doesn't have to be alone. It forgets that it could come to the village again and find people sharing art and music because they love it.

Tabitha leans back in her desk chair and sighs. "Is the muse still there?"

I take a deep breath. "It's out now. It just needed music to make it strong and happy again."

"But . . . the storms closed us down. We would've been back later that same season if only the lightning hadn't made it impossible."

"I have an idea that might fix that," I say.

"Fix the storms?"

Obsidian sits on my feet, pressing against me like he's trying to glue us together. I rub his soft fur and whisper, "Good boy." Then to Tabitha, I say, "I'm hoping you can reopen the amphitheater—bring back the concerts and shows. I think so long as the muse is happy, you won't have so much trouble with storms."

Aunt Maggie is smiling at me. Wisps of her reddish-brown hair have fallen from her loose bun.

"I noticed when I came here that the canyon feels alive," I say. "It wasn't just all the talk about the muse, but something else. It felt comforting. Like when you're sad, but it feels a little better if someone else is sad with you."

Aunt Maggie and Tabitha both have soft eyes, which assures me they know what I'm talking about.

"I think the animals felt it, too. Marco's hawk is con-nected to the muse, and it flew to that spot at the theater. And Obsidian tried to lead me into the canyon so many times. When I was out in those canyon storms, the lightning and rain felt like what I've had inside me for a long time."

Aunt Maggie has tears in her eyes. I know she's thinking of Mom, like I am.

"I think the sky over the canyon stormed like that," I say, "because the muse was sad."

They both let out a sigh. Obsidian rests his head on my shoe. The sun slants in through the sales office windows, angling across the carpet and Tabitha's desk. I pull the folded paper from my pocket—something I drew last night. I lay it on Tabitha's desk, right in the sunlight.

"You think I'm a good magician, right?" I ask, smoothing the paper flat and sliding it in front of her.

"I definitely do." Tabitha smiles and puts on her glasses to look at the paper. It's a design for a show poster—a tribute concert, featuring the music of Tess Winterrose.

"This time, I need your help with another sort of magic."

CHAPTER 34

TIP THREE: LEARN FROM OTHER MUSICIANS

"Okay, Harrison. We're ready for you." Chloe's voice comes over the speakers.

I run my fingers over the mic tape on the back of my neck, smoothing it down to be sure the wire is secure. It's been three weeks since we brought back the muse, and I haven't once felt nervous about this concert. Since it was my wish, I've known it would work. I never doubted. But now, with people gathered in the plaza, waiting for the house to open, excitement tickles my stomach. I step out from the stage-right wing. Tabitha and her partners brought in a crew to clean up the mud and resurface the black-painted stage. They have some wealthy donors and a previous grant for the arts to pay for it, but a lot of people in town also volunteered. It's as good as new. I stop at the orange X in reflective tape at center stage and look out at the empty seats that'll soon be full of people.

"Talk normally into the mic first," Chloe says from the back of the house.

"Do we have a big crowd? Can you tell?" I ask.

"Yes!" Chloe gives me two thumbs up from the sound booth. It's a big control panel behind the last row of seats, and it's open to the theater, so Chloe will hear the sound as the audience does. She has a professional audio engineer there with her, showing her the ropes. And she's a natural. "It's going to be a pretty full house, I think."

"I'm glad. How does the mic sound?"

"All good. Now, sing a few lines so I can check the levels." Chloe's wish is coming together just like mine. It's amazing what she's done with sound production and lighting design in just a few weeks. She already had a knack for it, but with a little backup from the pros, Chloe is running a lot of the tech for this show—her very own art.

I take a deep breath. The sky is turning orange to match the cliffs as the sun sinks low. It'll be nearly dark by the time the show starts at seven. We need the darkness for the projections on the giant scrim—a large piece of fabric stretched across the stage like a screen.

I think of the images that the crew will be projecting

on the scrim behind me, and I sing a few bars of "You Are." The tiny microphone taped near my mouth captures my voice, and the speakers send it out to the cliffs.

"You're all set," Chloe says, giving me two thumbs up again.

"Thank you. Meeting in the greenroom in ten minutes?"

"You got it."

I take a deep breath and scan the empty audience seats in the twilight, imagining Mom standing on this same stage and singing for her mic check as the sun set in this same canyon. I walk into the wings and down the stairs that lead to the tunnel under the stage. I found the tunnel a few days ago, when we started our tech rehearsals, but I wanted to wait until now to really check it out.

The lights in the tunnel are already lit, and the walls on both sides are full of painted murals in memory of past shows and performers: *The Music Man, Ragtime,* Ryan Shupe & the RubberBand, *In the Heights,* Bernadette Peters and the Utah Symphony, *Grease.* In the middle of the tunnel, on the left side, is the one I knew would be here.

Tess Winterrose.

The mural is a painting of Mom. She's wearing a long green gown with gold flecks in it. The background is navy blue with silver stars and a giant light-blue moon above her. Paint handprints surround the outside, and people have signed their names to them. The smallest one is mine. It's low to the ground. I remember Mom telling me to choose a spot, and then she placed her handprint next to mine. I kneel to touch our handprints and notice the one next to them. Calvin Boone. Dad was here that summer, and he worked on a lot of Mom's shows. It makes sense he worked on this one.

I told Dad about the concert and the muse. It was a weird conversation to have on the phone. I didn't expect he would want to come, since he can't bring himself to listen to Mom's music. He said he didn't think he could do it, and now he's in Sacramento with the Striker show. It still surprises me that this concert was my wish. I thought I would wish for Dad and me to be together, but I knew what I needed when the muse showed up, and this was it. A way to remember Mom in this place and feel close to her. I do wish Dad could be here, part of this new show, which reopens the theater where Mom performed.

I pull out my phone. I have two new texts from him that came in before my mic check.

Dad: Break a leg today! I know you'll do great!
Dad: I'm proud of you.

I immediately try a video call. Just in case he can talk for a minute. Maybe we can look at this mural together. But I only have one bar in the tunnel, and the call fails. I place my hand over my little five-year-old handprint and then over Dad's. Then I hold my hand over Mom's handprint. I match my fingers and thumb to hers against the wall. I imagine the long string of time folding together. These two events could exist at once, and I could have my hand on hers and be with her here right now.

"I miss you," I whisper. I can almost hear her whisper back, *I miss you, too, Harrison the Magnificent.*

My phone rings. It's Aunt Maggie. I can hardly make out the words.

"You won't . . . musicians from . . . want to . . . greenroom . . ."

"I can't hear you. You're breaking up," I say. "I'm going to the greenroom. I'll call you when I get there."

I stay with Mom's mural for a few more seconds and then hurry out of the tunnel. I'm about to call Aunt Maggie back when a large crowd approaches the greenroom building. They're wearing concert black clothes. Most of them are carrying musical instruments and have guest performer badges. I didn't plan for any guest performers other than a dance team and Marco and Byron opening the show with their birds. I wonder if Tabitha sent them.

"Are you Harrison?" A red-haired man wearing a black tuxedo holds out his hand to me. He's carrying a cello case.

"Yes?" I shake his hand. "Do we know each other?"

"Well, we've met. But I wouldn't expect that you'd remember. My name is Tyler Brandt. A bunch of us just spoke with Tabitha, and she sent us back here to talk to you."

"Okay." From the other end of the back lot, Tabitha's SUV approaches from the Authorized Vehicles Only road. She parks outside the building.

Tyler Brandt motions to everyone with the guest performer badges. "We were friends of your mom's, and we've all played in orchestras that accompanied her performances. We learned about your tribute show, and we came here, hoping we could play the music live for you."

"I . . . That would be wonderful. That's so nice of you to come. Um . . . the show starts in thirty minutes. We've had all our tech rehearsals using just the recordings. So we need to find out if the crew can add you in with microphones and lighting."

I sound like a director or a producer or something, but I've been around this stuff my whole life. I've watched Dad behind the scenes and crews with their headsets pull together all the elements that make a show run. I've seen how a good crew can organize every piece without the audience realizing how difficult it is.

"I'm sorry it's last-minute, but we only heard about the show yesterday."

Tabitha, who is dressed very fancy and is talking

into a headset, strides toward us. Tyler introduces me to the other musicians. They all want to shake my hand.

"Your mom was as kind as she was talented," says a white guy with a gray beard and a guitar.

"It was my pleasure to work with her," says a violinist with a French accent.

"Tess knew how to be a friend," adds a woman wearing a hijab and carrying a clarinet.

"I'm so glad you're doing this memorial concert," says an Asian woman in a black pantsuit. She's holding a string bass. "I got on a plane immediately when I saw it on the internet."

I wonder what was on the internet as I shake hands and meet these people from around the world who loved my mom. Tabitha finishes her headset conversation, and some of the crew comes and takes the musicians to the stage. The crew begins adjusting lights and setting up risers and chairs for our last-minute orchestra.

Tabitha hands me her headset. "Chloe's got to stay in the sound booth. She wants to talk to you."

"Thanks." I take the headset from Tabitha and speak into it. "Chloe? How are you doing?"

"I'm fantastic! Have you heard? We've got a live orchestra!"

"Yeah, I just met them! It's amazing that they came."

"You can probably thank Marco and Leon for that."

"Really? Leon?"

"Yeah, but we gotta talk about that later," Chloe says. "I can't help get the sound ready to include new mics for the orchestra and also make it to cast meeting. We're gonna do this, Harrison. It'll be epic. The orchestra is going to accompany your big number. Just do it like we rehearsed. It'll be practically the same for you, except that the live music will play on top of your mom's recording. I have help, and we'll adjust the levels. You've got this."

"*We've* got this."

"We do," Chloe says. "Break a leg, Harrison."

I smile. I never imagined someone would say that to me. And now both Dad and Chloe have said it. Mom was the performer, not me. But right here and now, it feels good to be the one taking the stage. I'm still not even nervous—well, not too nervous. I feel like I'm about to show a card trick, a very good one, to a theater full of people. But I don't even need to summon Harrison the Magnificent to do it. I think I can just be me.

"Thank you for everything, Tabitha," I say, handing the headset back to her.

"Don't thank me yet," she says, looking uncertainly at the sky. So far, there are no clouds in sight. "Let's see how it goes, first. Also, I have a surprise for you in the greenroom."

"Really?"

Tabitha and I enter the greenroom together and

walk through the kitchen into a crowd of people. Almost immediately, someone slams into me and wraps me in a hug.

"Harrison!" Kennedy exclaims.

"Kennedy! I thought you couldn't visit until next week!"

"Yeah, well. When the coolest kid I know is pulling off a tribute concert for my mom's best friend and favorite client, we're not going to miss that!" Kennedy's black hair is in long braids now, and she's wearing heels that make her taller.

"Are your parents here, too?"

"Yep! When you told me about this, my mom got us all plane tickets. I wanted to surprise you."

"Well, you did." My cheeks hurt from smiling. I can't believe Kennedy is here for this.

"And I have one more surprise for you." She taps something on her phone. "Come look at this."

I lean in to watch the screen. It's a video of James from the Mall. He's holding his guitar and standing in front of the Art Collective with a crowd of people.

"Harrison, I told you that one day you'd want to sing for her," James says. "Today's that day, and I'm so glad. We'll be singing for her here, too." He plays his guitar for a few seconds and then waves before the video ends.

"Thank you, Kennedy," I say. "I'm glad you went to visit him."

"You're welcome," she says. "Well, you've got a show

to do. I'll go out in the audience with my parents and wait on the edge of my seat. Break a leg."

"Haha, thanks."

"And Harrison?"

"Yeah?"

"You're amazing." She points two fingers at me and winks.

"Am I . . . *magnificent?*"

"Definitely." She gives me one more hug and leaves.

The greenroom is loud and buzzing with excitement. Tabitha brought back some of the old stage crew that used to work at the Red Cliffs Amphitheater. The rest of the crew is made up of volunteers from Muse and nearby towns. I find Marco standing by the far wall, next to a bookshelf of games and puzzles. He's wearing a blue suit and his falconer's glove.

"Are you guys all set?" I ask him.

"Ready as we'll ever be. Pepper and Blossom are here, and they're rested. Mostly they're hungry, which is a"—he pauses as his next word gets blocked—"good thing." He laughs, but the laugh sounds a bit nervous.

"It's going to be great," I say, trying to reassure him.

At the start of the show, Marco is going to stand center stage. Pepper and Blossom are going to fly from his glove, over the heads of the audience members, to Byron's outstretched glove and a morsel of meat at the back of the theater. But I don't think that's what Marco is nervous about. He's nervous about that little microphone taped to his cheek. He's going to speak to the crowd. Somehow, this has to do with his wish. He hasn't told me everything, and I haven't asked.

Tabitha holds up her hand and whistles. The room quiets to silence.

"Tonight is special for many reasons," she begins. "Not the least of which is that we get to pay tribute to Tess Winterrose and her talent. But also, all of you get the unique opportunity to be part of the show that re-opens the Red Cliffs Amphitheater."

People cheer, and then someone hushes them.

"A lot has gone into this production," Tabitha continues. "And we have Tess's son, Harrison Boone, to thank for that."

People start clapping. I didn't expect that.

Tabitha motions for me. I move through the crowd, around tables and chairs and the dance team Tabitha brought in from the nearby university.

The dancers cheer as I walk past.

They are going to dance during "Love's Old Sweet Song." Suddenly, I realize the new risers for the un-planned orchestra are going to be partially in the danc-ers' space on the stage. But before I let the worry build inside me, I remember the muse and our wishes, and the talented people who are making this happen. I think it's going to work out.

I stand next to Tabitha in front of the crowd. Mom may not have known all of these people, but they're here doing this tribute concert because they feel something about her, about this concert, or about this theater.

The room quiets down, and everyone is waiting for me to say something. "Thank you all for being here and for being part of this."

I pull out my deck of cards and hold them up. "My mom used to say that magic is real, and it's our job to find it. All of you being part of this show has been some of that magic for me. I hope you find more in the show tonight."

"For Tess!" someone calls out.

"For Tess!" others shout, and everyone moves to the center of the room in a jumbled circle. Tabitha and I join the circle as each person places one hand in the center.

"What's the word, Harrison?" asks someone on stage crew.

This is something Mom and Dad used to talk about. Someone in the cast chooses a word for the night. It's supposed to bring everyone together and inspire the performance.

I spot Marco smashed in the circle, smiling as he holds his gloved hand out.

"The word is 'wish,' " I say.

The cast counts down, "Three, two, one . . . *wish!*"

CHAPTER 35

TIP FOUR: SHARE THE MUSIC IN YOUR SOUL

The orchestra plays an overture before the show starts. The musicians know it because it's a medley of Mom's songs that many orchestras used before her concerts.

The stage manager, a woman named Kelsey, is calling light cues from the prompt corner, where Marco and I wait in the wings on stage right. On a table reserved for his birds, Marco has placed two giant hoods, with Pepper and Blossom waiting inside them. Mrs. Swift stands by the table to watch over the birds and help out if we need it. I wave at her, and she gives me and Marco an enthusiastic thumbs-up.

"Chloe must've figured out the microphones, because that sounds great," I say to Marco, tilting my head toward the orchestra onstage. "By the way, she said you might've had something to do with the orchestra. What did she mean?"

"Oh. I was doing some research online—it was something for my wish—and I thought it m—might help the show if we had ads on the internet. I was talking to Leon about it."

"Leon? Really?"

"Yeah."

"And he said he could help us with online marketing."

"Leon?" I say again, surprised.

"Yeah. Apparently, his m—mom did marketing for the theater before it closed. I talked to Tabitha about it. She hired Leon's mom to get the website going again for ticket sales."

"I'll have to thank her, because having this orchestra here is amazing!"

"You might want to thank Leon, too. He got excited to help and took the show posters his mom printed to businesses all over Muse and Ivins. He even got some of the businesses to help sponsor the show."

"Wow." I'm shocked. And grateful.

"Yeah. Well, we wanted the show to be a success. You know, for *all* of us."

"Me too." I glance at the small microphone taped to Marco's cheek and wonder what he's going to say during the show tonight.

One of the rules of theater is that if you can see the audience, the audience can see you. Marco and I stay hidden behind the "legs," or the curtains in the wings, but I can feel the full-house energy coming toward the stage. I can almost touch it—the anticipation, the crowd settling in, ready to be entertained. I understand why Mom loved this. She said it connected her to people and that every show was an experience that could never be repeated.

On the wall in the prompt corner is a flat-screen monitor that shows what's happening onstage and in the audience. The sunlight is fading, but it isn't dark yet. The audience will get a great view of Pepper and Blossom as they fly overhead. As I watch the monitor, I think I can make out Aunt Maggie sitting next to Mr. Bradley in the center section where there's a space for his motorized chair. I watch them for a moment. Someone in a brown jacket has walked down the aisle steps and has stopped to talk to them.

"You've got five minutes, Marco," Kelsey the stage manager says, cueing him to get the birds ready.

I put on the extra glove from the table. It's my job to hold one bird while Marco sends the other bird flying to Byron at the back.

"Here we go," Marco says as he opens the first giant hood and brings out Blossom. I've never held the falcon, but I've watched her in practice. She's white and gray, and a leather hood covers her eyes to keep her calm. She perches on Marco's gloved hand, very still. He grasps the leash that's threaded through her anklet.

Mrs. Swift opens the other transport box, and I reach in. Pepper feels my glove in front of him and steps onto it. I pull him out slowly. Marco waits until I have a hold on the hawk's leash, and then he moves to the edge of the side curtain, waiting for Kelsey's signal.

Tabitha enters the stage from the other side and walks to the center with a handheld microphone. Her silver high-heeled shoes catch the spotlight that follows her path.

"Welcome to the grand reopening of the Red Cliffs Amphitheater!" she starts.

The audience erupts in applause that echoes off the sandstone.

"It's a nice full house," Kelsey says to us. Then, to the crew in her headset, she says, "Jarom, stand by for light preset two. Chloe, mic one."

And with that, Marco's mic is live. Anything anyone says around him will be broadcast out of the enormous speakers, so we stay silent. I wonder again about his secret announcement.

"I think we're going to have good weather," Tabitha says to the audience, pointing to the clear sky with the orange and pink streaks of sunset. The audience cheers again. "We'd like to remind everyone that there is no flash photography and no video recording allowed during the show. The public performance of the music and recordings tonight is provided with permission from Bright Light Productions."

Bright Light Productions is Mom's record label. She and Dad created it. I didn't know we needed permission to play my own mom's music in front of an audience—especially when my mom owned her music. I don't know what's happened to the label since she died. I wonder who's even running it now, since Dad's stage-managing Dorian Striker's show.

"Now please enjoy 'Soaring: A Tess Winterrose Tribute.'" She exits left, and Kelsey cues Marco to enter. She also cues the lights, which turn the stage into a man-made sunset that matches the canyon sky. Marco stands on the orange X on the stage. The opening music begins just as it's supposed to. Chloe is doing a brilliant job in the sound booth. The onstage orchestra joins in with the music track, playing Mom's song "Soaring over Sunset" as video of her on the stage at this very theater shows up on the scrim.

Marco looks straight ahead, over the audience, to the top of the lighting booth, where Byron is in place with a lure.

Before the first line of the first verse begins, Marco says, "As a person who stutters, I learned something from Tess Winterrose the summer she performed here. First, n—no m—matter how long it takes for you to say them, your words are important and should be heard."

He sets to work loosening Blossom's hood. It takes one hand and his teeth to do it, so there's a slight pause in what he's saying. He pulls the straps but doesn't remove the hood just yet.

"And second . . ." Marco pauses. I don't know what it's like to stutter, but Marco seemed nervous to go out in front of all these people. I don't want this to go badly for him.

Kelsey gets to work, doing what a good stage manager does. She speaks quiet orders into her headset. The video on the scrim and the music recording both pause, right before Mom's first note of the song. The orchestra director, who is wearing an earpiece to hear Kelsey's cues, slows her baton and raises her other hand palm up. The musicians hold the note in a gentle fermata, to give Marco the time he needs.

Marco relaxes, and the word comes out smooth. "Music has a way of making words soar." He pulls off the falcon's hood, and right when the video, the recording, and the orchestra begin again, Blossom spots Byron and the lure at the top of the theater. She launches from Marco's fist and flies over the audience just as Mom sings the words *We'll go soaring.*

The audience gasps as the falcon breezes over their heads. I watch the monitor, holding my breath until Blossom reaches the lure and is safely on Byron's gloved fist. Marco comes into the wings. He taps Pepper's talons, and Pepper steps off my glove and onto his.

I don't know if Marco's mic is still live, so I mouth, *You were awesome!* He nods a thank-you and smiles at his mom, who stands out of Kelsey's way by the birds' empty carriers. I think Marco has discovered what he needed to tell his family and everyone else about his stutter—maybe *that* was his wish.

I had no idea that Marco remembered my mom from that summer or that he might have even met her. Knowing that just one more person has a warm memory of her makes me feel like Mom is more here than gone. Marco returns to the stage. He removes Pepper's hood so the hawk flies over the audience as Mom's voice and the music builds at the chorus: *Soaring over sunset, where the day and evening meet.*

The live orchestra playing makes it feel like Mom might actually step onto the stage at any moment. Maybe she *is* here, standing next to me in the wings, even though my eyes can't see her.

The opening number finishes, and the audience cheers. We're off to a great start! I'm relieved the daylight lasted until after Pepper's flight. Including the sunset in your show takes some careful planning, and it takes some faith in the weather. So far, my prediction that the canyon storms would ease off has been correct.

The show continues without any noticeable problems. I wait in the wings, staying out of the dancers' way when it's their turn to go on, and watching everything on the monitor. It's almost time for my part, and my insides wind up like a spring the closer it gets. I practiced this in tech rehearsals, and it was thrilling to sing with Mom in this canyon. Sharing the music with an actual audience—the way Mom used to—is what *I* most wanted. But with Tabitha's permission and the approval of her partners, the profits from ticket sales are going to the homeless shelters around southern Utah, in Sylvania's honor. I think it's what *Mom* would've most wanted.

The stage lights go dark, and the audience applauds "Love's Old Sweet Song" as the dancers hurry offstage. One of them pats my head as she goes by and wishes me good luck. I don't even mind the head pat as much as usual, and I whisper, "Thanks." I step to the edge of the wings, and Kelsey cues my microphone and the special effects to stand by.

"It's time, Harrison," she tells me.

I smooth the front of my suit jacket and walk onto the darkened stage. The evening canyon breeze is light but chilly this late in the fall. I watch the floor for my glow-in-the-dark X. I imagine Mom walking with me, her hand on my shoulder. I stand on the taped X and think of her watching me, smiling. I can almost hear her talking to me softly:

We can sing together, Harry.

I nod.

You start, and I'll join you with some harmony after a few bars.

I feel the warmth of the spotlight rising on my face, and I remember Sylvania's wrinkled smile as she waited to hear my voice. I begin singing a cappella—just my voice without any accompaniment. The words have new meaning in this place.

> *Bright light in the dark night*
> *Soft glow in the day*
> *Music rings when I'm near you*
> *It has something to say*

The music track, which the sound crew has queued up to this spot, fades in slowly, and the orchestra joins in. Mom's voice soars from the speakers, and I sing a third lower than her, the way she taught me to sing harmony. Her image appears on the scrim, just like when we practiced. It's from her last performance at the Kennedy Center. She's wearing her sparkling green gown, and her hair is down around her shoulders. I watch the screen as we sing while trying not to turn my back on the audience.

> *These hands are small, but they can hold*
> *A bigger world*
> *A heart of gold*
> *You are the breath, the light that makes me whole*

As I hold out the long note at the end of the verse and the music builds to the chorus, a wave of color passes over the projection on the scrim. At first, I think it's a stage effect—something the lighting designer fig-ured out—but it moves like an ocean wave in greens and blues. The colors of the muse brighten and flow over the screen like in a Dutch pour. It's exactly like when I used the hair dryer to move the paint across the canvas for *Inside the Mirror Stone.*

The audience gasps as they realize what I already know. This is not a stage effect. And what might nor-mally distract me instead makes my voice stronger. I find harmony with Mom's notes without even trying.

You are
You are
You are the promise I keep

And suddenly, I'm not watching a projection of an old performance anymore. Mom is looking right at me. She's closer, as though the camera has zoomed in, and she motions for me to stand beside her in the frame, like I'm on the Opera House stage, too. As I approach the scrim, where normally the image would become blurred, everything gets sharper and more real. It's still an image on a screen, but something is moving it. I'm able to see deep into my mom's eyes as she looks into mine.

I'll never be lost or in darkness at all
When I have the light that
You are.

We sing the next verse, the second chorus, the bridge. Although Mom is a two-dimensional image on the scrim, she moves like Mom and her eyes recognize me. She smiles at me like only Mom does. The connecting thread of music I imagined is stronger with the muse's power; it's like a ladder that can reach from this canyon to the place we can't see—a heaven for musical souls. And if Mom's soul is here with me in this moment, then this place, right here, is heaven.

I'll never be lost or in darkness at all
When I have the light that
You are.

We hold out the final note, which comes all too soon. Mom reaches her hand out to me, and I lightly touch that spot on the scrim.

I'll always be just a song away, I feel her say as she smiles, her eyes twinkling with life.

A tear runs down my cheek, and my heart feels like my mirror stone painting. The darkness of grief has burst open, and the colors inside are pouring through me. They don't completely eliminate the dark, but I'm pretty sure I'm three-fourths light and only one-fourth shadow now. I know that although it's smaller, the shadow will stay, because you never stop missing some-one. And that gives meaning to the light.

The music ends. The theater is silent, and the scrim

fades to dark as the muse's light ascends into the night sky. I'm still in spotlight, and the whole thing has made me forget what to do next. As I stand there, not moving, the audience erupts in thunderous applause, like I've never heard before.

I can make out the figures of Aunt Maggie and Mr. Bradley clapping wildly. Mr. and Mrs. Taylor are near the lighting booth, and I think they're clapping for Chloe as much as anything. And near the front, Kennedy and her parents are wiping their eyes. I spot a row of kids from Red Cliffs Middle School: Marisol and Simone are here. And Leon is with them. They're all cheering. The ushers, the backstage crew, the people in the lighting and sound booths—they're cheering, too. And as I notice Kelsey, who's jumping up and down in the wings, I see my dad.

He's *here*. He *came*!

Somehow, I still remember to bow to the audience before I practically run off the stage, hurrying straight toward Dad in the dark wings.

He's not cheering or even clapping. His mouth is set in a flat line, and his hands are stuffed in the pockets of his brown jacket. He seems shorter. Or maybe I've grown a bit. When I reach him, by the glow of the monitors I notice tears shining on his cheeks.

"Dad . . . you made it. I didn't think you would."

He nods.

Taking the stage to sing with Mom, and having the

muse give her back to me for just a moment, showed me that I don't have anything to shove down and hide anymore. It's just me being my real self. And I think that's what Mom saw in me when she called me a magician name in the first place.

Dad's mouth trembles a little. I've never seen him cry—not even at the funeral. It looks like a million thoughts and memories are crossing his mind.

"I've missed you so much," I say.

He wipes his eyes and takes a deep breath.

"Harrison the Magnificent," he says.

"Calvin the Incredible."

And he pulls me toward him in a hug that feels like it holds enough love for three people. It's big enough to hold Mom, too.

Part Four

HARRISON'S
TIPS FOR LIFE

The new path you need might be
the one that leads you home.

—CALVIN BOONE, MY DAD

CHAPTER 36

LOOK FOR THE MUSES AND TELL YOUR STORY

I told Dad about Sylvania, and how she inspired Mom and even inspired me. I explained how Sylvania chose her name from the lighting company's holiday display, and how I think she might have been a different kind of muse. Or, maybe, she knows the muses.

Dad agrees with that immediately, because it turns out a woman with weatherworn, wrinkled skin and bright-green eyes showed up at the Dorian Striker show in Sacramento, the same night Dad got a call for the Bright Light record label. The Red Cliffs Amphitheater was requesting rights to show a public performance of Mom's music. The green-eyed lady had approached Dad, taken one of his hands in both of hers, and said, "Her music is what you need." And then Dad got on a plane to Utah.

I told Dad that James had said Sylvania was thinking about heading to Sacramento.

It's Christmas Eve, and Dad and I finished decorating the Cactus Gulch model home just this morning. It isn't the model home anymore, though. It's ours. After the tribute concert, Dad decided to find and train his replacement on the Dorian Striker show, and he came back to live in Muse. He finalized the sale of the home a week ago and bought the furnishings with it. It turns out that the wish I needed came with my original wish coming true.

Dad and I placed our painting where we could always see it. *Inside the Mirror Stone* sits in what Tabitha calls a display niche—a part of the wall that's pushed back, with a shelf and a light above it. I keep the obsidian and calcite crystal next to the painting, for anyone to pick up when they feel like it. Aunt Maggie says that calcite can help you let go of the past and move forward into the future.

She and Mr. Bradley arrive early for the party, bringing veggie wraps and vegan cheese dip and kombucha. Dad is still making an effort to like Aunt Maggie's food. Mr. Bradley tells me I can call him by his first name, Sam, when we aren't at school. I still call him Mr. Bradley, and I'm hoping that their relationship doesn't make things weird in art class. But he is a nice guy to have around.

Mr. and Mrs. Taylor and Chloe arrive next, followed by Marco and the Swifts, some of the amphitheater stage crew, and some of the dancers from the show. The house is full of new friends and people Dad will be working with as the new artistic director of the Red Cliffs Amphitheater.

The person Dad will be working with the most, Tabitha, is the next person to show up, with hot apple cider. She says that she melted Red Hots candies into it, and I think it's my new favorite holiday drink. Dad smiles a lot when he's around Tabitha. The same way Mr. Bradley smiles at Aunt Maggie. It's still kind of new, but the grayish look is gone from Dad's face, and I don't think he's so lonely anymore.

During dinner, Chloe, Marco, and I go onto the back deck and sit on the steps, sipping our hot apple cider. Even though it's the desert, it's cold at night in the winter, and a light dusting of snow has covered the ground like powdered sugar on red velvet cake. The sandstone cliffs glow red and green from the Christmas lights Dad and I strung through the backyard.

"I like what you did with the cactus," Chloe says.

"Thanks," I say. Dad and I wrapped the tallest cactus in holiday lights and topped it with a large red Santa hat.

Marco laughs. "That's great."

"I'm running the sound and designing the lights for the spring musical at school," Chloe says. "You wanna help me, Marco?"

Marco swallows a mouthful of cider. "M—maybe. I

usually have more time in the spring, because we keep the birds penned."

"Oh." Chloe looks confused. "I mean, that's great if it gives you time to hang out with us, but why?"

"In the spring, the birds have mating urges and nesting tendencies." Marco says it like a scientist on a documentary. Chloe and I can't help it; we burst out laughing. Marco laughs, too.

"What did your dad say about that camp?" I ask Marco when I get myself under control.

Soon after we freed the muse and Marco made a wish, he found a summer program called Camp SAY. It's for people who stutter and their families. I think Marco's wish was to tell people that what he has to say is important and worth waiting for. But it seems his wish also included more support from his family and to connect with other people who stutter. Marco showed me the camp's website and videos, and it looks like a really fun place in the mountains.

"He said yes," Marco says.

"Yes! That's awesome!" I exclaim.

"I'm happy for you, Marco," Chloe says. "That's great news."

Obsidian, who has been wandering the neighborhood like he often does, trots into the backyard. The Christmas lights give his black fur a colorful glow. He still likes to wander, but he always comes home, and he knows this is where he lives now. He bounds up the steps and sits next to Marco, who rubs his fur.

"Thanks," Marco says to both of us. "It's a big deal, because it's tough for falconers to leave their birds. But my dad was able to find another falconer who agreed to care for them while we're gone."

Chloe shifts on the step a little. "What is this camp *for,* exactly? I mean, is it about *fixing* . . ." She stops, and it's obvious she doesn't want to say the wrong thing.

"It's not about *fixing* something in myself. M—my speech therapist says I can learn techniques for dealing with my stutter and that connecting with other kids at the camp could be . . . good. It's nice to not feel alone in this."

"I didn't know you had a speech therapist," I say.

"I meet with her at school sometimes. She's the one who told me about Camp SAY."

The sliding door opens from the kitchen, and Tabitha steps onto the deck. She has a small wrapped package in her hand.

"Sorry to interrupt you three," she says, "but, Harrison, I have something for you."

"Thanks. Do you want me to open it now?"

"If you'd like," she says. "I have something else to give you for Christmas. This is a gift for helping us reopen the theater."

"Oh." I stand up and take the package. She's tied it

nice with a ribbon. I open it carefully, because it feels like glass through the paper.

It's a picture frame. In it is a picture of Mom. With Obsidian.

"What?" I ask, surprised. "Where did you get this?"

"Remember, I knew your mom when she performed here? Well, that's Obsidian when he lived at the theater. We all called him Onyx back then, but both are lovely stones. You found a dog who knew your mom, and you gave him a good name and a home."

My heart feels like it's too big for my chest. Mom with Obsidian. She hugged and loved this dog, too.

"We take a lot of pictures of the cast and crew in every show. Obsidian is in a lot of them. I just went back and found the pictures of the year your mom did her show. I have more pictures of her to give you, whenever you'd like to have them."

I hug Tabitha. "Thank you."

Aunt Maggie, Adrienne, and Dad come out onto the deck.

"Your friends have arrived," Dad says.

I peer through the sliding glass door. Simone, Marisol, and Leon are in the living room with the others. Leon still has this way of trying to be the best or know the most sometimes, but I think he just wants people to like him. The more he feels liked, the less he tries to show off. I made sure to thank him for what he did to help with the concert.

"Come inside. I'm getting out my guitar," Aunt Maggie says.

Adrienne's eyes go wide. "And maybe later, you can show us some more of those card tricks," she says to me.

"We'd like to sing some songs, Harrison," Dad says, smiling at me and then at Tabitha. "Mr. Taylor's already got a request list going. Want to join us?"

I breathe in the crisp December desert air and soak up the feeling of Dad asking that question. Obsidian follows us inside and shakes off the dust and snow. I leave the sliding door open a few inches, making sure the canyon and the muse can hear us sing. I set my deck of cards on the counter for later. I don't need Harrison the Magnificent to cover up how I feel anymore, but I can still do some believable tricks for a good audience. Dad says I'm a natural performer.

I think of the tips I learned this year—for magic, art, and music. Of all the tips, I think my favorite is this: a master magician tells a good story. This house is full of friends who are part of my life now, all because of Mom. I have Dad back and know that music will always keep Mom close, and I finally know the story I'm telling.

ACKNOWLEDGMENTS

Many magicians and muses contributed to this story and helped shape it into the book you hold in your hands. I learned some of my own tips for magic from my amazing agent, Danielle Burby. She believed in my writing from the day we met, and it has been her encouragement, cheerfulness, and professionalism that paved the way for me to do what I love. Thank you for making wishes come true.

Thank you to my editor and the co-publisher and VP of Crown Books for Young Readers, Emily Easton. Harrison's story required careful consideration of him and everyone in his life, and you knew exactly how to help me find the nuance and the joy. I am incredibly lucky to have a brilliant editor who is also a cherished friend.

My gratitude goes to Claire Nist and the Crown team for everything you did behind the scenes to bring this book to publication. You had to do much of this remotely and through virtual meetings to stay safe in a pandemic, and I appreciate all the ways you made things happen. Thank you to Chelen Ecija for the breathtaking cover that tugs at my heart every time I look at it. Thank you for showing Harrison's own version of magic, his strength, and his willingness to be brave and vulnerable.

I'm incredibly grateful for the friends I found among the talented authors in the Roaring 20s Debut group. Together, we navigated debuting with closed bookstores, canceled book tours, and writing second novels in quarantine. I'd specifically like to thank PJ Switzer (Gardner), Arianne Costner, Sarah Allen, and Jenny Esplin.

Thank you to my supportive husband, Paul, for encouraging me, for handling family challenges such as a bike accident and broken bones while I was on deadline, and for making sure I eat when I'm stressed. Thanks for the many Blue Apron dinners. I could not have written this particular story without the emotional support I have from you.

Thanks to my amazing daughter, Victoria. Your genuine joy, enthusiasm, and creativity show the magic of your soul. Watching you connect with an audience as a dancer and listening to you create music definitely inspired much of this book.

I owe a debt of gratitude to my mom for amazing cheerleading and for spending long hours on the phone with me discussing plot, art, and life. I watched you paint your way through grief, and it never left me. Thank you for answering my questions about what it means to help and advocate for a child who stutters and for being the reason that I know unfailing love from a mother.

Thank you to my longtime friends and critique partners, Kate Coursey and Melanie Jex. Thanks for sending virtual hugs and emotional support and for reading my work during a pandemic. I owe you both a cup of tea, mounds of gourmet chocolate, and another trip to St. George without a plumbing disaster and shows canceled for lightning.

I could not have learned what I needed to know about falconry without the generous assistance of Craig Boren, a master falconer. I also learned much about Harris's hawks, Saker falcons, and bird abatement from Jamie Stride of Island Falconry Services on Prince Edward Island, but Craig guided me to understand falconry as it applies to the Utah desert.

This story developed as I had the unique opportunity to experience the healing power of the arts and the desert as I watched my son perform professionally for a season at Tuacahn Amphitheater, also known as Broadway in the Desert. I want to thank my son, Maxwell, for that seven month experience that strengthened our relationship and inspired much of this story. Thank you for being my first reader and for your expert notes. You bring light into the world when you share your talents, and I believe you will write your own stories one day.

Thank you to the cast and crew of the regional premiere of *Matilda the Musical* and the employees and directors of Tuacahn. In particular, I'd like to thank Mindy Smoot Robbins for her brilliant performance of "My House" as Miss Honey in *Matilda the Musical*. The tears I shed while listening to that song became the first seeds of this story.

This book was partially born of grief and healing through the arts in my own life, so I must acknowledge my loving father, Harley Russell. Not knowing he would die young in an accident, my father still made every effort to be sure he was in photos and videos with me, so I would "know he was there." He made many recordings of his voice on cassette tapes, which I treasure. I've learned I can be close to him through my creative pursuits, and without his influence, I'm not certain I would have found my voice to be an author today.

ABOUT THE AUTHOR

CELESTA RIMINGTON is a musical theater performer and an advocate for wildlife and the arts. She grew up in an Air Force family and lived in many regions of the United States, but she didn't truly discover the southern Utah desert until her son performed at a professional theater there for a season. She witnessed lightning storms, explored lava tubes, participated in art festivals, and watched over fifty performances at the canyon amphitheater as she worked on the idea for *Tips for Magicians*. Celesta holds a degree in sociology from Brigham Young University and is a graduate of the Institute of Children's Literature. She's the author of *The Elephant's Girl* and a member of the Society of Children's Book Writers and Illustrators. *Tips for Magicians* is her second novel for middle-grade readers.